Praise for
The Origins of Benjamin Hackett

"*The Origins of Benjamin Hackett* by Gerald O'Connor is a raucous and riotous coming of age story that is brutal, tender and hilarious."

—Paul D. Brazill, author of
A Case of Noir and *Guns of Brixton*

"O'Connor doles out killer dialogue that adds oodles of character to this hero's journey. Told with the lilt and panache of Joseph O'Connor and Dermot Bolger in their novels of the '90s, Gerald O'Connor is the new and improved voice we've been waiting for."

—Gerard Brennan, author of
Undercover and *Wee Rockets*

"Visceral writing that inherits a long Irish tradition. O'Connor's narrative contains sharp characterisation, and has an assured voice, while dramatising conditioned guilt with humour and style."

—Richard Godwin, author of
Wrong Crowd, Buffalo and Sour Mash, and others

"If you're expecting the usual coming-of-age tale, you're in for a big shock. This is a tale big on heart and one which the author, Gerald O'Connor, has hied religiously to the advice of Harry Crews for writers, to 'leave out the parts readers skip.' None of those parts remain in these pages. An auspicious debut!"

—Les Edgerton, author of *The Genuine, Imitation, Plastic Kidnapping, Bomb,* and others

D0161982

THE ORIGINS OF
BENJAMIN HACKETT

GERALD M. O'CONNOR

THE ORIGINS OF BENJAMIN HACKETT

Down & Out Books
3959 Van Dyke Rd, Ste. 265
Lutz, FL 33558
www.DownAndOutBooks.com

Cover design: Khent Rick Tobil

ISBN: 1-943402-46-9
ISBN-13: 978-1-943402-46-5

For Rosemarie, with all my love.

Chapter 1
Whitehaven, Cork, 1996

It was a Saturday in June when life turned its savage eye on me. Up until then, I, Benjamin Hackett, had amassed eighteen years of solid idleness without a bother in the world, bar a questionable name and this itching wanderlust of youth that remained unsatisfied. I was just a regular Corkman lying spread-eagle on the floor of the Brehon Pub, enjoying the mild dementia that sets in after a stack of pints.

A vivid dream had roused me. In the midst of my drunk-sleep, I'd felt my bladder contract and the warm gush of urine flowing as free as the tides, and I swore upon waking I was wet to the neck. When my eyes opened, I padded the ground and sniffed the stout-soaked air above me. No damp patches met my fingers. No fug of ammonia fouled my nose. I smiled weakly at the absence of my nocturnal shame. It was a dream after all—a tiny victory—but I'd celebrate it nonetheless. Morning afters could be monstrous bears.

My throat begged for water. I swept my tongue around my mouth and hunted for spit. The soft lining of my cheeks was crusted. My lips wilted flesh. When I drew in a lungful of air, I coughed from the ash and smoke on the tail of it. Phlegm rattled high in my chest. Something unnatural squealed on exhaling. The night, it seemed, had rusted my lungs.

I propped myself up on my elbows and winced at the glare that met me. The light bleeding in through the shutters was an innocent enough sight. Some might have even called it a blessing—a rare burst of warmth that'd have a man fit for life. But to me, it was venom spat from the skies.

Here it came. The drunkard's penance. An anvil struck in my skull. I bent forward, buried my face in my hands and cursed. This one had teeth, all right. Big ridgeback jaws on it. The stabbing peaked and then faded, but I knew it'd return with the persistence only time could heal. I'd been this soldier before. The tricksters were simply resting before sending another salvo of pain my way. I nearly cried for the thought of it. Last night was a mistake, and I'd revelled in its stupidity. In truth, I'd little choice but to go along with the madness. A Corkman's passage into adulthood was much like a wake—drink-filled, mournful and with attendance obligatory. Happy eighteenth indeed. The cost was proving to be huge.

I slunk back down on the floor and coiled my knees to my chest. Sleep would cure me, if it could be found at all. With my eyes closed, I decided to listen to the welter of sounds gathering nearby. Coals hissed in the grate to my right. Drips pinged off a metal sink. A grandfather clock played its march of tick-tocks. All soothing noises, sure enough, but it was the burr of a hedge trimmer outside that lured me. The drone of it was monotonous, hypnotic, and I dialled into the sway of it, praying for its blades to lull me into a trance. And I'd have lain there corpse-like for ages, but when Mam's warning popped into my mind, I groaned at the memory.

"You'd better be dead or dying," a voice said. "Because you've my pub humming."

I turned to spy Connie, the barman, emerge from the gloom. The tap, smack and slip of his walk told me his gout must have been crucifying him. Connie and his limp was some sight to behold. He'd claim ground out front first with his walking stick, land the good foot heavy and snap the lame one forward with a quick thrust of his hips.

"Come on and get out," he said. "I've a load of work to do to right this mess before opening." He folded away the shutters and flung the window open, releasing a scut of a day on us. Drizzle lashed my face. Sunlight blazed my irises. Ripe gusts swept over my skin.

I bolted up from under the table and staggered back from the horror of it all. "A warning would have been nice, Connie."

He turned and smiled. It wasn't one of his usual watery efforts, I noted. Instead his expression was borne of pure delight; one of those instinctive eruptions of gums and teeth conjured up by your face before a laugh.

"You really did do it," he said.

"Do what?"

He jabbed his stick out the window. "That."

I followed his gaze towards Whitehaven far below, past its Market Square with its canopy of trees, past the green copper cross of St Michael's, past greasy roofs and ivied walls, until the ramparts of the castle appeared, and the whole affair came rushing back to me in fits. The lock-in at midnight: shutters drawn, lights dimmed to a soft beating light, pints and whiskey chasers and that devil's own chartreuse, rowdy songs of the Black

3

and Tans igniting the flame in us. Then all it took was a drinking bet lost, and off I went half-wild until I was tearing the flag down to the hoots of the lads and running up my clothes to replace it.

I glanced at my reflection in the mirror hanging over the fireplace. Sure enough, there it was—the goddamn parish flag—all blue and red and covered in grime. And wasn't it wrapped around me like a toga.

"We got a bit out of hand there, all right." I toed some shards of glass away from me. "Do we owe you anything? For the damage?"

"Don't sweat it," Connie said. "I've had worse nights. And anyway, you and your friends drank gallons, so I'm covered." He slipped behind the bar, ran the taps and began gathering up the empties from the counter. "You're some men, though. Complete lunatics, the two of you." With a quick flick, he slung a sopping wet rag at my buddy JJ asleep on the floor. It landed with a loud squelch, and JJ reared up, heaving in an emphysemic breath.

"What's it to be?" JJ asked, waking up at a canter. His words came slick and fast, his legs, though, not so much. He clutched the bar for support and puffed out his cheeks. When the clock's bell tolled nine times, he gasped and charged for the door.

I smiled wryly as he fumbled with the chain. He'd the air of a man too afraid to slow down. JJ always acted as if he could outrun the misery of his hangover. "Where you racing off to now, Lazarus?"

The latch clacked back and the door swung open. "Work," he said, shielding his eyes from the sudden shock of daylight. "You coming? I can drop you back en route. If you're spotted walking home in that rig-out you'll be skinned alive."

I clutched at the tattered flag. It was stained with dried blood and beer, and had managed to cling to every sweaty crevice of me. Not the most stylish way to stroll home in the morning. JJ was right—the flag was sacrosanct to Whitehaven. Robbing it was one thing, but soiling it with bodily fluids was a mortal sin to the locals. All in all, the offer of a lift was heaven sent given my current dress.

"I'll tag along," I said. "I'm late for my folk's little tête-à-tête anyway."

Outside, the weather came at us at from all angles. Sun, rain and wind swallowed us whole. It was a day for all seasons, another schizophrenic summer. We ducked low, sprinted over to JJ's car and jumped in. His maroon Fiat 127 was a sight. Welts of rust blistered its skin, and the exhaust hung so low it clipped anything heftier than a pebble. But it was the engine that wasn't to be trusted. Anytime it didn't fancy the look of a hill, it would throw a tantrum and splutter to a stop.

JJ pulled the choke and fired her up. The Fiat coughed briefly, and we hared out of the car park and down the hill towards town. The welcome sign for Whitehaven blurred past, and a corner jumped up out of nowhere. JJ made a weird clucking noise as the wheels clipped a kerb, and the rear of the car fishtailed violently. He hammered the brakes with both feet, and we jolted to a stop next to two old women who slapped the roof twice in disgust.

"What did we hit?" he asked, panting.

I glanced back and shrugged. "About sixty near the end?"

We both shared a laugh then—a loud rumble in our chests—but it lasted all of two-point-something seconds. My ears thrummed in time with my pulse, and my head-ache crushed all the fun of the moment. I reached into the glove box to retrieve some of Mam's arthritis pills. I'd stashed them there the night before as I'd a hunch I would need them. Popping two into my mouth, I chewed until they dissolved into manageable bits. The chalki-ness, the unnatural bite to them. The taste was foul, but I swallowed them greedily. They were the heavy-hitters of pharmaceuticals after all. Real morphine-grade anal-gesics. If they didn't have me right in a jiffy, the day would be gone to rot.

"So what do your parents want to tell you then?" he asked.

"I don't know. Who can figure out the minds of parents?"

JJ nodded knowingly, slipped in behind a tour bus, and we coasted downhill toward the quay. "It's very hush-hush, though, isn't it? Bit Black Ops and all that." He swiped dust from the dash. "I've a bad feeling about it. If I'm honest."

I pictured Mam lingering by the door as I wandered out for the night. She was normally the perpetual opti-mist; always quick with a warm and inviting smile no matter the trauma I conjured. But she'd a rare look of sadness in her yesterday—as if I were tramping off to Flanders to face a hail of German bullets. "Be back early tomorrow morning, won't you," she'd said, which was bizarre given how she knew my form on drinking my years in pints.

I slumped back in the seat and watched the quayside slide by with a worm of worry creeping over my skin. "They've probably a surprise cake planned or something. Bet when I get there they'll be crouching under the netting, waiting to pounce with those gaudy paper hats and confetti."

JJ gave a vacillating shrug. "I'm not sure, Ben. Don't think your folks are the partying type. Do you? And anyway, your birthday was yesterday."

I ignored his statement. It wouldn't do to second-guess my family, and my head wasn't set for the challenge of complex thought. I cracked the window down an inch, leaving the air rush in thick with the brine of the sea. Despite the sourness of the smell, Whitehaven had its buzz on. Fishermen aboard bobbing decks baited crab traps with practiced hands. Men clustered by the corner-shop and leaned into the weather, their shoulders shifting to the beat of their mouths, sharing a smoke and the gossip. People often commented how Whitehaven had a soulful pace to it; one that would allow a man to tell the time of day by the swell and slide of tides. I could see that easy flow of life in my birthplace, then. The leisurely pace to it all was soothing to me.

A few minutes later we cleared town. Home was less than two miles journeying along a boreen of muck and bramble, so it wasn't long before we rumbled over the cattle grid and crunched to a stop in front of my farm.

"See you later," JJ said, revving the engine to stop it from conking out. "Enjoy the cake and candles."

I stared at our two-storey cottage with its render

puckered by the weather and the net curtains dressing the glass. It looked all grey and bleak and ancient, a yawning monument of mediocrity despite the bloom of colour Mam had added with her baskets.

"Do you want to meet up in Brehon's about seven?" I asked. "I fear I might need a cure."

JJ nodded. "A sound plan. Best of luck then."

With a quick salute, I jumped out and strode around to the back of the house. I paused for a moment with my hand hovering over the door handle and glanced seaward in the habit I had from a child.

Our house sat on the brow of an isthmus of land surrounded on three sides by the Atlantic. It was a small dairy farm of fifty acres with barely enough grass for our thirty head of cattle. When a high tide rose, it would cut the road off from the mainland, and we became temporary islanders. According to Dad the sea was in our DNA. Had been for generations. But Mam had more of a crawly attitude to it; one borne of old wives' tales and warnings passed down through generations.

She said the ocean had a way to it, said it could dial into a fella's future, and a keen mind could tell of portents of ill tidings. She used to stand at the end of the garden and read the rains sweeping over it like they were leaves in a teacup. I never believed those old superstitions, but today doubt slipped over me at the sight below our fields. Clouds hung low on the horizon, mercury black and heaving with badness. They rushed towards land, drawing a veil of black shadow in their wake as they went. The sea sat impassive below them with its waters slate grey and brooding. The Atlantic harboured little respect for the seasons. When the westerly blew over its waters, it'd bite at your skin no matter the month.

I cupped my hands and blew heat into my fingers, smiling as my nerves gave way to sense. There were no hidden premonitions arriving on shore; no secret whispers buried in the bawling wind. Just greyness and gales and piddling weather. And with a shiver settling on my skin, I drew a steadying breath deep into the pit my lungs and stepped quietly inside.

Chapter 2

The usual racket greeted me when I entered the kitchen—the lub-thump of the washing machine hammering away in the corner, the grill spitting fat, pots furious with the heat sending their lids hopping wild. And there was Dad, sitting at one side of the table, slurping a mug of tea and reading a quartered newspaper. He frowned when he spied me.

"Was it worth it?" he asked.

"Think so."

"And your clothes are where?"

"Up a flagpole?"

He tutted and rolled his eyes. "Your mother's got a late breakfast for you there. You'd better eat it before it gets any colder, or she'll have a canary."

I slid along the bench opposite him, and we both sat in mutual silence. Dad wasn't much for talking at the best of times. It would take a life-changing tragedy for him to string sentences together. I guessed the silent brooding type worked for most in his family. You could spy the cuteness in his two younger brothers by the way they used to communicate. A quick nod or flick of the eyes was all they needed. There were certain subjects immune to their silence. The weather, of course, was worthy of a word or two. And the politicians up the Dáil could rouse them into an uncivilised rant for five minutes. Other than these, though, the three of them could sit in a room like monks after taking a vow of silence. It drove Mam mad. Years of marriage, and she hadn't managed to carve a single slice of his mother's raring from him.

"Where's Mam?" I asked, noticing her absence. You could always tell when she was missing. The house grew still and lifeless, as if she took the soul of the place with her when she went.

Dad dipped the paper and peered over the rim of his glasses. They looked so delicate perched there on the tip of his bulbous nose—the thin-rimmed bifocals. He never wore them in public. "Just eat your food. She'll be in when she's in."

Ten minutes passed, and all I'd managed was to stare at the fry-up whilst newscasters spouted static from the radio, wondering if the sip of tea I'd sent down would send my insides into a spasm until they chucked it back up. Then a shadow ghosted past the window, and in through the back door stepped Mam wearing a smile nearly splitting her cheeks.

"There you are. My child, now a man. And how's the head? Do you need a painkiller?" Over to the medicine cabinet she went with her trademark *shush* of slippers and perfume trailing in her wake. "I've some Paraceta-mols here somewhere, if you need them."

"Aren't they months out of date?" I asked.

"Sure everyone knows that's only a cod to make you buy more."

Despite my misery, I laughed at her logic. "You're probably right. But I'm fine. Taken a few tablets already. I should be flying in an hour or so."

She nodded, turned the heat down on the cooker and

folded her arms. "What's with the flag?"

Dad snorted derisorily. "Don't ask, Peggy. For the love of God."

It must have been the spotlight above, but I really only copped on to the state of her then. In all my life, I'd never seen Mam fully made-up so early, like she was stepping out for a night in Cork city. Yet there she stood dressed in her finery, with her face gleaming from all the rouge and lippy and her hair set immaculately in a bob. I studied her face a while longer. Her lips wore the smile well, but it was her eyes that made me swallow. They were red and moist and sat in puddles of black. Even with all the makeup on, I knew she'd been crying half the night.

"You're looking well, Mam. Is there a mass or something?"

"No, no mass."

"A day out with the ones from the choir, then?"

"If only I were so lucky." She fussed with her bracelet for a moment. "Too much to do around here to go gallivanting around town. How's the fry-up?"

I stuck a fork in a rasher and wiggled it. "Just the ticket. Thanks."

"You meeting JJ again later? Going for day two of a three-day bender no doubt?"

"Maybe for a swift few. Got the minor match tomorrow, so we've to take it easy tonight."

She smiled again, but it came faker than those prissy grins you'd see sprawled over the cover of glossy magazines. "We were young once ourselves. Enjoy it while you can."

I crinkled my brow. "You all right, Mam? Anything wrong?"

"Oh, we're grand. Aren't we, Pat?"

"We are," Dad said without looking up. "All hunky-dory here."

"You see? Now, do you want a fresh top-up of tea?"

"No, thanks. Stomach's a bit queasy, so you won't mind if I only manage a bit of this?"

"Well, eat what you can. I've a beer in the fridge, if you fancy a cure. What is it you and your pals call it? The hairy dog?"

I laid the cup down and stared straight up at her. "What's going on, Mam? I mean...you're never this nice to me the morning after a session."

The smile slipped from her face, and her shoulders tensed up slightly. She sloped over, sat next to Dad and twisted her wedding band around and around on her finger, before jabbing him in the side. "Go on then, Pat."

"Go on with what?" He shook the paper once and raised it ever so slightly.

"You know damn well with what."

"Do I?"

She grabbed the newspaper from his hands, sat on it, and the two of them locked eyes. It was a worrying sight, to be honest. With the weighty stares on them, it looked like they were either going to score the face off each other or fight.

Dad broke away first and clasped his hands on the table. "You fancy your chances with those Glenbridge boys tomorrow? Word has it they're strutting about the town like cocks of the walk, thinking they'll wipe you off the pitch."

"Stop stalling," Mam said, clipping her ring off the edge of the table.

"I'm not...I'm easing into it. I can't just—"

"You can too."

"All right, calm down." He sipped his mug, winced and reached for the teapot. "That's stone cold. I need a hot drop first before I—"

Mam yanked it out of his hands and slammed it on the table, sending some of the tea lipping out of its spout. "You're adopted," she said, quick as you like, and slapped her hands over her mouth.

The words had barely reached my ears when everything went north of normal. Mam erupted into a shaking mess of tears. Dad recoiled with a feverish look to him; his ruddy face deepening to purple and his eyes enlarging to the size of cue balls. Even the washing machine beeped and shuddered to a stop from the shock of the moment.

I held up my palms defensively. "Rewind for a second there, Mam. Could you repeat what you just said?"

"Benjamin..."

"Yes."

"You are...a-dop-ted."

Jesus Christ.

Mam tilted her head and cupped my chin in her hand. "I'm sorry, Benjamin. I didn't want to blurt it out like that. But it's done now. I love you. You hear me? That's all you need to know. And now..." She glanced about briefly and nodded. "Now I've got to hang up the washing." And with that, she gathered up the linen basket, hemmed it against her hip and barged out the backdoor into the yard.

"Peggy," Dad said, leaping up and running after her. "You can't let the lad hanging like that."

A sour wind full of rot swept in just then. It scooted about briefly and buffeted the blinds, before sucking the door shut with savage force. For the next little while, I sat motionless in slack-jawed silence, staring at the tea-stained tablecloth until Dad crept back inside and slipped in opposite me once more.

"Right so, Benjamin," he said. "I can tell you're confused. So while Mam's busy with her hissy fit, let's try this again."

Chapter 3

Life was lived in the quiet moments; all the rest was pure bluster. I was paraphrasing of course. I hadn't the foggiest who'd said those words, or whether they were ever uttered out of the mouth of anyone at all, and if by happenstance they had it probably was more succinct. But the thought cropped up in my head then, watching my dad visibly stutter less than the width of a jab away from me.

"There's no way in hell I'm adopted," I said.

"You are a bit."

"You can't be a bit adopted."

Dad seemed to consider this for a moment, before shrugging and smiling wanly. "No...I suppose you can't."

"This is a pile of unadulterated nonsense. You're both having a laugh, right? Some twisted revenge for me not applying to college?"

Dad reached inside his shirt pocket, pulled out a manila envelope and laid it on the table. "This," he said, tapping it twice with his index finger, "contains your adoption certificate. We decided to keep calling you by your birth name, Benjamin. Seemed the correct thing to do at the time."

"Did it?"

He held up his hand to hush me. "It's the original document we received the day Father Brogan brought

16

you here and made it all official." He slid it over to me. "It's yours now."

I picked up the envelope and tore it open, unfurling the paper inside and laying it flat on the table. My eyes skimmed over the document, flitting from word to word—adoption, adoptees, dates, signatures and the official diocesan insignia on the envelope. They were all there, all the bureaucratic paraphernalia of the state and church.

I held his stare, neither of us flinching. "Am I really adopted?"

"Yes."

My throat turned to dust. Call it the formality of the letter, or the way the word cut short on his breath. I thought of Mam's delicate frame and barley-blonde hair. We looked nothing alike. But Dad? He was meant to be the exception. We both towered over her. We both had lanky frames. Hell, we even shared that same terrible torture of walking on long, flat feet that no shoe, no matter the cut or cobbler, could fit comfortably.

Reams of memories of years gone by played on a loop in my head. "Sure, isn't Benjamin the spit of his old man," they'd said. "Dug from the same field, no doubt about it. Oh, he's a Hackett all right, this fella." And my parents had lapped it up. Like the time in Hay Street, in the bustle of market day, when they nodded in tacit agreement at some hunched-over old coot as she tousled my hair and told them how my curls were the carbon copy of Dad's.

"But we look alike?" I said.

"Do we?"

"You know we do."

He leaned in closer, dropped his voice to a whisper. "Truth is, we've been secretly dying your hair since you arrived. You're actually ginger."

I shoved the table into him and threw my hands up. "Jokes? You think now is the time for messing about? For having a bit of a laugh?"

"Sorry, sorry," he said, showing his palms in surrender. "It just snuck out...but seriously, you're not going to make a big deal of this, are you?"

"And why shouldn't I?"

"Because it's not what Hackett men do."

"Well, I'm clearly not one of them, now am I?"

My comment flushed crimson high in his cheeks. He balled his hands twice and relaxed them flat on the table. "You've been long enough on the farm," he said, quieter now. "Long enough to know that animals of all sorts adopt strays and nurture them as their own. And there's not a blind bit of difference in them when they mature. Attitude is more in the rearing than the genes. You're my son *and* a Hackett. Adopted or not."

"So you're calling me a stray animal now? Christ, Dad, you're some piece of work."

"That's not what I meant and you know it. Don't go all melodramatic on me now. We've enough histrionics happening outside already."

I shook my head in disbelief. "I think we're allowed this one time to have a bit of a barney."

"Well, you're not. No son of mine is going to throw a tantrum over something like this. Adoption happens all over the world, every day of the week. Just because you came out of another doesn't mean we're not your parents. And let me tell you this now. If I hear any of that sort of nonsense when your mother's about I'll—"

"You'll what?"

"Ah, nothing." He leaned back, folded his arms and studied his feet for a while. His standard move whenever his mood blackened. "You know," he said after a while. "I never wanted to say anything. But your mam wouldn't have it. Have you any idea how difficult it was for her to keep this a secret all this time?"

"And if it was such a burden on you two, why didn't you relieve yourselves of it sooner?"

"Because we thought if you knew too soon it'd mark you, hang over you like a shadow looming large. Scar you for life. Father Brogan advised us to tell you early, but your mother thought it was best you didn't know. She thought you'd settle better and handle it easier as an adult rather than a child. I don't know...maybe we should have taken the priest's advice and told you sooner?" He stroked his stubble and sighed. "It was bad enough you'd that birth mark on your face without lugging this around as well."

"Nice one, Dad," I said, and instinctively I felt for the port-wine stain on my face. I couldn't help myself. It was an old habit, hiding behind my veil of fingers and thumbs. "An Angel's kiss" Mam had called it when I was finally tall enough to catch sight of myself in the mirror. Even at three years of age I knew it'd be a burden. Angel's kiss was such a pile of nonsense. It was more like ten of them took turns to give me a six-inch hickey from cheek to chin. I stopped wearing camouflage since the age of twelve. No matter how you applied the green-tinted clay, it always came out a weird shade of vomit.

"Okay so, Mister Automaton," I said. "Tell me this, then...who are my real parents?"

"Not a clue. All we know is what's in that letter, and we never felt a need to find out more. Do you?"

"Ah, I don't know what I want to do with all this. I mean...who would? Springing it on me now after all these years with my head all over the shop."

"Well, if you do, Father Brogan's your man. He knows all about this revelation today. I expect it wouldn't be a surprise to him if you turned up there later." He pushed up and away from the bench. "Right so, that's that."

"Seriously? That's all you're going to give me?"

"Well, as much as I'd like to stay and chat the farm won't work itself. Fancy helping me spraying weeds in the paddock?"

"What do you think?"

"Suit yourself, then." He buttoned his overalls, swung his arms into his mac and zipped it up to his neck. With a hand on the door handle, he inched it ajar, before turning around once more. "You know, Benjamin. We've farmed this patch of land for near on ten generations. And do you know what I've learned from the three decades I've held it together? Tides come and tides go. Every bit of sand laying on the beach below us today will be somewhere else entirely tomorrow. Nothing stays the same. All this is just noise, a glitch in your life. By tomorrow, or next week, or ten years down the line, today will be a distant memory to you. Hell, you'll probably even laugh about it."

"I doubt that."

"Well, whatever your plans are from here, don't go

leaning on your mam too much. Do what you have to do, but do it gently." He fixed his cap on his head and held a finger up as if he'd just remembered something. "Oh, and make sure to collect Ella from Nell's before you trot away into the day. And get her home before the high tide. It's a spring one and it'll cut the road off. If Ella misses her lunch, there'll be hell to pay."

I snorted. "And we can't be having that."

"Nope. You're right on that point," he said, the trace of a smile brightening his face. "You see? We are alike after all."

Away up the yard he pottered, hands tucked into pockets, shoulders hunched forward, with a host of grey clouds looming above him. I raced upstairs and changed out of the flag into a plaid shirt and black denim jeans, and a whole load of questions kept buzzing about in my brain. One kept barging its way towards the front and trampling over the others. "What you gonna do, Benjamin?" it said, over and over again, mockingly.

I looked through the attic window and spied Mam down in the yard with pegs clipped to her blouse and her sheets being harassed by the weather. She must have sensed me staring because she glanced up and immediately gestured me down.

"You going out?" she asked, when I appeared.

"I am. Going to pick up Ella from Nell's."

"Thanks for doing that..." Her voice trailed off, and she turned away, and I knew she was lining up the sentences in her head.

"And then?" She picked up a duvet cover and laid it across the line.

"Then I'm going to see Father Brogan."

A peg fell from her grasp, and she kicked it away across the yard. "I thought you might."

She nodded over towards Dad. "Did he handle it okay? Explaining things, I mean."

"I suppose so."

"Any jokes?"

I shrugged. "Just the one."

"Ah, I'll wear him up the road—"

"It was a pretty good one, though, in fairness."

"Still…"

The wind stiffened. Wisps of hair slipped across her mouth. She tucked them back behind her ear, and her eyes met mine. She looked scared standing there and frailer than her years. "You won't stop until you find them, will you?"

I shook my head. "I'm the odd man out. I have to find out why."

And with that I turned on my heel and strode out of the farm and away from the people I thought were my family. The weather seemed to match my mood; a gale rose up and blew in my face. In the distance, the seas roared thunder.

I stopped by Mosses Point and walked out to the ledge where the whole sweep of the coast stretched out beneath me. The isle of Inis Saor stood less than a mile from shore as a tall and immovable mule of rock. Normally, a quick glimpse of the place would take the breath clean out of my chest, pulling any bit of foul mood with it. Not today, though. For some unknown reason, I thought of Dad, of him leading me into the fields with my wellies two sizes too big and the chill of dawn biting at my skin. I remembered the shakes I'd felt, as I stood rooted to his side with one tiny hand clutched in his. The black-and-white giants plodding toward us with their teats swollen terrified me.

"You have to be brave, Benjamin," he'd said. "If they rush you, wave your hands, stand tall and make as much noise as humanly possible."

And I did. I was only five, but I'd waddled over to the nearest one with my boots sticking in the muck, and I'd barked until they clomped the ground with their hooves and shied away back down the farm. When I'd looked at Dad he'd this honest-to-God warmth to his smile that had me brim with happiness.

"That's my boy," he'd said, like the big liar he was.

All the frustration in me erupted. I opened my mouth wide and screamed into the winds until my throat ran hoarse. One thought played over in my head—I'll find my rancid parents. And when I do, I'll punch them square in their goddamn noses. And with the fire in me stoked up nicely, I cinched my shirt closed and headed up the road to Nell's.

Chapter 4

The hill up to Nell's wasn't built for speed. A man would need the constitution of a goat to get up it without having a coronary. I had three breaks on the ascent such was the monumental weakness in my legs from the boozing. By the time I'd reached the crown of it my lungs were fit for transplanting, and I'd gladly removed Kilimanjaro from my bucket list.

I never really understood why Nell lived all the way up here on the headland and it poking out to sea like the nipple of Ireland. Especially being so keen as she was on traipsing down to the pub most nights for a bit of fun and a bunch of drink. Only on a clear day could you spy it from the quays in Whitehaven; the house looked nothing more than a teensy white dot high against the rocks with seagulls squabbling over which one of them was due a perch on her chimneypot.

I crossed over the narrow road, jumped the stile and stopped by the gate. In fairness to Nell, the garden was singing. Every manner of flower bloomed—blood-red dahlias, jasmine, roses—and a load more with names recently rinsed from my head. Each one had been planted and pruned randomly with neither rhyme nor reason to the layout. But the madness of it worked up here. Hell, even the weather seemed more inclined to spoil you near Nell's. The moment I'd climbed the brow of the hill and the coast reared up on the horizon, it'd calmed down beautifully. Only a faint breeze remained from the squall I'd stepped into.

I turned seaward briefly and let the wind lick the heat from my skin. Waves fizzed far below, bees buzzed in the gorse, and the sea calmed to sheet steel. Truth be told, I felt like slipping down the path, balming out on the beach and forgetting about the whole adoption affair. But there'd be none of that for a while. Not with priests to question, ghosts to chase and abandoning parents to punch in the face.

I'd barely stepped in through the gate when my sister Ella came barrelling around the corner squealing in her usual excited way; the flush of pink high in her cheeks, and her yellow Brownies shirt soiled with stains. I stayed stock-still and watched Boots hare around a laurel bush, leaping up for the sash she trailed in her wake. He was a terrier breed and a right little gurrier to boot. Two years ago, we'd all gone to Dooley's kennels to pick out a puppy. The place had been teeming with bundles of doggy perfection, but it didn't matter to my sister. By rights, any normal four-year-old should have fled screaming when this blizzard of spittle appeared with his mangy coat and freakish lower jaw jutting out a mile. But not our Ella. No, the moment he cocked his leg, peed on her shoe and licked it, she was smitten. And no amount of showboating by the others could sway her from wanting him.

"Benji," she said, when she finally saw me.

I smiled widely when I heard her. I hated that version of my name, and only Ella was allowed to call me by it. It was our private in-joke. Benji—after the dog in those children's films. We used to watch them when our parents headed down to Whitehaven for their monthly game of bridge. They were God-awful movies, but Ella always giggled at the similarity of our names.

She ran, jumped into my arms, and I almost collapsed from the weight. A lump of sadness caught in my throat at the sight of her. It took me by surprise that feeling; hit me like a sucker punch smack in the gut. But I knew the reason why. If I were adopted, Ella wasn't my sister. It was as simple as that. And of all the thoughts I'd suffered, this one cut me to the core.

"Jeez, Ella," I said with the mask of a smile on my lips. "You might need to stop leaping for me like that. You're not a little baby anymore."

"No. I'm a big girl now. I am six." She counted them off on her fingers before pinching my cheeks. "And you're eighteen. Which is ancient."

I laughed. "It's hardly that old."

"Ancient," she said again. Then she knitted her brow in the way she did as a baby. "What happened to your face?"

I touched my forehead and found the rough edge of a scab. I'd no real notion where I'd earned it, but the previous night's booze-athon probably had a hand in the matter. "I fell."

"Where?"

"Down the road."

"How?"

"I tripped. Okay? No need for an inquisition."

She studied me for a second. "We'll need to put bandages on that."

I put her back down and patted my pockets. "I cannot seem to find any. If only—"

"Here's one." She pulled out a Mickey Mouse-patterned bandage from her pocket and held it in her palm. "You see?"

"Do it quick, then." I kneeled on the path. "Or I could bleed out and die here this instant."

She peeled the tabs off, laid it across my brow and slapped it down with the heel of her hand. A pain shot through my temples, and my hangover ignited once more. "Thanks for that, Ella. It's just the job."

"You're welcome. Now, follow me. I've something to show you."

We went into the kitchen, where Aunty Nell straddled a stool with her hair rolled into curlers and dressed head-to-toe in her usual black. She didn't look up when we entered, just kept scrubbing at the insides of a press with all the cups and saucers and silverware arranged in neat little bundles on the sideboard. However crazy my aunty looked, it was the heels that made me think she'd a bit of a want in her. Nearly fifty years of age, and there she was clicking a pair of black stilettos in sync to the radio whilst scouring the life out of surfaces already clean enough to be buried in.

"Cleanliness is next to godliness," she'd said, "but booze would have you seeing Him sooner."

Had to admire a woman with a mantra like that.

Ella screeched for Nell to get down and raced into the bedroom.

"Be sure to keep away from my trunk," Nell said. "There are heirlooms in there dear to me. Not for grubby hands that haven't had a wash."

"Will do," Ella said from behind the door. "Just get him ready, please."

Nell turned around slowly, her eyes boring into me. I knew by the seriousness in them that she'd at least an inkling of the goings-on in the house earlier.

"Benjamin," she said, nodding curtly.

"Nell."

"You look awful."

"As do you."

She slipped down off the stool and gestured at the sofa. "Take a seat, like a good man. Ella wants you to have the best chair in the house for this. She's got a surprise for you."

I slumped into the seat and waited, drumming my fingers to the ticks of the clock. I felt the heat of Nell's breath on my ear as she leaned in close, and her humming of neat bleach and fags.

"And be sure to make all the right noises when she shows you," she said quietly. "She's been working on it all morning at Brownies."

I didn't answer. I never really had a chance to; because in stormed Ella with her hands behind her back and an impossibly wide beam wedged high on her cheeks.

"Close...your...eyes," she said, clipping the words. She was a stern little general for her age.

I shut them tight and covered them with my palms. "Now what?"

"Ta-dah."

I opened my eyes and saw a birthday card held up in front of me. It had all the hallmarks of Ella—garishly pink and glittered to the hilt with gluey thumb-prints smudged on the corners. I took it carefully and laid it on my lap.

"Open it," she said.

I peeled the pages apart. A slew of glitter fell out onto my jeans and trickled between the floorboards.

"Pixie dust," Ella said, whispering mysteriously. "I made it in Brownies today just for you. Got my artist merit badge for it and all. So...do you like it?"

"I absolutely love—"

"Because it was really tricky," she said, babbling away excitedly. "Had to use string for your hair and dried pasta for the shoes. The glue got all over me. Mrs Looney said, 'It has to be a Brownie's activity.' But I said, 'No way.' And she said, 'That that was fair enough,' and here it is anyways. What do you think?"

I studied the card again, giving it a fair bit of attention. My head was four times too big and by all the misspellings of my name, I reckoned there was a glut of crayon casualties before she'd spelled it correctly. But for all the horrors of my day, it was a moment of sheer happiness, a pause in the lunacy, and for the briefest while I forgot about the rigmarole in my head. I caught her under her arms and threw her up in the air with her screeches ringing in my ears.

"I think," I said, pinching her lips to hush her up for a second. "That it's possibly the greatest piece of art the world has ever produced."

"Do you?"

"I do. Better than Picasso, or Goya, or any of those artists. It'll go on my wall of fame. Hand on heart."

"And your Liverpool posters?"

I screwed up my nose. "No place for them anymore. Not with your masterpiece."

That did the job, all right. Ella's face scrunched up so

much her eyes almost disappeared, and she slung her arms around my neck and squeezed with all her might.

Nell slipped in, took her from my arms and carried her to the door. "You see? I told you he'd like it. Now, go outside and play because I want to have a word with your brother for a second. All right?"

"Okay," Ella said, ducking out the door to the yelps of Boots.

Nell slid onto the chair opposite me. Within seconds, she'd sparked up a cigarette and sent a haze of smoke curling above her. "A hyper one that girl. She'll need a firm hand to stop her when she reaches puberty."

"I don't think you've to worry about her. Far as I can tell, she's the sanest one among us."

The clock over the sink whirred briefly and chimed twice. No sooner had the bells died down to a hum than Nell removed a naggin of whiskey from her apron and poured some into her silver quaich. Ever since Dad had brought the two-handled cup back from his trip to Scotland, she'd latched onto it like it was a priceless relic.

"Two o'clock?" I said, nodding at the drink. "That's a bit early for you, isn't it?"

"That depends."

"On what?"

"On what the hell you think you're doing telling your mam you want to find your birth parents." She tapped the glass on the edge of the table and knocked it back in a single gulp. A second shot followed the first and red butterflied her face.

"I'll do whatever I fancy," I said.

She horsed another one into her. "Will you, now?"

"I will."

"And have you thought what might happen if you manage to actually find them?"

"Bar them getting two bloody noses?"

"Typical Benjamin. Raging against life." She rapped my skull with her knuckle. "Any ounce of common sense lurking around in there?"

I laughed dismissively. "Says the woman getting drunk for no particular reason."

"It's the weekend. What else is there to do? And anyway, I've more reason than you know."

"Meaning?"

She slammed the glass down and jabbed a finger in the air like she was looking to stab me. "Meaning you should let sleeping dogs lie. Nothing good will come from digging up the past. It happened. It's done. It's ancient bloody history. Grow up and move on."

"So that's the consensus then, is it? Bet Mam was on the phone before I'd made it to the end of the drive. Had a good cry did she?"

"Your mam's my sister. Women talk. Women cry. And funnily enough it's normally down to men. So nothing new there then." She settled back in the chair and clasped her face in her hands. "If you'd even one iota of experience with our fairer sex you'd never have asked such a question."

"You know, Nell..." I stood and slipped the card under my shirt. "I thought you'd be on my side on this one. Thought you'd understand me a bit more than that pair of liars down below. But you're all the bloody same, aren't you? It's not my fault I was adopted. Not my fault they lied to me for eighteen years. You can hardly blame me for wanting to find out."

Nell stretched her neck until it clicked and folded her arms high on her chest. When she looked at me again there was a flash of iciness in her smile. "Well boo-hoo you. Do you know what I learned about life, Benjamin? Rashness is for fools. You should take some time to think about all of this before you go up scuppering everyone's life."

I laughed wryly. "There's really only one life I'm worried about right now...mine."

"That'd be you all right, Benjamin—selfish to the core. What if you find them, and they don't want to know? You'll end up ruining five people's lives; your own included."

"You see, the problem with you is your bitter and twisted view on the world has you only ever seeing the worst of life. What if this, what if that? I'll give you another hypothetical. What if I track them down and everyone gets on like a house on fire, and I've two per-fectly functional sets of parents who end up richer for my efforts? What then? Sounds sweet enough, doesn't it?"

"Oh, that sounds sweet as a nut all right, Benjamin." She sucked the cigarette down to the filter and lit another. "Sickly sweet."

"Doesn't matter. It's a possibility."

"Ah, it wouldn't happen in a month of Sundays. Not even on *Little House on the Prairie*—for Christ's sake. Life's not so generous, not so keen on happy endings in my experience—"

The screams of Ella playing cut her short. Nell fell silent and set her hands palm down on the table while the creaks of the cottage filled the void. "Best you get that child home now. I'm sick of all this drama. It'd be nice to see an end to it. So go on and get out. Go chase your ghosts."

I headed for the door and stopped to watch her. She looked so sad sitting there, this lonely spinster who was the image of my mam, but with none of the happiness.

"It's like the story you read to me," I said. "When I was little. You remember it?"

Her eyes met mine, the flicker of recognition. "*Pandora's Box*?"

"Yeah, that's the one. All this adoption malarkey...It can't just be put back. The secret's out now. Squirreling away something like this? It isn't for me. Know what I mean?"

For a moment she didn't answer. She simply stood and walked to the sink, filling it up with suds and staring out the window at the Atlantic far below. When she spoke, her voice had that far away whisper to it. "I do," she said, finally. "Just leave me be and go wherever you fancy."

I opened the door, closed it quietly on the latch and waved at Ella to follow me.

"Did you have a nice birthday?" she asked, as we strode away down the lane with Boots marching out in front, barking at the wind.

Whitehaven town appeared below us, sitting down snugly between a cluster of hills. In the middle of it all, the church rose high above the buildings, its limestone spire glinting in the sun, like a beacon guiding me home.

"That depends," I said.

"On what?"

"On Father Malachi Brogan."

Chapter 5

Rain. Jesus, the rain. It didn't come bucketing down. No, that would have been too simple. A fine soft drizzle frittered from the clouds, the kind that hitches a lift on the wind and soaks you sideways. I'd barely beaten the tide back home when I dropped Ella off. Didn't dare to enter the place for fear of Dad hectoring me again. After dealing with Nell, I was done with bickering. I simply watched Ella and Boots to the door, waded back down the lane with the Atlantic slipping up over the walls, and then I hurried the two-mile stretch back to Whitehaven.

It seemed my day was cursed for merciless hills. And here I was once more, leaning into another, soaked wet and with a bear of a hangover. In fairness, it wasn't the canniest way to meet a priest. They were ninjas when it came to secrets. And Father Malachi Brogan was a 10th Dan master of the stuff. His parochial house sat at the end of a row of terraced buildings, perched right on top of Market Street. It lorded over Whitehaven, with the Holy Cross church to its left, like its big brother daring you to have a go. With its grey brick walls and pebblestone garden, it pretty much matched the bleakness of the man.

I paused by the front door and shook out my hands. I never imagined I'd be hanging around here looking for some guidance from a priest. A sense of dread took root in my gut. I pictured a Bible randomly opened and unleashed against me, like a cluster bomb of parables layering on the guilt in sweeps of Father Brogan's clap-trappery. I shuddered and flicked my fringe from my eyes. It had to be done. He held the key to finding my parents, and I'd be damned if I left without it.

I plucked back the knocker and rattled it off the plate. A single, brassy note hummed. For the longest while nothing happened. Not even the streets showed any hint of livening up. It seemed like a fair clip of time to be stuck in His shadow and nothing moving but swollen clouds in leaden skies. The air grew heavy, as if I were breathing through damp cotton. I shook the rain from my eyes and was about to give the knob another rattle when the door creaked open, stopping on a chain. An elderly woman peeked out, whey-faced and gaunt.

"What do you want?" she asked, eyeing me up and down like I was a beggar.

She wasn't his usual housekeeper. Miss Maguire was a real dote, always happy in her world sporting that cartoon smile of hers, always keen to get the priest to save your soul. Not this one, though. With her hawkish eyes and biting tongue, she seemed more like a miniature bouncer.

I cleared my throat and threw my best film star smile at her. "Where's herself today?" I asked.

"Away on holidays." She looked to the skies and grimaced. "And it's a right dirty day out there to be on a break."

"And you are?"

"Busy." She clicked her fingers twice. "So come on. Tell me your business?"

"Is Father Brogan in?"

"Is Father Brogan in, what?"

I'll admit this threw me. I wasn't expecting riddles.

"Is Father Brogan in *please*, ma'am?"

"He might be. Depends on the reason you're here."

"It's a personal matter."

"Aren't they all?"

She tried to close the door, but I jammed my foot in the gap. "He's expecting me."

"If he were, I would be. And I'm not."

I clicked my teeth and breathed deep. "It's an official church matter. I doubt Father Brogan would be happy with you delaying important information from being delivered to him."

I held up the envelope and fanned it under her nose.

"And what's this supposed to be?" she said.

"Letter from the Bishop. He had me swear I'd hand-deliver it myself. And I came as soon as I received it, despite…" I pointed at my neck, "being off duty myself."

She grabbed the envelope, held it at arm's length and studied it intently. The second her eyes copped the official diocesan stamp on the back, she gasped.

"Why didn't you tell me you had word from the Bishop?" She slipped the chain off the latch and swung the door open. "Come away out of the rain immediately, Father."

"Father in training," I said, correcting her. It seemed more appropriate. "Not quite there yet. A year still to go in the seminary."

"And which one are you at?"

I thought for a second. "Maynooth."

"A fine establishment. I know you're trying to be all

modern and the rest, but the absence of the collar confused me. You'll pardon my shocking manner?"

"Don't give it a moment's thought."

Before I'd a foot in the door, she began sweeping the rain off me with a brush. I'll admit I'd never been swept before, or had any all-body grooming in any form whatsoever. It was a strange experience, to be honest. I held my breath as she turned me about to do my front. When her hands approached the way-hey zone, she stood aside and pointed at a heavy mahogany door to our side.

"Why don't you make yourself comfortable in the drawing room, and I'll let Father Brogan know you're here."

"Will do."

The air inside hinted of incense and cloves. I sat on an old wooden chair with its arm worn down by centuries of parishioners looking for salvation. It sent a shiver of dread through me. I pictured a sinner picking the varnish off and him pouring out his heart, looking for his soul to be spared the short hike downstairs.

The room was composed of the usual religious iconography. A wooden cross hung by a nail on the wall. A picture of Christ in the Garden of Gethsemane took centre-stage on the shelf. His eyes peered down at me, probing, his face drawn a porcelain white. I'd asked about his skin colour before. Apparently religion wasn't open for discussion, and a bowsie like me should know better than to cause the Almighty sufferance with my ignorance. And I should be flagellating myself every night rather than using His gifts against Him. They were all-round champion people my teachers. I shook my head to clear away the slew of religious dogma stuffed in there by the priests. A man wouldn't do well to focus on those high tales for too long.

A draft slipped into the room. Father Brogan appeared with a large Bible in hand and ebony rosary beads coiled thrice around his fingers. Armed to the hilt already, it seemed. His eyes were his true weapons, though. When the look of recognition came over them, they tore holes in me in an instant.

"Benjamin," he said in that booming, preacher tone of his. "I understand you've just celebrated your eighteenth birthday. Well, to be young again. It must have been a serious session, judging by the colour of you."

"Cheers, Father. Got a bit lairy there for a while last night. But we survived."

His smile was all teeth and no eyes. There wasn't even the slightest hint of mirth in the gesture. "You do know," he said, "impersonating a man of the cloth is a sin?"

"Sorry, Father. Your stand-in housekeeper kind of came to that conclusion by herself."

"Really?" He sat behind the desk and loosened his collar. "Now then, young man. What can we do for you today?"

"Well...my parents told me today that I'm adopted."

He nodded. "Go on."

"And Dad suggested you could help me track my real parents." I gave him the envelope with my certificate. "That's all I've I got to go on. So I was wondering if you knew how I'd go about it."

He studied the document for what seemed like an age, eyes zipping down the page, lips sticking out in an exaggerated pout. "Tell me, Benjamin," he said finally.

"Have you decided what you want to do with your life?"

"Not exactly. No."

"How about university? A bright boy like you should be able to secure a place fairly easily."

"I can't decide what I want to do, Father."

"Can anyone?" He dipped his head in close. "Have you ever considered the priesthood?"

I swear to God my shadow tried to leg it. "To be honest, I haven't. Never got the calling, as you say. I suppose I'm not the calibre of soldier Himself is looking for."

"Pity. You'd make a fine bearer of the Word."

Would I heck—maybe if the Word wore heels and had hips.

"Anyway," I said. "Any idea about the parents, and so on?"

"Confession," he said suddenly. "I notice it's been a while since I cleansed you of your ways. Why don't we wipe the slate clean before we go on?"

My hands gripped the arms of the chair, and I picked off flecks of varnish with my nails. "Shouldn't we do it another time? You know...somewhere a bit more private?"

"There's nowhere more private than here. After all, it's only us and Himself listening." He dragged his chair around to my side and shuffled in close. "On you go, Benjamin."

The walls of the room seemed to shrink in towards us. Clamminess set on my skin. He was so close I could smell the soap on him and see the rivulets of sweat beading his top lip. "Bless me, Father, for I have sinned."

"Yes, yes."

"It has been two months since my last confession."

"That's it...go on."

"I did not love God when I..."

And I rattled off the usual litany of lies every child learns will satisfy the priest without annoying him.

Lied to my parents; check.

Cursed; check.

Used the Lord's name in vain; check.

Had improper thoughts about Mrs Coveney the shopkeeper's breasts; double D and the rest; check.

I finished it off with a few whitish ones, nothing too serious, misdemeanours really. Guaranteed to get a few decades of the rosary at a stretch.

By the time I finished the act of contrition, the sweat had soaked me through. Father Brogan had his eyes closed, listening to every syllable like it was his final fix. He mumbled my absolution, and for some strange reason I thought once more of Mrs Coveney's breasts and my groin twitched. I tinkered with the idea of mentioning it, but decided it might ruin the moment for him.

"God forgives you, Benjamin. Despite your black deeds, He forgives you. Say three Hail Marys and four Our Fathers." He made the sign of the cross and tapped me on the chin. "And make sure you play in the match tomorrow, won't you? We need your skills against those Glenbridge lads. I hear they're tricky ones."

I nodded.

"Good man. Now off you go"

"Any chance, Father, you could possibly track back to the original question about my birth parents?"

He bolted up out of the chair, a foul mood reddening

his skin. "Back to that nonsense again?"

"I...I didn't think we'd left it."

"And are you sure you want to go tormenting your family with this business? Aren't you happy where you are?"

"Of course I am. It's just since they told me I was adopted I kind of had a hankering to find out."

"No good will come of this." He pointed his finger at me. "Heed my words."

I pretended like I was, but it was hard to act heeded. All I managed was to clasp my fingers together and stare forlornly at the floor. "In order to go forward, Father, I need to exorcise the demons of my past."

Call the Army. Genius had invaded.

"Well now. That sounds like the mind of a cleric." He hemmed his hip against the edge of the desk and chewed his lip in thought. "You may be saved yet."

"God willing."

"Indeed," he said, arching an approving eyebrow. "So is this really what you want?"

I nodded.

"Well, so be it. All I know is you were born in Barnamire Convent in Cork. The nuns there arranged your adoption and matched you up with your parents. I've no clue as to who your real parents are. Bring your paperwork with you and ask them there. They'll probably redirect you through official government offices, but it's worth a punt going there first."

I stood and shook his hand. "But just so you know, Benjamin, whatever the circumstances *they* cast you astray to the world without so much as a by-your-leave. And it was your fine folks back up the road there, honest-to-God Catholic stalwarts, who took you in as their own. If you ever forget it, God help your soul."

"I won't, Father."

"Good. Oh, and by the way, the convent is being closed down by the diocese next week. So I'd hurry up if I were you."

The door slammed shut, and I stood alone on the road thinking if Father Brogan were the employee I'd hate to meet the Boss. He was hard to get the information from, but I had it. I'd sniffed out the name of the nunnery where I'd been dragged into this world and cast aside like the runt of the litter. A buzz of adrenaline seeped through me. It jettisoned the sting of my hangover. Only one thing would stop me—the place closing down. God knows where the files would end up.

I needed to get there fast.

I needed wheels.

I needed JJ.

Away from the church I went, scooting through an archway and down the brooding Speaker's Lane with its psychedelic shop frontages. The footpath was thick with tourists plodding about, peering at maps and sporting those garish jumpers with shamrocks embroidered on the front. I threaded through them and nearly bowled into Don, the local tour guide, as he herded a group of tall Scandinavian types into the back of his beaten-down Volkswagen.

"Where's the fire, Benjamin?" he asked, with the gritty voice of someone hungover.

"Have you seen JJ lately?"

"I have. Spotted him piling kids into the bus down by the school gates earlier. Think they're all going to the summer camp up the road in the Mansion House. Probably be there all day I'd say."

I nodded at the van. "Fancy dropping me off?"

"Sure. If you help me guide this lot around the Fort first." He jammed a finger toward the mob inside. "They're mad for questions. And to be honest, my head's not up for probing today."

"Heavy night?"

"More like a heavy decade."

I laughed a conspiratorial laugh. "Sorry. I'm a bit up the walls right now. But I'd appreciate a lift."

Don cocked his head back and fidgeted with the keys. "Ah, I don't know about detours. And there is the delicate matter of maximum passenger capacity to contend with."

I got the hint. I dug into my pockets and threw him a tenner. A minute later, we were racing through the streets of Whitehaven, half-choked to death by diesel fumes seeping up through the floor. I sat with my back to the door and swayed with the motion of the van.

We'd barely crawled up the hill when the *oohs* from the Swedes grew to a new high. I'd heard the same gasps from many a tourist as I led them on a tour of the Fort. They were always composed of the same old lot—a bunch of well-heeled Yanks or jabbering Asians, combing the ruins, clicking away with cameras at every broken rock strewn here and there, cataloguing anything that sounded, smelled or feigned of Irishness. And just as the rain doused their mood, and they'd a notion to duck back to their hotels for a lick of the black stuff, the clouds scurried away, and the whole of Ireland erupted in a dress of greens and blues.

I looked down below as row upon row of waves slipped under the keels of boats anchored off Curtles Bay. Everything seemed to move in sync, bobbing and glistening in its own special way. It must have been the weird will of the weather, but for the first time all day my mind calmed. I closed my eyes, patted the envelope twice and let the *phut-phut* of the engine waft me away into a fitful sleep.

Chapter 6

When I decamped from Don's van, I heard the unmistakable crooning of kids off the leash. How JJ put up with the screeching was impressive stuff, despite it being essential for his survival. Ever since his dad had scarpered and left himself and his mam to their own devices, JJ'd been working every spare moment he could scrap together.

I couldn't recall a single school holiday since, when he hadn't been either picking fruit for punnets, or hawking programmes up Páirc Uí Chaoimh or giving grinds to students with questionable IQs. But it was working with kids that really filled his swag bags. Babysitting, child-minding and summer camp supervising down at the GAA club. He did them all, and with supreme gusto. I had to tip my hat to him. His industry may have been annoying, but taking charge like that was the stuff of heroes.

I followed the noises along the pathway and cut through a grove until I emerged onto parklands jangling with screams. Every snatch of grass teemed with activity. Picnicking families waged war for the blankets, teenagers flung Frisbees back-and-forth, dads booted balls in high arcs for twitchy looking toddlers to catch. And there, right in the midst of twenty or so school-kids stood JJ, trying to herd their short attention spans through the complexities of Rounders.

"How's it going, chief?" I said, ambling up beside him. "Your chinos are tasty. Those creases could chop wood."

He looked down, a brief spasm of a smile on his lips. "Cheers. I'm quite proud of them. What with the limited prep time this morning."

"Hair's a bit extreme, though. Did Val do it? It has her trademark lick."

He fussed with his fringe, scrunching it up with his fingers. "Ben. Why are—"

A boy with a buzz-cut unwound and flung a pitch baseball style. It zipped and skimmed the batter's head. JJ blew his whistle and jabbed a finger at the pitcher. "Third foul ball in a row, Charlie. Throw it high on purpose again and you'll be off. Got it?"

Charlie rolled his eyes in protest, picked up the ball once more and squeezed it in his hands. "But it's only soft, John Joseph."

JJ's full title always jolted me. I'd heard it for the first time during roll call in primary school. John Joseph Ryan. To my ear two first names sounded ridiculous, as if anyone had a need for a spare one. It didn't take long for me to rechristen the blond-haired boy sitting next to me. In the end I settled for JJ. Short and catchy and with a rapper's twang to it. He loved it. And his mam, Val, absolutely hated it. The natural order of things really.

"Rules are rules," JJ said. "Underarm only. None of that American carry-on." He waved at the lad batting. "Walk to first base. And next batter up, please."

A whippet of a girl sporting impossibly tight pigtails took her position. Judging by the dainty limbs and inch-thick glasses, I doubted she'd be running the bases.

When she waggled the bat behind her, the Charlie lad had one eye closed all ready, no doubt lining her up for another body shot.

"I'd watch him, JJ. Got a sneakiness in him that young fella."

JJ sighed. "They're eight years old. They're all sly at this age." He folded his arms and glanced at me briefly. "Now, what do you want? You hardly came all the way up here to help me."

"I want to ask you for a massive favour."

"I don't like the sound of—"

Another ball came. More fizz on this one. A loud cheer went up. The girl dropped the bat, clenched her fists to her side and screamed something about head-shots. JJ tooted his whistle twice and strode to the mat with his hand up in the air.

"Get off the field of play, Charlie. Go and stand over there on the sidelines with the subs and I'll deal with you later."

Charlie threw his hands up and stomped off. JJ knelt down by the girl whose face was all ready shining wet with tears. He chatted softly to her for a minute and then tapped her twice playfully on the chin. There must have been witchery in his whispers because when she retrieved the bat her eyes hinted of revenge and her lips struck up a feisty grin.

"Nicely handled," I said, when he'd jogged back to position. "What did you say to her? Some of Bull's pre-match specials?"

"I don't have time for you, Ben. There's a load of primary school rivalry playing out here. Lots of grudges being settled."

The sponge ball came floating through the air once more and the batter missed it by a county.

"It's dangerous stuff, all right," I said. "Real gangland brutality."

JJ tutted. "Don't belittle their efforts, Ben. Criticism at this age can crush confidence—not to mention their sense of adventure. Why don't you go back the way you came and leave me be? I'll catch up with you later."

Normally a jibe like that wouldn't have fazed me one bit, but the last few hours had mushed the confidence in me. I could have said how I was only hopping the ball, how I wasn't exactly screaming obscenities at them, how only the two of us were actually privy to the thing in the first place. I could have said all that, but I didn't, because my mouth caught a dose of verbal diarrhoea.

"I'm adopted," I said, spewing out the words like a greasy sweet.

The whistle slipped from his lips. "Is that what your parents wanted to talk to you about?"

I nodded.

"Right." He ran onto the field, caught the ball in mid-air and pocketed it. "That's it. Game over, line up with your buddies and prepare to sound off."

A chorus of moans rose up from the throng of kids.

"But we've only started," one said.

"And I didn't get a go at batting yet," said another.

JJ grabbed the groaners, paired them off with one another and clapped his hands to spur on the rest. "Come on, guys, rain is on the way."

"So?" Charlie said. "Rain is always on the way."

"It's time to have your lunch."

"Again?"

"Yes, again. Line up in twos behind the plate."

"It's a cone."

JJ patted him on the head and guided him forward, pairing him off with the pigtailed girl, who nearly wilted when she saw her partner.

"Be sure to pop 'power of observation' on your CV, Charlie. But in the meantime, get in line."

I strode over to JJ and grabbed him by the arm. "You don't have to stop the game. We can talk right here."

"No, we can't. This is huge, Ben."

It was either his placid tone or his doe-eyed stare, but I immediately understood why miss pigtails piped down.

"It is a bit of a shocker, if I'm honest."

"Mon-u-mental...we'll talk in the cafeteria. Can you pick up the cones and bits and shepherd them from the rear for me? And watch out for Dan there." He pointed to a blond-haired boy with a cast on his arm. "He likes to climb things that move. Don't you, Dan?"

Dan stared up at me with a sure-you-know-yourself look on his face. "Vans," he said. "I like to surf vans."

A few minutes later and we were all crammed into the café. Myself and JJ sat at the end of a long line of fold-up tables and plastic chairs with my ears ringing from the incessant chatter of the kids. It had a greasy-spoon reek to the place and a menu primarily composed of chips and meat, or meat, or just plain chips. Naturally, with a menu like that, it was jammed.

The waitress wasn't half bad, though. A foxy firecracker with a touch of meanness in her face that said she'd be game-ball for some freakiness. Despite the sincere way JJ'd ran in here to discuss my recent revelation, I was beginning to suspect he'd ulterior motives.

He'd spent the first ten minutes perched on the edge of his seat, trying to catch her eye, looking every inch the bunch of useless he was when it came to luring women.

I waved to get her attention, not wildly, though, just a brief flick of the finger as cool as you like. With a roll of the eyes over she strolled, hips all east-to-west, stilettos clicking, and her pad drawn out at arm's length like a shield.

"What'll it be?" she said with a bored drawl to her voice.

"Two white coffees, please." JJ said.

I smiled briefly.

She nodded at the rabble behind. "And this lot?"

"They're grand. They've packed lunches, so only tap water, if you wouldn't mind."

Game over, already. The tap water was the clincher. She clucked at the word.

"Busy in here today?" he said.

She didn't answer, hell she didn't even acknowledge him. She turned away and drifted to the next table, ripping the smile off his face as she went.

"So that's why you wanted this summer gig?" I said.

"That?" His eyes zoned in on her all needy and wistful. It was a cringe-worthy spectacle. I'd seen people rattle cans with more pride. "She's all right, I suppose. But don't forget the six pounds an hour they pay me."

The doorbell chimed and in strutted a lad wearing all the right brands and a blaggard's smirk. Pure flash Dan, this fella. The waitress cottoned onto him fast, snapping around the second her womb sensed his wallet. Her fingers caressed her neck, a touch of red raised up in her cheeks. I didn't need any more than that. Subtle as a boot in the head, this lass. Poor old JJ was on a hunt to nothing.

"Don't think she's the one, JJ, if I'm honest. You get anywhere with her?"

"It's a work in progress. Playing aloof at the moment. Playing it cool."

"Bet she doesn't even know your name."

"Course she does."

I raised an eyebrow, and he chuckled low in his throat.

"Anyway, we didn't come here to discuss my love-life." He shuffled his seat forward and laid his palms flat on the table. "Are you actually telling me that Peggy and Pat adopted you?"

I nodded.

He blew out his cheeks and shook his head gently. "What is it with the adults in our world?"

"I know, right? First your dad and then my—"

JJ raised a hand. "I'll have to stop you there, Ben. You know we don't mention the man."

"Fair enough."

"You all right, though? Head's a bit all over the place, I'd wager. I know it took me a long time to process the loss. You know, to start the whole charade again. To get on with living."

"I'm nowhere near that point, JJ. Too many unanswered questions."

"So what do you know?"

I told him the whole sorry tale, about my parents' botched attempt at telling me, about Nell and her crankiness, about Father Malachi Brogan and his recruitment drive avoidance tactic. That made JJ laugh all right. And then I told him about Barnamire, my only lead, my only raggedy clue I had for my efforts.

"Not much then?" he said.

"Nope."

"And I'd bet my bottom dollar these blessed creatures up Barnamire won't be too willing to dole out their little secrets in a hurry. And it's also probable that certain files won't reach their new destination intact."

"What do you mean by that?"

"Ah, don't be so naive, Ben. Adoption is a sore point in this country. Wouldn't surprise me in the least if the church decided to do a bit of shredding to cover their filthy little secrets." He points his finger at me. "Like you."

A sigh escaped my lips at the statement. I'd no idea what they'd do, but there was a hint of truth in his foreboding all right. I clasped my hands behind my head. "Not very many options left to me, though. Are there?"

"No, I suppose not. So...you actually want to hunt your real parents down, then?"

I nodded.

"And what are you going to do when you see them?"

I shrugged. "All I've got so far is an overwhelming urge to punch them in their noses."

"It's a stout plan. But what can I do?"

"You can be my wingman. I'd say I've a need for one of those for this. Religion isn't my forte."

"And my wheels?" he said, like the super sleuth he was. "You need my Fiat also I imagine."

"Yeah, that too. But it'd be cool if you could tag along. Maybe bring some money also?"

"Say no more, bud. I'll be there with bells on." The

waitress returned with a pot of tea and a steam-free coffee without even a lick of milk in it. JJ's eyes met mine, and I shared his defeated smile.

"But first," he said, "we have to play in the final tomorrow."

"Screw the match. This is far more important."

"No match, no JJ. No JJ, no wheels," he said in that matter-of-fact way he used when dictating to the kids.

He had me there, in fairness, the fat Mary Poppins.

Chapter 7

Mick "the Bull" Goggin stood in the centre of the dressing room, with a team sheet in one hand, a hurley in the other and his face sanguine. Rumour had it he'd confirmed the nickname upon himself years ago, but in comparison to my freakishly large teammates sitting on the benches beside me there was certainly nothing bullish about his stature.

He stood at just over five feet tall and possessed a weedy, wiry build. His hairline had receded decades ago, leaving only a few wisps of hair flailing about his head as evidence of their departure. We'd counted five of them, but God bless him, he must have loved the illusion they created, because he nurtured the poor strands until they grew to nearly a yard long and arranged them in a webbed scrawl on his head. It was shameful, really, to watch a grown man studiously fix his comb over by licking his hand and smoothing it into place—only to have the whole crop of hairs flap about his skull in the mildest of breezes.

A right poor excuse for a human being he was, and he notoriously hated every inch of land and anyone who'd ever had the audacity to breathe a single breath in Glenbridge, including his mother.

"Right, lads," he said. "You're already wearing the jerseys, so you know your positions, but for the benefit of the many among you who are a bit weak in the head,

I'll run through the team sheet."

He rattled off the team, barking the usual orders and threatening violence if his tactics were ignored. He cajoled and screamed in the same breath, and he swung the hurley at our fullback's head, stopping just short of his nose. There was no one on earth that quite matched our Bull in the dressing room before a championship match.

JJ sat opposite me playing the lickspittle serf as usual. He tested the spring in his hurley by bending it both sides—something you did when you were twelve, until you broke your favourite hurley because you hadn't figured out that ash was wood and wood could break.

Next, he clicked the visor of his Micro helmet shut, before finally drenching himself with a bucket of icy water and stretching his quads, or his glutes, or whatever those muscles are called that make you pose like a yoga instructor to work them. In fact, watching him readying himself for the match, I reckoned he was a high-five away from turning all-American.

I had to admire his dedication to the whole pantomime, though. For try as I may, all I kept thinking about was sixty minutes and we'd be out of there. Two tortuous thirty-minute halves, and we'd be off up the road into Cork chasing down my shambolic parents.

"The halfbacks are Mulls, Stacky and Jezz," Bull said, snapping me out of my reverie. "Now, Jezz, you may be borne from a gypsy brood, but whatever you do, will you mark your man and stop wandering away up the field like you're looking to pitch camp? You're there to stop scores, not notch up your own. If I see you anywhere near the halfway line, I'll replace you. Got it?"

He paused for a moment as the door of the dressing

room whooshed open, and the unmistakable figure of Father Malachi Brogan ghosted in all collarless and casual. The room quieted as he strode from player to player, flicking a bottle of the holy stuff at them and mumbling some words of protection, before shuffling back to the far corner of the room.

"That's just the job, Father," Bull said. "May the saints preserve us." He raced through the sign of the cross, before turning about on his heel and squatting down next to me. "Now onto midfield. This one is controversial due to the fact Benjamin here thought himself too fine a player to bother traipsing up the field to train with us for the last few weeks. But he's playing at number nine today because—despite the fact he's a lazy so and so—it's the championship, and we've to field our strongest fifteen. All right?"

"Grand," I said.

"And none of your dainty steps and solo runs, Benjamin. Keep the ball moving into the forwards. If I catch you showboating, I'll personally come on to the pitch and flake the legs off of ya."

"Got it, Bull."

He jumped back up and clapped. "And, JJ, you're playing alongside him, and your job is to make sure he doesn't get creamed by Humphreys."

A ripple of sniggers and taunts broke out.

"I can take care of myself," I said. "I don't need baby-sitting."

"Oh, don't you? Now aren't you a fiery lad all of a sudden. Well, why don't you go out there and prove that on the pitch by wiping the floor with him like any self-respecting Whitehaven man would?"

Before I'd a chance to answer, the referee poked his head in the room and said, "Two minutes, lads."

"Right then. Up, up, up," Bull said, smacking his hurley against his palm. "This is it. Get up on your toes and jog on the spot."

The entire team, togged out in the blue-and-red stripes of Whitehaven, bolted up and jogged on the spot. The sound of studs clattering the concrete floor had a hypnotic effect on me. When Bull talked, the walls of the room seemed to resonate with the gravel in his voice. Outside, the crowd chanted for Whitehaven and applauded in step with us. When Bull smacked his palm once more, we cranked up the pace, edging ever closer to one another. Two more smacks quickly followed, and we closed the circle, huddling around him.

The atmosphere in that knot of players had an intoxicating charge to it. We all knew the team talk would come next—those final few words that'd have the soul design of ensuring we were driven into a hysterical blood lust. If Bull was on form we'd be leaping out of the doors and tearing the skin clean off of those Glenbridge boys, and there wouldn't be a doctor in the land that'd revive them.

My hand gripped the handle and boss of the hurley, and I welcomed that familiar feeling of adrenaline coursing through me. It was a Godsend that stuff. It never failed to steel my nerves and shore up my will before a match. In those last few moments in the room, I forgot about my adoption, I erased the noise in my head that bandied the word endlessly about and allowed myself to be swept up in the frenzy.

"This," Bull said, with his eyes wide and face livid

with sweat, "is the Minor Hurling Championship final. There'll be no second chances. By the end of today we'll either be winners or losers. We've not won a single cup since nineteen seventy-three." He paused for a moment to allow the fact to sink in.

"When you go out on that pitch I want you to run and chase and fight until there's not a whiff of air left in your lungs, and your legs burn, and your hearts burst. Since the days of Brian Boru, your forefathers have fought and died to give you the chance to play in this game today. And when we're finished with them, and their corpse of a team scuttle back to whatever rat's nest they scurried out from, the town of Whitehaven will drink to your deeds, the history books will regale our battle here today, and you'll go down in lore as the men who battered the Glenbridge Blues and ended our twenty-three-year drought. So...you will not run. You will not walk. But you'll storm out of these doors, hunt these Glenbridge devils down and drive them back to that feral pit of a town."

He broke away and stopped breathless. With a slew of tears welling up, his eyes shone, and the last few words burst from his mouth laced with spittle and raging hate. "Will you do it, lads? Will you do it for those brave souls who ran with only pitchforks against a hale of British cannon shot? Will you do it for yourselves and your families?" With one vicious swing he smashed the hurley into the ground, sending splinters of ash spinning into the air. "Will ye do it for Whitehaven town?"

The roar that answered him practically fractured the foundations. JJ grabbed me by the back of the neck and slapped my face. "You and me, Ben," he said, hitting me again. "We'll rule the midfield. Just like we always do."

Bull yanked open the door, and we burst out of the dressing room, surging outside like a pack of wolves chasing traces of blood in the air.

The minute the crowd spied us a tumultuous roar lifted from the banks. There must have been every man and his dog from Whitehaven lining the pitch. They stood at least ten bodies deep on steep slopes circling the grounds. A sea of hands rose up and clapped in rhythm to a booming bass drum on which some loyal soul thumped out a slow, carnal beat. The wall of noise flowed over and around me like an audible shield. It electrified the air, charging the hairs on my neck and jangling my senses.

I ran into the centre of the pitch and swung the hurley, swishing at the wind and feeling the weight and power of my stroke. A few zigzagged bursts tempered my nerves. As I stood facing the crowd, with the Atlantic winds ruffling my back, my chest puffed out in pride, and the whole of Whitehaven encouraging me, I was invincible, godlike.

Then the entire Glenbridge team strolled on to the pitch like they were out for a Sunday saunter. It was a queer sight given our team's state of mania to see our opponents turn up with the urgency of a challenge match. They lumbered off in various directions, some chatting and laughing, some knocking the sliotar back and forth between themselves, each of them indifferent to the hecklers in the crowd. And then, right at the tail of them, appeared Humphreys. With a cigarette clamped between his teeth, he walked straight towards me, his eyes zeroing in on mine.

The fizz in me flat-lined. Try as I might, there was something in his nonchalant manner that spoiled my confidence. It was the persistent stare that did it; it cut to my core. When he finally reached me, all I could muster was to stare at the clump of grass in front of my feet and wonder which one of my old injuries I'd resurrect first.

I never really knew why Humphreys had it in for me, but I remember when it started—the first day of Junior Infants. I'd been sitting at my wooden desk, with my maroon jumper and gun-metal grey slacks all shiny and new, arranging my pens and sharpening my pencils, when in walked a boy with a bull of a head, buzz-cut hair and nails bitten down to the quick. I smiled, he growled, and that was that.

"Oye, Patch," he said. "Have you gone all shy on me? Are you blushing?" He stopped a few feet short and flicked the cigarette at my face. "My mistake. It's just that period stain on your face. No make-up today?"

Same old Humphreys. He'd probably practised those lines all night hoping his sieve of a head wouldn't scatter them like marbles once he spoke. It was common-as-muck, ten-a-penny, brainless twaddle from a man who once gazed slack-jawed at the blackboard when the teacher told him he'd emerged into this world from his mother, and not, as he fancied, by descending on the wings of angels.

Normally, I'd have thrown some smarminess back at him. Riled him in order to throw him off his game. He was always wide open. But my brain had seemingly decided right then that my tongue was due a vacation. I stood silent and unmoved. All the shrill of the crowd and the frenzied excitement Bull infused into us had wasted my reserves. I was a flaccid old man in a whorehouse. Completely dejected.

"I see your bodyguard's nearby," Humphreys said, nodding at JJ. "You two are right fond of yourselves, aren't ye?" He stepped closer and rammed the edge of the hurley hard into my ribs. "Does he tuck you in at night too?" He grabbed me by my neck and tightened his grip. Before I'd a chance to free myself, he shoved me back, yanked my hurley out of my grip and whipped it across my shins.

Whoever engineered the human skeleton was a cynical half-wit. If you were going to create a bone so vital as a shin, wouldn't a world where gravity was in cahoots with rocks, and Humphrey-like Neanderthals roamed about cracking skulls demand a more intricate covering other than skin? The heavens and light, the moon and the stars were all solid design constructs fair enough, but shins?

I'd have gushed tears from the pain, if it weren't for the fact I'd somehow managed to locate a bit of pride. I clamped my teeth down, gnashed away until the blood roared in my ears and decided it sensible to make my escape. It was a tricky move to pull off, though, especially with mangled shins. I attempted to run, but it ended up being more of a stumble. Within ten yards, I collapsed onto my backside and let out a string of blasphemes.

"There you go again," JJ said. "Thinking that Ben here is your personal piñata." He thundered past with the momentum of a panzer tank, sending Humphreys sprawling onto the ground. Humphreys clambered back up, and they both ran at one another once more. The crowd had obviously been watching the ruckus because the harder the two of them went at it the louder the whistles and shouts grew, until they reached such a din that the referee finally turned around.

"Couldn't you two have waited until the match had begun at the very least?" he said, driving a hand between the two of them. "Consider this a warning, lads, and you're lucky I didn't see how it started." He fished about in his pockets, pulled out a sliotar and spat on it. "Right then, let's get this show on the road, and for the sake of the match report I'll be writing later, keep the violence to a minimum."

The referee checked his watch and raised the whistle to his lips. When he threw the sliotar in, it came low and slow, and I didn't get a sniff of it. Humphreys darted out in front of us and swung at the ball as it bobbled on the turf towards us. The sliotar fizzed up field and into the hand of their corner forward, who feigned left and right, before slotting it over the bar.

"No worries," JJ said, patting me on the back. "You'll get the next one."

I didn't.

The first half passed in a haze of mistakes. It must have been cringe-worthy to watch me flounce about the place like some half-witted foreigner swinging the stick for the first time. When I jumped to catch the ball, it squirted out of my fingers. When I dived to block a swing the follow-through crushed my knuckles. The only free I took was a simple twenty-one yarder. And despite the fact that a blindfolded child could have nailed it, when I struck the sliotar it ricocheted off the crossbar and spun harmlessly away for a wide. If I were a horse

I'd have been marched up to the knacker's yard and summarily shot. I was that bad.

When the referee finally blew the whistle signalling half-time, I remained in the centre of the pitch whilst the rest of the team ran to the dressing rooms. Not even JJ bothered to console me. In fact, the only player to speak to me at all was Humphreys.

"Pathetic," he said.

Within moments a different kind of chant swelled from the crowd. It started in just one or two patches at first, but like the bunch of woolly-headed sheep they were, the entire bank of spectators quickly joined in.

"Take Ben off...Take Ben off..."

The bunch of turncoats. One bad half and they were looking to lynch me. And by the sounds of all the laughter and jeering accompanying their request they were having a rare old time of it. All in all, I had to admit my day had rotted to its core. My pride was having whatever remained torn away by my family and friends in their catty little chorus line. So I decided the only sensible thing to do was to lie down, close my eyes and take a moment for myself.

"Stinking up the place a bit aren't you, Benjamin."

Dad stood over me beaming with his usual Barbour jacket tied up to his neck. He was always a cooler for my moods. And I almost fell for it. It was that weird confessional-box aura he had to him; those quiet eyes and hushed tones out of odds with the sheer heft of him. Throughout my childhood I'd watched in awe as he'd enter the chicken coop and calm the hens spooked witless by a mink with little more than a wave of his hand. But then I remembered what an almighty two-faced liar he was.

"Not now, Dad. I'm taking a moment."

He pulled me up, and we stood eye-to-eye as a cheer rose up from the crowd. Near the dugout, Bull handed the referee a piece of paper and waved me off the pitch.

"Well," he said, shrugging his shoulders. "Do you want me to drive you home?"

A clap of thunder sounded in the distance. I gazed out at the horizon where clouds closed ranks and rushed towards shore, sweeping the sun away. Even the heavens, it seemed, had lost interest in my day. I looked back at my dad as the gloom washed the light from his eyes and a chill nipped at my skin.

"I can't go home yet, Dad," I said, sighing.

"Why not?"

"Because I'm going to Cork city with JJ to hunt down my parents."

Chapter 8

There wasn't a single soul bar me left in the car park. I'd watched as the crowd dispersed, singing their heads off and yapping on about the game in intricate details. I watched the slow march of the grandparents as they waddled with their canes and walking frames, pausing every yard or two and nattering on in their own blissful way. I watched in horror as a group of kids piled into Don's minibus, praying he'd left his silver canteen at home. Hell, I was still there when the local bowsie boys, who were never keen on leaving anywhere before anyone else, drank the last dregs of their flagons, climbed into their Imprezas and wheel-spun away. On and on I waited, amid the gravel and the grass, hoping JJ would eventually arrive so that we could drive to Cork.

He was always last out of the dressing room. Many times I'd waited, dressed and dried inside there, watching him watching himself with his face puce from his half-hour shower. He'd mousse his hair and dawdle while it air-dried. Then he'd tousle it, gel it sparingly and dry it once more, before tweaking little strands into some pre-designated shape. JJ running through this obsesssive routine was a soul-destroying experience. And the hair was only the beginning. His wash bag was chock full of a zillion potions and lotions, each with their own specific purpose, and each to be used in his precise military order; myriad moisturisers, eye drops, hand cream, Cool Water, or whatever eau-de-pimp he'd convinced his mam to buy for him from the supermarket would all be teased out one-by-one, and rubbed or sprayed or coaxed into one part or another of him. "Something for the ladies," he'd say as he sprayed half the final bottle around his nether regions.

You'd imagine he'd feel a little nauseous after staring at the male version of his mam in the mirror for so long. They were identical, the two of them, with the same Greek nose, square chin and fluffy blond hair. Exactly the same. But he never saw it, and I never told him. I was good like that. Unless you counted that time when I was howling-at-the-moon drunk and made up a nice three-line ditty in Brehon's hammering home the resemblance until the entire pub sang along with me. It was the only time he'd ever punched me in the guts. And on his birthday of all days. I still hadn't forgiven him for it.

I sat up and turned off the radio. Normally, a good song would have lulled me into better form in an instant, especially in the bloom of summer. All it took was an arrhythmic beat, or a bright-eyed key change, and I'd have been hopping about in my head, imagining myself landing on a dance floor and throwing some shapes at some girls. But my head wasn't into it tonight. So I decided to lie back in my seat in the silence and wait some more.

"How do?" JJ asked.

The sound of his voice startled me. I opened my eyes and watched him slide into the passenger seat with a chirpiness that'd have you thinking he was medicated. He didn't just sit into the car, though, no, he practically floated. He was dressed in one of those loose linen suits with the sleeves rolled up. His mop of hair had been slicked back like some greasy eighties chancer, and the waft of cologne coming from him had me sneezing in fits.

"Who said you could drive my car?" he asked.

"Ah, go on. I need the practice. I've my test coming up in a month."

"Fair enough. But if you break it…"

"I know, I know. Anyway, what's with the get-up?"

"I'm trying a new look. Retro is *en vogue* these days, don't you know."

I laughed a mocking laugh. "The eighties were never in fashion. Not even in the eighties."

"We'll see…It's not every day that we get a chance to head up to Cork city. Those urban foxes like a bit of class."

I sighed at the statement. He was the consummate optimist when it came to his chances of seducing women. In all the time I'd known him, I couldn't remember him copping off with a single girl. And there were some right howlers in his back catalogue of attempts that'd have taken any fella rather than mope off home solo at ten-to-two.

"When we get out of this car you can walk ten paces ahead," I said. "I don't want anybody in Cork thinking I approve of you. Got it?"

He took a comb out of his pocket and drew it slowly through his hair. "Wouldn't have it any other way."

I revved the car, stuck it into first and sped out of the car park. Within a mile we were clear of Whitehaven, and its harbour slunk down behind hills. I clasped the steering wheel lightly and feathered it left and right in time with the bends. It was mesmerising, following the white broken line in the centre of the road as it meandered in sweeping curves up and around the coomb and over the Mackey Mountains. The higher we climbed the more the air roared through the car. It nipped at my back and billowed out my shirt, making me shiver.

"I can honestly say, Ben," JJ said, shouting over the roar of the wind. "That was, without exception, the worst display of hurling I've ever had the misfortune of seeing."

"Way to ruin the moment." I rolled up the window. "You don't so much as rain on the parade as blow the bloody floats up."

"And in front of the entire town."

"Enough."

"I fear you may never get laid again." He paused. It was one of those infamous JJ moves where he'd look at you with his eyebrows raised for about five seconds, before delivering whatever rubbish line he'd cobbled together in his head. "Nell would have done better. In fact, scratch that, anyone at all, from any walk of life wouldn't have choked as badly as you did today."

"Did we lose?"

"Nope, we scrambled a very undeserved draw. No thanks to you. Just so you know, though. Whatever lies ahead in this master plan of yours, I'm coming back for the replay on Wednesday."

"Ah, come on. You can't put a time limit on it. It could take us weeks to track down my parents. You can't just abandon me after a few days. What if we are hot on the trail? You're hardly going to make us run back for a pesky match. This is far more serious than a game of hurling."

"True, it is more important from a purely emotional perspective. But if you come at this from a logical position, and not your current one, which is borderline crazy, you'll find that the discussion is moot."

"And why's that?"

"Because, wherever your parents are on Wednesday, they'll still be there on Thursday. But come Wednesday evening circa seven, this final of ours will flit away forever, never to be seen or played again, confined to the annals of history. And I want to be in it, not reading about it. So you've three days. No more. Agreed?"

"Agreed."

The miles slipped past without further comment. After a while we came over the brow of a hill by the airport, and the city of Cork suddenly loomed up in front of us. Far in the distance, a brace of cargo ships sat docked in their port, their hulls lying low in the tarry waters of the River Lee. As I picked up speed, the city stretched out for miles around us, reeling me into her bosom. In comparison to our little village of Whitehaven the place looked gigantic, solid. It was as if the Lee valley where it sat had formed from the sheer weight of the place.

"Right we're here," JJ said. "Where's this nunnery?"

"Far as I know it's on the south side. We'll hang a right on the circular and follow the signposts. There are bound to be some, especially for a convent."

There weren't.

Hell, there wasn't even a sign for the city centre. I'd forgotten all about the country's tendency to hide the whereabouts of anywhere from anyone who didn't know where it was, especially if they wanted to get there in a hurry. Even if you happened upon some sign, you could be confident it'd been tweaked by the locals out of badness.

So we circled about Douglas for a bit and asked for directions, which would have had us in Mallow—if it weren't for me spotting the two teenagers sniggering in the rearview mirror. When we decided to change tack and ask some reliable looking elderly woman, she just swore at us. After about an hour of blindly touring the south side, I swallowed my pride and turned to JJ.

"Map?" I asked.

"If you must," he said.

We pulled into a filling station and purchased one that needed a degree in engineering to operate it. JJ secretly loved the whole thing. He inspected it first to see whether it opened like a fan, or whether the pages collapsed down on top of one another in some sort of origami-style puzzle. "It's an eight-page, double-sided, triple-fold variety. Or accordion style, if you like."

"Just tell me which way to go, and stop highlighting why you're still a virgin."

"Go that way," he said, pointing back the way we'd come.

Rows of Victorian mansions flitted by in a blur of colours. They were hulking three-storey houses with manicured lawns all stuffed with azaleas and fringed with tidy hedges. It wasn't long before the elegant street devolved. First came those pebble-dashed bungalows and, finally, to what could only be described as huts. There was no mistaking the place we were then. We'd heard horror stories of beatings and drug busts, of stabbings and floggings and vandalised headstones. The legend of the place was stained in bloodlettings and gangbangers. We had somehow entered Parkmore.

"We're in Parkmore, JJ."

"Probably not as bad as those reports make out," he said, without even taking a cursory glance out the window. "You know they're all right-winged, middle-class journalists perpetuating the myth of the place. Fear sells newspapers, and sales are all that count. I wouldn't pay it much heed."

"I'm not sure about that. The legend looks bang on so far."

On every T-junction hardy-looking men huddled together, peering out from underneath their hoods and spitting as we passed by. The farther down the road we went, the tetchier I became. Every few blocks a car would appear either burnt-out or still smouldering from the fire. We coasted past estates full of boarded-up houses with token patches of parkland in the middle.

The place must have been purpose-built and full of good intentions once upon a time. I could picture the town planners looking at the original scaled-down models, patting one another on the back whilst gushing over the square of field and pristine social housing solution. The figurines of families picnicking and playing and frolicking in the sun was how they hoped the place would be. I don't imagine for a moment they foresaw the locals burning and gouging the place up with wheel-spins and filling the green up with abandoned shopping trolleys and grim, mean-looking people.

When we stopped at a set of traffic lights, a group of about twenty men walked in front of us and stared for a second before crowding together. It was a surreal sight to behold, watching the hardy bucks of Parkmore shrugging and pointing and nodding less than ten yards away with only a windshield to protect me. I could almost hear them rattling off a checklist: car, check; two blow-ins, check; a dandy-looking fella reading a map, *kerching*. Hell, I'd have been disappointed if they hadn't carjacked us.

"JJ..."

No answer.

"You wouldn't mind hurrying up with the directions, because this lot look as if they're discussing which one gets to assault us first."

JJ finally took his face out of the map. "Oh..." he said.

"I need more than that."

"Turn back?"

"You're some man for a crisis, aren't you?"

I slipped the car into reverse and pressed down hard on the gas. "For a man with his head constantly in the clouds you're a useless co-pilot."

Chapter 9

Barnamire. We'd made it. We stood halfway up the drive and watched the place for a while as the water lapped on walls and a faint breeze whispered in my ear. The building itself was immense. Its red-bricked walls wrapped around the grounds and faced out towards the harbour. It stood three storeys high like some sentinel guarding against the city. I took a step forwards, and far across the water Shandon Tower rang out. They made ominous sounds those bells. Their deep notes echoed across the expanse and reverberated the air around us. When they clanged their seventh and final time, it seemed to me as if the city itself was warding me off.

I paused and checked my watch. "Seven p.m. Late enough. What do you reckon, JJ? Should we rock up to the front door and knock?"

I knew as much about nuns as the next Irish man. They were a right old enigma. We just assumed they were put on this planet to keep all the schoolgirls safe from the carnal advances of our kind.

"What time do nuns go to bed?" I asked.

"Well, I don't admit to knowing much about the diurnal habits of the Sisters of Barnamire."

"Don't you?"

"But I'd hazard a guess that right now they're partaking in vespers, after which they'll retire to the cloisters for quiet contemplation, before retiring for the night."

"You seem to know enough."

"I never really had much of a call to examine the specifics of each order of nuns. But those few I mentioned seem to be fairly standard."

I turned and stared at JJ, a quizzical frown on my face. "And how do you know that?"

"Mam used to be one."

"You're joking me? Mad Val?"

"Yeah, I know. Doesn't seem her thing does it?"

"You're telling me."

"She hadn't quite made the final profession, but she was there for a while in Wicklow all habited up in her wimples and scapulars."

"Let's sneak up and see what they're up to."

"Is that your best plan?"

"I think so."

We crouched down and skirted along the shoreline keeping low and out of the glare of the lights from the building. We were ghosts. Walking on soft grass, on flat feet, controlling our breath…Ghosts.

Click.

"Stop…" a voice said from behind. "Or I'll shoot ye both in yer scrawny bollixes."

It was a strange thing to hear; the click of what sounded like a safety clip being released and an order like that, especially when you were attempting to sneak up on some nuns. I'd this trippy image of turning around and seeing a burning bush with the face of Himself cackling away at the state of the two of us. Time creaked on and we stood statue-still. Barnamire was less than a hundred yards from our spot. I had an overwhelming desire to throw myself into the lap of the gods and race to the door. We were so close to the endgame. So bloody close to getting an answer.

"Don't even think about it, slim," the stranger said. "I'm still coming down from a nice little buzz, and I always get jittery with any sudden movements."

The squelch of boots on grass. Something cool and metallic pressed hard against my skull. I glanced at JJ and mouthed a quick "what-the…" at him. He didn't respond. He just kept staring at some fixed point in the distance with his brow furrowed and his lips rigid. I went to turn, and the same metal edge clunked twice on my head.

"Now, now. How's about you catch a dose of cop-on and raise your hands to the sky. You were doing so well, I'd hate to have to waste a bullet on you."

The thought of it zipped through my mind—a bullet exploding out my forehead, crimson mists trailing behind as my body slumped to the ground lifeless. I swallowed hard and raised my hands high.

"Good boy," he said, clipping the back of my skull. His accent was local Parkmore brogue and rapid-fire fast. If you hadn't caught on at the beginning of the sentence you'd never catch up. "So which one of ye dainty lads has the keys?"

"What keys would they be?" I asked, my voice about five octaves higher than usual.

He pressed the gun to my temple and counted down. "Three, two, one—"

"I do," I said. "They're in my left trouser pocket."

"A right smart boy, aren't you? You afraid of

numbers, though? I never said what'd happen when I reached zero, now did I?" He fumbled in my pocket and fished the keys out, before checking my right and removing my wallet.

"And what about *Miami Vice* here? I tells you, I like your suit." He patted JJ down and whistled when he found his wallet. "Jackpot. Where were ye going with all this mulla, lads? Don't answer, don't answer. It doesn't matter, but ta very much, though, for the donation. Now, turn around and take a good look at my face. I hate to have people thinking someone else held ye two fools up."

Standing less than ten yards away was the weediest looking man I'd ever clapped eyes on. He stood five feet tall at a stretch with a nervy gatch and had two identical totem-poles tattooed on both cheeks. In his left hand he held a gun that looked like one of those snub-nosed peashooters you'd see being drawn by a prostitute in the saloon of OK Corral. And all the while we gawked at him, he kept spinning the gun on his index finger and pointing it at the two of us. Spinning and pointing, spinning and pointing. Just like I did when I was ten, when I used to pop shots at my parents with my spud-guns.

"Now, first things first," he said. "Introductions...My name is Mossy Deane, or Apache, as I prefer to be known. Ye got that?"

"Got it," we said.

"What's my name?"

"Mossy Deane."

He switched off his smile and cocked the gun at us. "Are you trying to be smart? Didn't I tell you only a moment ago I preferred to be called Apache? I did, didn't I? I mean, it was you I was talking to, wasn't it? Unless there's some other long stringy piece of spaghetti and his weird-looking sidekick who just got done in a convent. Now...one more time, what's my name?"

"Apache," we said.

"Nice one. And ye two are?"

"You're not the brightest spark, Apache," JJ said. "Allowing us to readily ID you?"

"Oh, I don't plan on getting nicked. The Gardaí tend to let us be, you see. But reputation...now that's everything up these parts."

"So what is it you want us to do?" I asked. "Write you a reference?"

He smiled a crooked smile. "Nice one, nice and quick too. Bet that mouth picks fights your fists can't win."

I shrugged.

"Nah," he said, continuing. "No need for references. I doubt ye two would be able to keep your little experience here quiet once ye get back to whatever little culchie hole ye came from. And there's only one Apache in these parts."

JJ stole an inch towards him, fists clenching tight.

"This guy's baloobas, JJ," I said as quietly as I could. "Just leave it be."

"Baloobas is it, a bit whoop-dee-do in the noggin," Apache said. "You being smart are ya, being a right funny fella? I tell ye lads, I met a proper funny fella once. He wasn't laughing when I shot him, though. No, boys, there was no hooting then. So let me tell you who I am— I'm a goddamn Apache, got it? A joyriding, drug-peddling Sioux warrior. I'm the Lord of this manor and you're my bitches." He spread his arms out wide. "And all the world will know."

"You can't be a Sioux warrior and an Apache," JJ said. "They're from two different tribes altogether. The Apaches are native to the east coast—"

"Enough...I can be an Apache, or a Sioux, or a Red Indian, or a feckin' Eskimo crossed with a Chihuahua, or anything else I choose. And do you know why? Because I've got a gun."

"Fair comment," I said.

"I tell you what'd complete my day no end, though." He winked at JJ. "That suit...I love that suit. Cotton is it?"

"It's linen actually."

"Whatever...take it off. I think I'll have that and all."

"Ah for Jes—"

"Are you going to curse?" Apache asked. "Are you actually going to use a dirty expletive in front of the Lord God here in the holiest spot of Parkmore? You'd better tie that tongue of yours, before I do his bidding and gun the two of ye down here where ye stand."

JJ hacked a laugh. "And armed robbery isn't a sin?"

"Ah, not really. You see ye have loads of stuff that I need. So consider it as me rebalancing all the injustice in the world. I'm a social pirate, you see. A modern-day Dick Turpin."

"And I suppose," I said, "you could just sidle up to confession and ask for forgiveness whenever you fancy it?"

Apache tapped the barrel of the gun on his temple. "Now you're thinking. Catholicism is handy that way, isn't it? But I'll not be witness to any more blasphemous remarks. Ye two got that? Any more and I'll shoot ye in the face." He closed one eye and peered down the sights of the gun. He panned it slowly between both of us, before zeroing in on JJ.

"Boom," he said in a whisper. "Just like that."

"I doubt it," JJ said. "Not with that gun."

"Don't be mistaken by the look of her. She's more than fit for the job."

"What you have there, Mr Apache, is a single-shot muzzle-loading caplock pistol from the 1850s, typically holstered in the garter or the boot-heel of one of those notorious courtesans you'd find in a Wild West boudoir. Possibly a replica, but they're hard to come by. And of course the ammunition has to be custom made by a master craftsman. Which I am certain you are not."

He took a step towards Apache. "No...it's probably a fake. But even if it were the real McCoy, you'd only get a single round off. And unless you shot us in the face at close range, there's a good chance you'd barely clip us."

A broad grin erupted on Apache's face. "Well, would you look at this fella, going all Sherlock Holmes on me." He clasped both hands around the gun. The smile slipped from his face, and his eyes halved in size. "I dare ya to take one more step."

He did.

"Zero," Apache said and shot him in the face.

It seemed as if the entire universe held its breath in sheer shock at the viciousness of the moment. JJ lay face up on the grass with splodges of blood on his temple without a twitch or a cry coming from him. Thoughts swirled about my head, flitting in and out of focus. The savagery of it all had fried the circuitry in my brain leaving my mind to pinball about. All I could do was stare at my lifeless buddy and wait until I rebooted.

Within seconds, the echo of the blast had faded into the night, and the city hummed once more. Traffic rumbled on roads nearby. Muffled voices of deckhands in the port floated on the winds towards us.

The sound of laughter jolted me. I glanced up and spied Apache about thirty yards away. He backed off some more and chuckled to himself with a leery sneer playing on his lips. There wasn't a trace of fear in his eyes, not the faintest hint of remorse at what he'd done. He just held my stare and calmly reloaded the gun.

"Give me a second there, slim," he said. "And I'll dole you out some lead of your own."

He was only a slip of a man, and I had at least fifty pounds and youth on my side. If I could get to him I was going to trounce him, tear him into infinite pieces. In that micro-moment all the previous days frustrations jumbled together in my head—my parents and their lies, the bull-headed Humphreys, my life-long friend gunned down by a spindly gurrier. All of them played on a loop, fuelling the blazing hatred in me.

The nape of my neck tingled, and a chill shuddered down the length of my spine. I ran at him, closed on him fast, but he reacted with lightning speed. He backed up smoothly over the grass, slipped a bullet into the chamber and aimed. It was all one swift, effortless movement. Instinctively, I ducked and zigzagged in the hope of throwing him off. He tracked me patiently, left then right, as if he was just getting a feel for the rhythm of my movement.

"Zero," he said again.

I flung myself to the ground. The muzzle flashed, the gun snapped back, and the bullet fizzed overhead. He cursed and went to reload once more. I leaped up to my feet and charged in a straight line at him. He backed up again, but I was too close this time. He stopped, pocketed the gun and bounced from foot to foot.

With only yards between us, I raised my hand and swung at his face. He sidestepped right and chopped me into the throat with the edge of his palm. The blow hit with such precision and ferocity that it nearly knocked me back. My legs buckled, and I stumbled onto my hands. I crawled for a yard or two and then collapsed to the ground, wheezing and scratching at my neck.

The pain burned. I tried to breathe, to pull in any wisp of air, but nothing came. I tried to shout, to curse him and his brood to hell and back, but my voice stayed silent. My vision clouded in from the edges, and the landscape swirled into a fuzz of blacks and whites. I clawed at the grass and dirt, desperate to pull myself up. A knee dug into my back. The brute force of it pinned me back down, driving the last trace of fight out of me. A hand grabbed my hair and yanked my head up hard.

"All in all, a bad day out for ye boys," he said, coiling an arm around my neck.

The wet of spit on my ear.

Foul breath on my skin.

Then nothing.

Chapter 10

It was the sound of hushed murmuring that coaxed me awake. For a moment I assumed I was dead, that my awareness was my soul floating about in the ether of the afterlife, awaiting either a fall to hell, or a lift up to heaven. I felt cheated by the possibility of it all. Just as I was about to pull the curtain back to reveal my parents' true identities and punch them square in the nose, Himself had decided it was best to smite me. And in the grounds of a convent, no less. I had to give it to Him; He was a fair old operator.

I listened for a moment with my eyes still closed for fear of what I'd see if I opened them. The voices became clearer. The accent was local through-and-through, and the panic died down inside me. Not dead yet. Despite what the inhabitants of the place thought, I doubted angels came solely from Cork.

Something cool wetted my lips. A glass prised them open, and fluid slipped into my mouth. Water. It'd never tasted so sweet. I swished it around for a moment and swallowed in minute amounts. I winced from the pain in my throat and the banging in my head, and I retched. Despite the discomfort, I sipped some more. With every drop of the stuff, the life force flooded back into me.

The image of JJ lying lifeless on the dirt with blood pooling about him stole into my mind. I saw the face of Val glaring at me as I told her the how and the why her only son had been killed. My gut twisted in on itself, and a wave of nausea rose up from the pit of my stomach. She rarely believed any of my high tales, and I doubted she'd see anything but blame in my story. In that second, I thought of my parents and wished that the whole blasted reality could be rewound and forgotten.

An impossibly gentle touch grasped my hand, and someone whispered in my ear. "You're safe now."

Safe? In another moment I'd have laughed at the lunacy of the word. I pulled away from the grip and opened my eyes. Bright lights seared into them, blinding me for a second. The throbbing in my skull pulsed even faster. Shadowy figures moved above me, their faces hovering overhead still dark and featureless.

Nurses or doctors or both, I thought. I must be in the hospital.

I blinked and waited for my sight to adjust. Slowly, the wooliness in my head eased, and the faces came into focus. Nuns—fully habited and all—stood two deep at my bed.

"JJ..." My voice croaked. I slid off the bed feet first and tried to push my way through them. I glanced around the room, searching him out, but there wasn't a hint of him anywhere, only a cross on one wall and the usual picture of Himself on the other, with His arms outstretched and His Sacred Heart bursting from His chest.

Hands pulled me back and pinned me down. "Is that the man who was shot?" one of them asked, tucking me back under the covers.

"Yes, he's my friend. Where is he? What have you done with him? And why are we not in a hospital?"

"Oh, he's in the kitchen."

"You're keeping him in the kitchen?"

"And, of course, being Sunday night in Cork," the nun said, going on, "the ambulances were busy."

"Busy?"

"So they said."

"But...he was shot."

"So we said."

I lay back down aghast. I couldn't believe it. We'd been mugged, JJ gunned down, and the best this poor excuse of a county could do was leave us festering with some nuns who'd only a few parables and fairy tales at their disposal.

"But," I said, "what if—"

"Now, now," an older nun said. "If 'ifs' and 'buts' were candy and nuts we'd all have a merry Christmas. They can't just magic up a vehicle on a whim, now can they? They'll get here when they can, along with the Gardaí. You need to rest until they do. You took a nasty blow to the neck with your brawling."

"I bet it hurts a lot," another said, jostling through the rest for a front-row look at me. "Would you like something for the pain? I'm afraid all we stock is Paracetamol."

I looked at the gaggle of women with their crosses, simpering smiles and genteel faces, and a wave of frustration exploded inside me. "Can someone...please tell me...where my buddy JJ is?"

"We told you; he's in the kitchen. He's been in there for a while now. Making a bit of a mess mind you, but the whole incident seems to have given him a fair appetite."

"JJ's alive? But he was shot in the face. I saw him lying dead with my very eyes."

"The bullet only grazed his cheek, it was the fall that knocked him unconscious. He was up and about within minutes of us bringing ye two in here. Wouldn't leave the room. Kept pacing around telling us what to do. So we sent him off for some food to distract him."

JJ was alive? The pain in my head didn't matter anymore. I leaped up and ran out of the room. The convent was a maze of corridors and stairs with nothing to clue me into which way was right. Up and down the length of it were only plain oak doors and whitewashed windows. The only furniture was a bench jammed into one corner, placed there, I assumed, to give the nuns somewhere to kneel if the lust for prayer overwhelmed them.

They youngest appeared at the door. "Hush now," she said, glancing up and down. "Mother Superior gave strict instructions you were to stay in the room until the Gardaí came along."

"But I need to see JJ."

The rest of the nuns shuffled out of the room and crowded together. A chorus of whispers emanated from them. Every now and then, there was some tutting and a nod in my direction.

"All right, come along," one said. "We'll bring you there for a second. But you have to come straight back."

"Will do."

We marched for an age, past toilets and lecture halls, classrooms and bedrooms, hanging lefts and rights and up and down stairs. If it weren't for their guidance, I'd have been lost for days. It was a veritable labyrinth.

"Who designed this place?" I asked. "The Mad Hatter?"

"Close enough," one said. "The British."

That seemed to tickle their funny bone because they all giggled together and congratulated the comedian for her wit. As we passed under an archway and into the kitchen, I had to admit, I was beginning to warm to them.

I stopped when I saw JJ. He sat wedged in between two nuns at the table, with a lump of bread in one hand and slices of ham clutched in the other.

"Ah, Ben," he said, when he spied me. "Me old wing man. Back from the land of nod I see."

I walked around him and stared in disbelief. "You're looking fit for a corpse." I went to lift the bandage wrapped around his head, but he batted me away. "I know we were wondering how to get in here, but feigning your own death...now that was a stretch too far." No sooner had the words left my mouth than a chill cut through the air.

The nuns fell silent. They lowered their gazes to the floor and scattered away into the shadows. I turned to find a grey figure looming in the doorway. The wind swirled around her, ruffling the folds in her veil. Rain pelted her back in plump missiles, but she just stood still on the threshold gazing straight at me.

"'Get in here,' you said...to what end, pray tell?" she asked.

For a moment, I simply watched her. There was something familiar in her dour face and hawkish eyes. Dread fussed my insides, and I lowered my gaze. It was the same sensation I'd suffered as a child when I saw monsters in the shadowy recesses of the night. Only one thought took root as I fumbled with my birthmark—she was the key to unravelling my secret.

I stepped confidently forward and clasped my hands behind my back. "Mother Superior, I presume. We need your assistance in a sensitive matter."

The words hung in the space between us. Seconds ticked by, but the only sound came from the chatter of rain on stone and the rumble of distant thunder. She remained immobile, mute. Not a flinch of a finger nor flutter of lashes. If it weren't for the slow rise of her chest I'd have had her measured up for a casket. But her eyes were alive all right. She trained them on mine like a seasoned hunter staring down a scope. Finally, she stepped into the kitchen and unhooked her cape, dangling it out at arm's length until a nun whooshed in to take it.

"Do not hang it from its tag like a rag on the line, child." She held it out of her reach for a moment, before dropping it onto the eager nun's outstretched hands. "Place it on a hanger in the armoire this time."

"Yes, Mother Superior," the nun said, and she scooted out of the room.

I had to admit, she ran a tight operation. The nuns obeyed her every whim like they were galley slaves afraid of the whip. Good honest-to-God Catholic fear it was. And she wielded it with ease.

"There are processes, Benjamin," she said, running her hands over her sleeves. "Rules, if you like, for approaching this convent and requesting our assistance in such delicate matters."

The mention of my name threw me for a second. I

touched my face again. It must have been the birthmark. Judging by the wizened face on her, she'd probably been persecuting the diocese for decades.

"How do you know my name?" I asked.

The hint of a smirk tugged at her lips. "Let's not frazzle your little brain with such mysteries." She glanced at the clock. "By my reckoning you have about ten minutes before the Gardaí arrive to collect you both. So, let us make the most of your impromptu visit and continue this chat in my office. We can assume, at least, a degree of formality and decorum, both of which are sadly lacking right now. So please tag along, and make sure you walk in silence behind me."

"Both of us?" I asked, nodding at JJ.

"Yes, both of ye. I do not want any more distractions for the sisters tonight. Come along."

We fell in step behind her, watching her move in her weird little way. There was no patter or shuffle of feet, no bounce in her step nor swish of her hips. She just glided across the polished marble like a spectre on tracks. And all the while we followed in her wake, around countless corners and up and down stairs, we didn't share a word or a glance between us. I'd been in funeral corteges with more spunk in them.

The further we travelled the more I became aware of the lack of life in the convent. There wasn't a potted flower or vase on a sill. The only items decorating the walls were biblical scenes, and the obligatory Padre Pio portrait with his hands bandaged and that "why-me?" look of anguish etched on his face. But it didn't surprise me really, given the sanitised manner to her. I imagined anything resembling colour and fun would have been immediately choked on the stalk on first sight.

We kept travelling up into the eaves of the building. The black, trussed ceilings hung lower with each step, giving the gloom of the hallway a claustrophobic quality to it. We stopped outside a set of doors housed in granite. Their panels were vertical strips of oak, gnarled and blackened at the edges. She pulled out a set of keys from underneath her habit and opened the right one up.

For a moment, I expected a colony of bats to scream out overhead, but the only noise that greeted us was the needle of an old gramophone clicking back and forth, trying to find its groove. She stood aside and gestured us in. JJ stepped in first and walked straight towards the sound. He lifted the needle gently and placed it back on its hook.

"An original HMV model," he said, nodding solemnly, as if he gave two flutes about it.

She paused and studied him for a moment. "Well, how clever your clogs must seem. I wish you could have put that brain of yours to work earlier and not made such a pig's mess in the kitchen. Sit down please, before your paws smear the shellac. After surviving two world wars and the equivalent of four of your lifetimes, I would hate to have it ruined by an over-eager know-it-all."

Any enthusiasm JJ had dissipated in an instant. He shuffled from foot to foot unsure of what to do, as if her disdain had rendered him demented. He'd played the same old card with my folks on many an occasion. He'd gush over an heirloom from some long-forgotten life of theirs, peddling his usual tripe about the quality of all things old, and they'd bask in the moment, nodding away and wondering why I wasn't as well-reared as him.

We took our seats on the stools opposite her desk. Even in that short time, I sensed a tactic at play. There was a gulf between the two sets of furniture. Where we sat on cheap pine stools, she'd one of those buttonholed chairs with the wings wrapping up around her head that'd lull you to sleep with one hug of its leather. Where we had the obligatory reed cross to gawk at, she'd the whole sweep of the courtyard and waters and twinkling city lights to view. Like any decent fighter she'd the height advantage all right, and judging by the cane lying on her desk she'd probably the reach to boot. It was an effective ploy, but I had her number.

"It was Father Malachi Brogan who informed you, wasn't it?" I asked, jumping straight in.

She smiled a cautious smile and placed her palms down on the desk. "Well, well, Benjamin. I must say you are full of wondrous reveals today. Such blinding insight. Truly wonderful. Yes, it was our esteemed Father Brogan who had the wherewithal to let me know you may be rushing up here to seek out your parents. But, if truth be told, we had hoped you may have had the good grace to educate yourself on the appropriate policies here, and made an appointment during normal working hours."

"Well, we had kind of—"

"What age are you now? Eighteen, nineteen?" she asked.

Her voice was mocking. It practically dripped from her tongue with each word that spilled from her mouth. I squirmed on the stool. My hand grazed its edges, catching a splinter. The sharp pain edged me to anger. I'd come here with good reason. She was the one in the wrong. She was part of the troupe of liars that had redesigned my life, wrapped me up in swaddling and handed me to strangers.

"Given how clued in you are already," I said. "I'm fairly certain you know I'm eighteen."

She slammed her palms on the desk and bolted out of the chair. "I'll let you know what I know, if I feel you have a need to know it." She grabbed the cane and paced back and forth behind us, smacking it into her hand.

My heart didn't jump, it fairly seized in my chest. Jesus, she didn't just have a short fuse, she'd none at all. I slouched down on the stool and waited for a caning. My jaw hung slack from the shock of it. Mental, that's what she was.

"Can I just apologise on behalf of my friend," JJ said. "He's a bit stressed out at the moment and hasn't really been himself. We know you're a very busy lady and—"

"Enough. No more vacuous platitudes."

"Yes, ma'am."

"Now, as I was saying, I will hazard a guess that you would have celebrated this illustrious passing into manhood by having the news of your adoption revealed to you...Yes?"

"That's right." I said.

"And in a flurry of righteous indignation, you took it upon yourself to flee from your duplicitous parents with immediate effect, setting off to uncover the truth as soon as was convenient for you. Yes?"

"Em, yes, more or less."

"And through no fault of your own, you managed to

get your friend here shot, assaulted and robbed, and scare the wits out of our sisters, whilst your adopted parents are left spitting in the wind until you decide to come back, or not, depending on how wonderful your meeting with your real parents may pan out. Is that about right?"

"Well, not really."

"Oh, come along now, Benjamin." She stopped pacing and whispered into my ear. "I must say I do not blame you really, knowing what I do of your ignominious beginnings. But let us just say, the apple really does not fall far from the tree."

"Now that's a bit harsh," JJ said suddenly. "We were—"

"Was anyone addressing you?"

"No, ma'am."

"Then be quiet."

"Yes, ma'am."

"Now, before we go any further." She returned to her seat, laid the cane to one side and closed her eyes. Then she breathed out in one long, continuous breath and opened them once more. The flush drained from her cheeks, and her lips twitched into a plastic smile like some second-rate actor on cue. "Would you like to know the real protocol for acquiring the information I have in the room next door?"

"I thought we could ask you," I said. "And you'd kind of tell us where my parents live?"

She laughed. Or at least, I assumed she laughed; it was more of a piggish snort, as if an alien had possessed her and was still getting to grips with the machinery. "Not quite. First you need to take your identification, driving licence or passport, and your birth certificate to the local authorities."

"But they're in my wallet, which was robbed by—"

"They will then process the application through the correct channels and contact us. Well...me. I shall ensure the paperwork is bona fide, cross-referencing it with our own records here. On completion of this process I shall draft a response to the local authorities, who in turn will draft a response to you outlining what information we have and what information you are allowed to have."

The more she prattled on, the more I realised that she was taking too much pleasure in it. She'd wrap my application in mountains of bureaucracy.

"And how long will that whole process take?" I asked.

"Oh, we really are getting better at the whole merry-go-round. But I am sure you appreciate the sheer number of enquiries we get here from places as far remote as the West Indies makes it impossible for us to return any request for information quickly."

"How long?"

"Our quickest time yet? Six months."

"Six months?" I couldn't believe it. I jumped up and swore.

My reaction didn't faze her one jot. She sat back, placed her head on the leather headrest and drummed her fingers on the arms of the chair. "And that doesn't take into account the possibility of a no-contact request being made."

"So you're telling me," I said, my face hot from the fury of it all. "After all this time and effort, I might not have any chance of finding my real mother and father anyway?"

Before she could answer, someone knocked twice at the door. She rose and walked over to it, pausing for a moment. "Possibly not, but that is the wondrous nature of life—you may be participating in the game of life, my dear Benjamin, but others are rolling your dice."

She yanked it open, and two guards stomped into the room. I recoiled when I spotted them. They'd the look of men lured down from the mountains by the scent of meat. I'd seen plenty of these types before; loved the city beat they did, what with the violence and buzz of kicking fifty shades out of some young fellas for simply messing about. They probably did it for fun until they'd discovered the Gardaí would pay them for it.

They stood for a second and surveyed the room. They were dressed in the usual Gardaí outfits—high-visibility rain jackets tied up to their chins, utility belts, and caps perched on top of buzz-cut heads. No stab vests for these boys, I reckoned, far too hard.

They were a rare breed of gentlemen, all right. And judging by the way they made a beeline for JJ and myself, I'd a notion that they weren't here to see whether we needed any medical intervention. The first one grabbed me by the wrist and swung me around. He forced my elbow up to my neck, rushed me to the wall and slammed me into it.

"What the hell is wrong with you?" I asked. "We were the ones mugged and nearly killed."

"Quiet, now, smart boy." He slipped his boot between my feet, parted my legs and frisked me. He rummaged up and down my sides, along the length of my arms, patting away, desperate to find something.

"You'll find nothing on me. We were the ones robbed at gunpoint. We're the victims here."

He slapped the back of my head. "I said shut up, smart boy."

I squirmed when his hands ran up the insides of my legs and under my belt. I turned for a second as Mother Superior stood by my side with a savage little smirk on her face.

"Unsolicited visitation," she said in a tone haughtier than ever, "after the official hours of business will be treated as trespassing. And trespassers will be prosecuted. Plus, as I mentioned to our two Garda friends here, when our sisters heard the gunshots we feared for our lives, and although it's not a crime to scare, it surely is against the guiding principles of Christianity to torture the wits out of us poor servants of God. And to that there must be an answer. Am I correct in my assumptions, Garda?"

He finished frisking me, slapped on some handcuffs and yanked me back from the wall. "That you are, Sister. Whatever these two latchicos were up to, we'll get to the bottom of it. Rest assured." He spun me around. "Now the good news, smart boy." He shouted towards JJ, who had the other Garda's knee on his head. "And this is for the benefit of both of you. I am arresting you on suspicion of trespassing with intent under section eleven of the Public Order Act of nineteen-ninety-four. You have the right to remain silent, anything you say, or do, will be taken down and may be used as evidence."

He marched me to the door, stopping at the threshold for a moment. "Rest assured, Mother Superior," he said. "These two won't be bothering anyone, anytime soon."

Chapter 11

Sunday night must have been fight night in Cork, because when we arrived at the station the place teemed with drunken yobs, bleeding and screaming their heads off. And the rancid smell of the place. There was sick in the corner, sick on laps and a patch of urine pooling about one lad's feet.

JJ and myself sat on a bench with our hands purple from the handcuffs, waiting for our turn at the booking booth. Judging by the numbers, we'd be there a while, but that wasn't in any way the worst of it. Our arresting officers had decided to upgrade the experience to torturous by hemming us in between two of the rowdiest girls I'd ever clapped eyes on. They'd had a go at breaking the ice with us by spitting, crying, swearing and making up with each other, whilst all the while trying to jam their tongues down our mouths. And God, of all the girls I'd cosied up to in my time, these two scored top-trumps for mouldy. Scrawny limbed, pockmarked ladettes with faces on them like they'd caught a dose of the plague. I spent the whole time wishing Apache'd had the foresight to shoot me in the head.

"It's only a bit of jailhouse fun, Ben," JJ said, luring his one up onto his lap with a nod. She'd one of those sashes draped around her that said "Bride in training" and had angel wings strapped to her back. Bláthnaid was her name—pronounced "Blaaaaw-nid"—and a fine traditional one it was at that. But I didn't imagine when the priest poured holy water over her infant brow that he'd have signed her up if he could catch a glimpse of her now, especially as the name meant flower.

"She's a game girl," I said, struggling to find anything else of worth in the moment, but JJ didn't have a chance to respond. The instant she mounted him, they locked lips in a blur of slobbers.

"Did you hear her telling me how *garjess* I look in my suit?" he said, briefly coming up for air.

"She'd cop off with your granny, that one." I said.

"You got a granny?" Bláthnaid asked.

"I do," he said. "Two of them."

"God, I loves men who got grannies..." And off she went again, snogging and grinding into him like one of those terriers humping a leg. The lads opposite us spotted the display and jeered. Within seconds, two female guards rushed over, yanked the two girls up and frog marched them both away.

I finally relaxed and turned to find JJ staring at me with an eyebrow cocked high and a smug grin on his face.

"Has it been that long since you scored?"

JJ jostled his shoulders. "I suppose being shot in the head makes you more aware of the frailty of life. Carpe diem and all that."

"And why so bloody perky? Take a look around, will you? We've been mugged, shot, arrested, and, by my reckoning, the hunt for my parents has come to a dead end."

He sighed one long, low time and fell into a contemplative silence. The bandage hung loose from his ear and flapped with every movement of his head. Patches of dried blood and mud stained his suit, and every time he turned around, I could see a lump on his skull the size of a baby's fist.

"Oh, I don't think we can write that off just yet," he said.

"And how do you figure that?"

I opened and closed my fingers a few times to try to get the circulation back into my hands. No joy, though. Despite my efforts, I couldn't even wiggle my wrist free. All I managed to achieve was a dose of pins and needles. The cuffs seemed welded to my bones.

"My birth cert is gone, ID gone, money gone, judging by where we are our freedom could be gone. Zip, zilch, zero. That's what we've got. Even if we get out of here now with it all in our possession it'd take six months to get any information in the first place." I looked to the heavens and sighed. "Six lousy months. And that'd only match the record, apparently."

He angled his head towards me and whispered. "How badly do you want to find them?"

"You know the answer to that."

"Well, you're ignoring one obvious, though slightly questionable solution. We steal the information."

"Steal the information?" I rolled my eyes and shook my head. "That's the obvious fix for two young fellas sitting in a Garda station awaiting a trespassing charge is it?"

"Well, as I said, I'm here until Wednesday, after which you're on your own. Logic dictates if you want to find them in the next few days—robbing the info is the only solution. However canny Mother Superior is, she did let it slip when she pointed out that the room next door held the pertinent information. And anyway, it's hardly a crime if you only take what's rightfully yours."

"So you're suddenly a master criminal? How do you propose we do it then? I don't know about you, but I'm fairly ropey when it comes to breaking into convents and nicking stuff."

"Just happens I was mulling that over—"

"Were you? Whilst you were scoring with Bláthnaid, I suppose?"

"Correct. And I concluded that we're equally crap at burglary." He bowed down closer. "But riddle me this. Who do we know, from our most recent history, who appears astute at the whole mugging, stealing and criminal behaviour kind of thing?"

I stifled a laugh. "No way, JJ. Apache's a maniac! He nearly murdered us both."

"Think on it for a second. He may be mental, but I reckon if he wanted us murdered we would be. And money does seem to form the cornerstone of his motivations."

"Something we don't have."

"A minor detail. He's a thug for hire. No doubt about it. And anyway that Mother Superior...I don't know about you, but she kind of has it coming. Don't you think?

"Definitely."

"So again...the question is, quite simply, how badly do you want it?"

I sat back against the wall and closed my eyes, breathing deeply through my nose and trying to block out the racket around me. JJ's plan was anything but easy. Bribing Apache to help us? It was a fantasy. In that poxy booking room, with my head lifting from the pain, and the hallions of Cork for company, I briefly wished to scuttle back to Whitehaven. It'd have been so easy, but then I recalled those faceless ghosts of my adopted parents and Mother Superior's irksome smile, and an overwhelming desire to see them suffer surged up inside me.

I butted my head against his. "I'm in."

"Excellent."

"But first we need to get the hell out of here."

He stared straight at me, and I felt what twins must feel when they claim they're psychically connected.

"Call him," I said.

A single, curt shake of his head. "I am not calling my dad."

"He's our only way out of here tonight. And you're still seventeen, technically a minor. The minute they cop on to that they'll be ringing Val."

He looked away and banged the back of his head against the wall. "They will. Won't they?"

"And Val will definitely ring my pair. And you can't be having the three of them traipsing up here in the dead of night, bailing us out of jail after being shot at and arrested for trespassing in a convent."

"They'll probably only slap a caution or a fine on us, if we shut the hell up and behave."

"They're obliged to ring your parents, JJ." I dropped my voice down low. "You know it's a fact."

He didn't respond. He nibbled his lower lip in the way he did when he was nervous until a Garda loped over and dragged me up by the cuffs.

"Come on, your turn to have a little chat," he said and shoved me through the throng towards the desk.

"Call him, JJ," I said over my shoulder. "You know it's for the best."

Chapter 12

Garda P. Byrne was the arresting officer's name. I'd no idea what the P stood for, but it was certainly not for pleasant. He was the same hands-on savage who'd roughed me up in the convent. And I must say, this whole questioning thing had ground him down a tad. He'd been going at it for about an hour now, wandering down the same dead end, and he was a far cry from the man who'd entered. He practically skipped in all kitted up with a face full of smiles and friendly chatter, holding brimming mugs of tea for the two of us—as if we were two auld biddies about to catch up on the goss.

"Don't worry," he'd said. "Sure, we'll be done in a jiffy." He clicked on the tape recorder and peppered me with questions about the shooting. Why were we there? Who else was with us? Where were our wallets? What'd we do with the gun? How did we get there? On and on he went, one after another, a never-ending series of questions to which I mostly answered "no comment." Name and address were the only tidbits I'd let him harvest from me.

"What do you mean 'no comment'?" he asked, for about the twentieth time. He must have ploughed a groove in his skull from the way he kept sweeping his hand over it. "This is an informal interview. Not an official statement. You haven't even been cautioned."

I gestured once more at the tape recorder and slowly shook my head. "No comment."

To be fair, my approach was a bit of a bluff. I'd no notion how long they could keep me, but so far there was only one pertinent fact—they hadn't actually charged me. It didn't take a genius to figure out that they'd had little in the way of any hard evidence to corroborate our apparent intent to cause criminal damage, or harm, or whatever other trumped-up charge they'd imagined for us. This whole event was little more than a fishing expedition. JJ was right about it all. Yes, we were trespassing, but criminal intent? No chance.

"Look, it's clear as day you two were in a ruckus, at least tell me who did this to you. You said you were a victim earlier, tell me about that then."

I was still in the same position I'd adopted since he arrived—leaning forward with my hands clasped, staring straight past him. After every question I'd busy myself tracing shapes from the stains on the wall until I decided to answer.

"No comment." I said again, my voice the same monotone drone.

"We haven't even charged you yet. Tell us what went on, and we'll have you chasing skirt around Cork within the hour. The sooner you answer, the sooner you can go."

"No comment."

He stretched his head back and stared at the ceiling, the sinews in his neck pulling taut against his skin. He was an easy read. His face was a colour-coded chart to his mood. Pale, then puce, then purple. He'd raced through them all. I was no psychologist, but even to my eye he was fit for bursting. He hung his head low for a while and hunched up his shoulders, his back rising and falling with each lungful of breath.

"You listen here," he said, hissing the words. "If you don't start answering some of my questions you'll be locked in here for the next twenty-four hours." He stood and paced around. "Administrative delays are an inevitable complication of a short-staffed station. If you don't cooperate with us, I'll have no other option other than to place you in the holding cell until I get around to processing you."

I tilted back onto the hind legs of the chair, stifled a yawn and let my gaze wander. A single bulb dangled on a cord from the ceiling. Every time he'd stood to pace it bumped the top of his head. I watched it for a while then as it swung around and around in ever-decreasing circles. Its soft glow faded for a second before sparking back to life. Slowly, I counted off ten of its erratic revolutions. When you'd a pike hooked on the line you always made it suffer.

"No comment," I said finally, with as much nonchalance as I could muster.

He clicked the tape recorder off. "Jesus feckin' Christ." He shoved the table into me with the heel of his hand, rushed around by my side and kicked the chair from beneath me. I hadn't expected him to go postal so quickly. I flailed for a second with my hands grabbing at the air, before landing head first with a crack.

"This is your last chance," he said, practically spitting in my face. "Speak, or I'll get my supervising officer to extend your stay here for as long as the statute allows."

I'd my mouth opened and primed to give him another

serving of "No comment" when a knock on the door had him wrenching me upright and sliding me back into the desk. He was some shape shifter. With a quick flick of his head, his hair slipped back in line and with a grin on his face he strolled to the door, yanked it open and left.

About two minutes later he arrived back into the room towing a familiar-looking fella in his wake. He wore a trendy suit, had his grey hair dyed to jet-black, and the sparkle of silver cuffs peeked out from his jacket. I knew I'd seen those threads before, and I'd certainly seen that shiny hairdo and face. My stomach lurched at the sight. It was JJ's dad.

"Hello, Mr Ryan," I said, feeling some guilt for the perkiness in my voice. However much JJ despised the man, it was wonderful to watch Garda P. Byrne look every inch the squirming midget by his side.

"Here ya go now, Paul," Garda Byrne said. "I told you Benjamin was safe and sound."

"Get out," Mr Ryan said without taking his eyes off of me. "And never refer to me as Paul again."

Garda Byrne muttered some apology and ducked away out the door. He didn't disappear completely, though. When he clicked the door closed he still had his face at the window, drilling his stare into mine.

"Doesn't he have to leave us alone?" I asked.

Mr Ryan strode forward, set his briefcase down carefully to his side and cleared his throat. "You, as the arrestee, have the right to legal counsel without them overhearing, but not them overseeing. You understand that anything you say to me will be treated in strictest confidence once you instruct me as your legal representative."

"I do."

"Well then, why don't you give me a brief synopsis of your version of the goings-on tonight? Trespassing is nonsense. With intent, a bit more serious, but it's still an innocuous crime that's notoriously difficult to convict, unless you two were caught with maps, floor plans and a diary outlining the criminal intentions…You weren't were you?"

"No."

"Well, at least there's that. So go on. I've heard my John Joseph's version—"

"JJ," I said, correcting him.

Mr Ryan stared at me for a second. He'd the eyes of a shark. He reminded me of my uncle, an impish slip of a man who'd an uncanny knack of deadpanning you into betting your house on a pair of sevens. I expected him to correct me, to run me over with that tongue of his. Still as sharp as ever, with an even shorter fuse by the looks of things, but he simply widened his eyes slightly and waited.

"Well, we were walking up to the convent in Barnamire when—"

Mr Ryan rubbed his face and slapped the desk once. "All right, I can't listen to any more of that, not at this ridiculous hour in the morning. No doubt yourself and my son have already corroborated your stories." He swivelled around and waved a lazy hand at Garda Byrne to return.

"But don't you want to fact check—"

He cut me off with a snort. "Whatever you say is moot. This pantomime has gone on too long now. Just hush up and let me do the talking. It won't take long, Benjamin."

Garda Byrne slipped into the room and stood above us with his hands clasped out in front. "Are you finished already, Mr Ryan?"

"You'll be releasing him now, Proinsias."

"Proinsias?" I raised my eyebrows.

"It means little French man," Mr Ryan said with the faintest of winks.

I mocked a laugh. "Proinsias? That's a bit of a bother isn't it? A hefty bundle like you with a name like that."

"It's Garda Byrne to you," Proinsias said, the colour snapping back to his cheeks. "And to you as well, Mr Ryan." He jabbed a finger towards him. "It may be two in the morning, and you might be a flash barrister, but you'll keep it formal. All right?"

I went to speak, but Mr Ryan tapped my hand and shook his head briefly. "Release him now, please, Garda Byrne. I will not ask again."

"And JJ?" I asked.

"In the car all ready. Now, keep quiet."

In fairness, he may have been a bigamist and a cheat and an all-round filthy mongrel of a father, but he got the job done.

Garda Byrne shuffled from side to side and mumbled some words about the poor nuns and the shock they'd been after suffering, but Mr Ryan cut his excuses off on his tongue.

"Irrelevant, inadmissible, pathetic posturing of a Garda who should know better. As far as I can ascertain, Benjamin and John Joseph—my son by the way—were both found injured in the grounds of a convent, arrested by you without any real evidence of intent. Then you held my clients without charge, questioned them half the night when they should have been granted rest, and the only reason you can spew out of your mouth is that the nuns were a bit scared. Is that the limit of your evidence?"

Garda Byrne grew the wilted face of a boy who'd just had his sandcastles trampled. "That's not the whole story. There was a gun."

"Did you find it?"

"No, but—"

"Then it's irrelevant. Anything else?"

"There were witnesses to the shooting. Honest, God-fearing nuns—"

"I don't care if Jesus himself resurrected to bear witness with them. Did they see my clients firing it?"

"No."

"Or holding it?"

"No."

"And as you alluded to, you didn't actually recover said weapon for ballistics and forensic examination?"

"Well no, but they definitely heard it. Loud as day. Two savage smacks. One closely following the other, and close enough to know they could be only coming from the grounds."

"Come on, Proinsias. Your only evidence of intent is that of nuns hearing gunshots...in Parkmore of all places?" Mr Ryan laughed then, a horrible mocking rumble in this throat. "There are more bullets than paperclips up there, for God's sake." He stood until he was eye-to-eye with Garda Byrne. "I'll give you two choices now, my friend, so listen closely. Either I formally report this to your superiors and immediately begin legal proceedings for this grievous harm and insult to my clients. Or you release him now. Without charge or blip on either of their records. I want the whole incident erased—right this merry instant. Got it?"

"That's not how this works—"

"As a man with country origins, Proinsias, if you spot a fool knee-deep in crap would you advise them to keep on digging?"

"No."

"Well then, this is exactly how this works. Ready their release, without charge or fine. Or we go to door number two. And do you know what prize is lurking behind it?"

Garda Byrne shrugged.

"Your job, your future, your family's security, your pension, lawsuits, court dates, Garda disciplinary hearings, unemployment and house repossessions and just pile after pile of goddamn shame that even your ample girth couldn't possibly swallow...in short, your whole pithy little life."

I'd never seen anyone eviscerated with such surgical precision. Mr Ryan had filleted the man on the spot with word after word of confidently delivered threats that would have had me feeling half sorry for Proinsias—if there was even a single grain of decency in him.

After a while he sucked in a soulful breath and nodded. "Fine. Thanks for clearing that up, Mr Ryan. Apologies for dragging you down at this hour of the night. The exit is this way. I'll sort the paperwork myself."

Chapter 13

When I was young I thought adults were so darn clever. I used to sit on my dad's lap while he danced his huge boots over the tractor pedals, working the wheel and the gearstick all at once as we chugged up and down the fields above our farm. Later that night, I'd lie in my bunk-bed dressed in my fancy Superman PJs with the ceiling lit up by my private-eye torch on the desk, and I'd while away hours trying to unravel the steps. My limbs would mimic his movements, my mouth the moans of the engine as it fought the hills like some asthmatic monster. By simply buzzing my lips, I'd get the sound of it down pat. But the symphony of clicks and pushes required to make it trundle forward remained an impenetrable mystery. For reasons such as these, my dad was solid magic to me growing up.

JJ's, not so much. Unless by magic he meant disappearing up his own arse.

Ten minutes must have flown by, and JJ hadn't even thrown a cursory nod my way, even though we were sitting less than a foot apart in the back seat of his daddy's tidy-looking BMW 5 Series. It was a cracking machine, though, and had that new car hum to it and all. The seats were hand-stitched black leather and a touch nippy at first. But when Mr Ryan started her up, the air conditioner whispered warmth through the cabin, and it wasn't long until the air turned tropical. There

THE ORIGINS OF BENJAMIN HACKETT

was even one of those deodorisers dangling from the mirror in the shape of a Christmas tree, infusing some forest glade essence into the mix like perfume onto the nose. All in all, there should have been sparse justification for JJ's swollen silence.

Mr Ryan wasn't found wanting of a few words, though. He'd driven us all to the bottom of Patrick's Hill, near the centre of Cork city, so he could find the only sweet spot for that monstrous mobile phone of his. For ages, he'd been prattling away in a fine and fanciful voice to his new bit of fluff, and, by the sound of things, there was no easy way out of his predicament.

"But I *have* to drive them back home to Whitehaven," he said for about the fifth time in as many minutes.

"See that woman again and when you return the locks will be changed."

Despite the phone being strapped to his ear, we could hear every word of the woman's screeching. Her name was Darcï, with an umlaut over the 'i', apparently. I'd caught a glimpse of it on the mobile phone screen before Mr Ryan had started this whole forlorn pantomime. As a Cork man, that told me all I needed to know about her immediately. Her singing nasally tone that'd rise up to a near shriek whenever she got her posh little knickers in a twist confirmed my suspicions.

"I can bring them home for the night, then. Get them on a bus in the morning, that would—"

"Oh, my God. Are you serious, like? Imagine if the neighbours saw you. We could never show our faces down Fota clubhouse again. You dare bring him and his criminal friend back to our home and you'll never see your Beatrix walk…" Her words died on her breath, and she sobbed quietly.

It was all too quick for my taste, as if she were responding by rote from some script. She was a trickster all right. A right puppeteer. And she was yanking Mr Ryan's strings like a good one.

"Paul," she said quietly. "You know I love you."

She practically purred the words and despite my noblest intentions, an image of her took form in my mind. Forty at a stretch, I'd say. Probably lying in bed with her perfumed hair spread around her like wings, her satin nightdress hitched up past her thighs, her smooth, supple skin aglow in a soft light and that sumptuous edge of sleepiness just pure hunger in her eyes.

I shook my head and smacked my cheeks. Enough of that kind of malarkey. It was bad enough I'd brought the wrath of her onto JJ without falling for a made-up version of his dad's mistress. She probably had fetid breath, a wonky eye, hirsute back and dubious toilet habits. Probably had rolls of pregnancy fat still hanging off her sides. Yeah, that was more on the money. That calmed me down for a while. Flatlined the hormones in me.

"And I understand why you went to get him out," she said, continuing. "But just leave it at that, why don't you? It's enough for now. Drop them off and come home to Rochestown. They can make their own way back to West Cork by themselves."

Mr Ryan caught me glimpsing in the rearview mirror. He blew out his cheeks and shook his head as if to say, "Look what I'm dealing with here." I slipped down until he no longer saw me. I didn't want to be a bit-part player in his act. It was bad enough his girlfriend turned my traitor gene on with her pouting lips, her writhing body, her tongue curled up at its tip in a—

God, there I went again.

"I can't abandon them on the streets in the dead of night like two stray alley cats," he said. "They're only children."

"They're eighteen years of age. Men, for Christ's sake."

"Well, technically John Joseph's still a month away from his birthday."

"Don't you start your legal pedantry on me."

"I'm just saying—"

"Well, don't. Him and his mother have been nothing more than a hex on our lives."

"Now come on, there's no need—"

"There is so a need. And remember, Paul, you wouldn't be squat without me and my father's influence."

"I know, it's just…"

His words petered out, and for a moment nobody said anything. It was a harsh thing to hear your dad bow down to some pretentious woman who'd flashed her bits and stripped him away from your family. Why Mr Ryan had decided to stay in the car and risk sharing the conversation with all of us may have been a conundrum to JJ at that moment. But it was no mystery to me. Blame Darcï and ease his guilt. A tricky move and stinking cruel to boot, but it was playing out perfectly for him.

I turned to JJ, who'd remained in the same exact spot since I jumped in next to him. He'd slumped down into the soft leather, with his arms crossed on his chest and his gaze away in the streets, and a whole load of guilt swept up and stuck its talons into my throat at the sight of him.

"What do you think of those mobile phones, JJ?" I said, trying to rally him some. "Figure they'll catch?"

He didn't answer.

"I reckon they're only a fad. First off, you can only use them in about a single square mile of the entire country. And who in their right minds would want to be contactable at all times?"

I left the lure dangling out there. It normally didn't take much more than the slightest exhibition of my technical ignorance to have him gushing forth with elaborate words on how I was such a Neanderthal, how the world was moving on at such incredible pace, how I'd be left behind bemoaning the death of Betamax and searching out second-hand stores for Commodore 64 game tapes if I didn't pay attention to the advancement of all things digital. But the trap stayed set. Save for him trying to murder me briefly with his eyes, he didn't utter a single syllable.

The connection crackled with static and the line went dead. Mr Ryan cursed and punched some buttons, holding the phone up to the windscreen. He drove down the street chasing the reception, circling the block once more, until a dial tone *dringed* and the whinging of Darcï came back into earshot.

"...and so what if he's your son. I mean seriously...you've a new daughter now to think of. Or have you no time for your darling Beatrix asleep in her cot, who wants nothing more than her father to be home with her now. She's *our* daughter, Paul. And she doesn't need one of her earliest memories to be her half-brother holing up here after being arrested in Parkmore...Parkmore of all places."

She was really singing now for the pitch of her.

"I've an obligation to see them home," Mr Ryan said.

She laughed in a confident and quiet way, a trace of huskiness in her sigh at the end. "I'll tell you what, Paul. You always adore your ultimatums in the courts. Well, I've one for you now...it's either them or us."

The line died again, and Mr Ryan chucked the mobile into the drinks holder and stared at JJ in the rearview mirror. "Sorry."

It was a pathetic apology and pointless really. Any father worth his salt would have driven us right up to our doors without a second's thought. There was no reason to subject us to the back-and-forth and general nastiness of their comments. Unless, of course, you wanted to come across as blameless and weren't bothered about slicing open another gaping sore in your son and drip-feeding acid on it like they'd been doing for the last half an hour.

"Want to scram?" I said in a whisper to JJ.

He stared at me for a second before shifting forward, his shoulders rising up and down in a slow shrug. With his mouth turned down, his chin doubling up on his chest, and a load of hurt dulling the eyes, he cut a doleful character just then.

"Well? Do you?" I asked once more.

He nodded.

Mr Ryan slipped the gear into drive. "I'll bring you two home. Or as close as I can without upsetting Darci.

And anyway, it is probably best if we all keep this to ourselves. If we arrived back at Val's she'd—"

"Why don't you pull over here, Paul," I said, mimicking the posh lilt of the girl as best I could. "Let you get home to Darcï and your new baby."

Mr Ryan ignored me, ramped up the speed and drove down Patrick Street.

I shifted forward and slapped the back of his seat. "Let us out now."

The car roared onto Grand Parade, past the English Market and onto the South Mall, slipping around cars and in and out of lanes with silky ease.

"You'll get out when I say so."

Gone was the benign sadness, the concerned daddy, the ruse of caring. He'd that same sniping malevolence to his voice when he was lording over Garda Byrne down the station. Mr Paul Ryan may have been JJ's dad, he may have been a powerful lawyer, he may have been all suited and booted and driving a BMW with a gormless posh queen for a girl and a bouncing new baby, but at his core he was always that same country shyster who'd wrecked an innocent family. Mr Ryan was a liar and a bully. And I'd had my fill of grownups like him.

A car full of teenagers screeched in front of us and slammed on the brakes. The passengers in the rear stuck their heads out the windows and gave us the finger. Mr Ryan leaned on the horn and darted around until he'd drawn up level with them. As he rolled down the window to fire off some insults, I shunted forward, grabbed his phone and slipped it into my pocket. JJ caught my act and the briefest smile tugged at his lips. I gestured at the door handle, and we both sat forward primed to flee. When the next set of lights came up, the car slowed, and we threw open our doors and leaped out.

We hit the asphalt with the car still rolling to a stop and weaved our way around the cars gathering up behind us. The night filled with screeches of brakes worn thin and idle threats aimed at us from bleary-eyed drivers. We ran across the three lanes of the road and onto the footpath.

The hint of rot lifted off the River Lee and spoiled the night air. Cork city was in graveyard mode, and the smell seemed to suit its mood. A drunk-looking couple with hips welded together waddled towards us, hands still clasping half-empty glasses of something. They mumbled some gibberish at us as we passed them by, but we ignored them and continued forward.

We struck out over the bridge towards the City Hall. Its granite walls were ablaze in the spotlights from below, but up high near its clock face only shadows twisted. I looked east and spied the faintest touch of blue bleeding into the horizon. Dawn would be upon us soon enough. One day less to track my parents. The thought had barely registered, when someone pushed me viciously from behind. I tumbled into the rails of the bridge, hands raised out in front, knees clattering against the hard edge of iron. A needle-sharp pain juddered up my legs.

I groaned and sat on my backside, rubbing my legs gently, coaxing the hurt to calm down. When I looked up, Mr Ryan grabbed JJ by the shoulders. He'd wild eyes on him now and rows of sharp lines wrinkling up his brow. In the wash of white from the street lamp above, he looked cadaverous, a once-upon-a-man.

"Get back in the car." His words were full of fury, and spit glinted on his teeth.

JJ shrugged him away and went to help me up. "You all right, chief?"

I nodded and stood gingerly.

"I told you we shouldn't have called him—"

Mr Ryan barged between the two of us. "Get into the car right now, or I'm finished with you, John Joseph."

JJ stopped and stared him straight in the eye with a swagger in his smile and this look of pure disdain on his face. Gone was the little boy skulking in the rear seat, gone was the blond-haired ten-year-old who prayed to all the saints to return his daddy in the night. JJ stepped closer, his chest swelling with each breath, his fists clenched tight by his side. By the looks of him, he could have plucked Mr Ryan clean up, swivelled him over his head and dropped him in the river with the rest of the garbage.

"The next time I'm in a jam, Paul," he said. "I'll tell my mother. However bad the fall-out, it will be easier to deal with than watching you fail repeatedly as a man."

"Thankless brat," Mr Ryan said. He poked JJ hard in the ribs with his index finger. "After all I just did for you."

"Three months," JJ said. He hissed the words, his breath visible on the cold. It wafted between the two of them, lingering only briefly until a gust whipped it away.

Mr Ryan took a step backwards and curled his lip into a sneer. "What are you going on about now?"

"My birthday...it's in September."

And with that JJ pushed him casually aside and

gestured for me to follow. I wasn't certain whether Mr Ryan got the reference. It wouldn't have surprised me one bit if he hadn't, being the toe-rag of a father he was. But I was a weeny bit disappointed that JJ hadn't smacked him about a bit. So with him half-paralysed on that bridge and the gnawing pain in my knees egging me on, I tapped him on the shoulder and feigned a punch.

"Flinched," I said as he stumbled back from me. "Cowards always do."

He gripped the rails and regained his balance. He swiped a hand over his hair, settling it back into his nauseatingly perfect quiff, and straightened his tie back up to his neck. He looked every inch the ageing sugar daddy just then. Punching him on the nose would have been a sweeter release I fancied. But I was sparing my knuckles for my own parents. Wherever the hell they were hiding.

I waved him away, caught up to JJ and slung an arm over his shoulder. "Well done, bud. Guy's a full-out asshole anyway."

JJ stopped walking and shook out his hands. "God, I don't know how I didn't smash him."

"You played it cool. Just so damn cool. Do you feel better for it?"

He held his fingers to his nose. A huge grin erupted on his face. In all the years I'd known him, I don't think I ever saw such happiness pink up his cheeks. "One million times. I know I haven't seen him in years...but God, what a rat. And that Darcï one. I mean, how plastic did she sound? With her Beatrix and her daddy issue. Can you fathom waking up next to that moody cow everyday?"

God, yeah.

"No, no…not a chance."

"We're better off without him. Myself and Mam."

"No doubting that."

We rested our elbows on the wall and gazed down-river. JJ sighed loudly and clapped his hands together. "Right so. That's *my* thing tucked away forever. What about you, Ben?"

"You still want to continue?"

"You helped me exorcise that demon shit of a dad. So yeah, I do want to go on. I owe you."

"Well, if that's the case we go track Apache, get him to help. Maybe we'll win back your car and some money."

He laughed briefly. "I doubt that somehow. But how will we find him?"

"A guy like that's not exactly incognito. Just give me a moment."

I ducked around a corner down a dark and narrow lane edged with garbage bags, rotten vegetable peels and gunk. The smell was as ripe as an open sewer. I crept down the middle of it, breathing through my mouth, trying to block out the stench. A tramp appeared on a step just beyond the back entrance to a restaurant. He sat on an unfolded cardboard box and wore a tattered green parka jacket. By his feet sat a bag of tinnies, the empties crushed and discarded to his side. He looked up when I approached, eyes hidden in shadows, his tongue dragging across the thin paper skin of a rollie. He sucked the tip, lit it and left a thick fug of smoke waft from his mouth.

"Where can I find Mossy Deane?" I asked. "Goes by the name of Apache. You know him, right?"

"Na, boy," the old man said with a slurred drawl. He picked some tobacco from his teeth and spat. "I've no notion who you're banging on about. You got any spare coins on ya? A stag would do."

I removed the phone from my pocket and held it in my palm. His eyes suddenly appeared from the darkness, jaundiced and webbed with age. He stood with his cigarette clenched in his teeth and his gloved fingers twitching nervously.

"Any notion now?" I asked.

"Does it work?"

I flicked it open and hit redial, praying it'd connect us. Darci answered, her voice sounded coarse and groggy. "Hello...Paul...wha—what is it?"

I snapped it shut once more and held it aloft out of his reach.

He stared at the phone and gave a hungry lick of his lips. I caught a waft of his breath and retched. When he smiled, I looked on in horror at the whole display of his mouth; angry, swollen gums riddled with sores and ground-down tobacco-stained teeth.

"Sounds tasty that one," he said. "She come with it?"

I shook my head. "You wouldn't want her, trust me."

"Fair enough." He shifted his feet, rubbed his nose and sniffed. "Apache holes up in the Tenns, a mile past Barrack Street. Can't miss it. But I'd try to—if I was you. He doesn't have much mass on strangers, if you catch my drift."

I lowered my arm and unfurled my fingers. The old man grabbed the mobile phone and cowered away back to his cardboard perch, smoking the rollie deep and flicking the phone open and closed.

The rain set upon us then. It came lashing down in sheets, slapping the bins and sending static into the air. I tucked my hands deep in my pockets and slipped back to JJ.

Chapter 14

A decaying blister on the cityscape was how the Tenns appeared when JJ and myself arrived after traipsing through the quarter-light of dawn. We'd sat there for hours just looking at it, frozen solid and sore with hunger, wondering if this was indeed the right place. It looked as if a crew of blind men threw it together in a week. All four storeys had the plaster ripped off exposing the breezeblocks below. Mounds of rubble blocked access to the yard. And in their valleys, oil drums still smouldered from whatever fire sacrifice had occurred the night before. Even as the night slipped away and the sun inched over the rooftops, the only trace of colour was an ominous sign staked in concrete by the entrance with three blood-red words scrawled across it.

"Trespassers will die," it read.

"That seems fairly unambiguous," JJ said, squinting at it and smoothing out his hair with the palm of his hand. "So, what has your keen mind decided to do to overcome the pickle of why our would-be murderer might help us for free? Far as I see it, we've no money to bribe him, no gun to force him and no time to fanny about trying to figure it out by ourselves. In fact, now that I'm standing here looking up at it, this seems more like the inane hatchings of a loon. There ain't no sensible move here."

"Well, we did come all this way. It'd be rude not to

pop up in for a chat." I cinched my shirt closed and picked my way over the rubble.

"Hold on there a moment, will you?" He ran in front of me and grabbed me by the shoulders. "We can't simply ramble up to Apache with empty pockets and expect him to help us out for nothing."

I shrugged him off and stepped back. "We do what the Don would do."

"Now's not the time for cryptic references."

"You must have seen those shows on the box? You know...those Mafioso ones. *The Godfather* with its vice cops and bribes, RICO and decapitated horsies. All that kind of stuff?"

He closed his eyes and sighed. "First off, we're not gangsters and they are *fic-tion-al*. And I doubt Apache's crew pay heed to rules created by scriptwriters."

"Look, it's simple really," I said. "We'll head on up to our good friend Apache and *ask* him for help in return for a favour. I can guarantee you a fella like him has a whole heap of stuff that needs doing. And besides, we both know there's no other move here."

"Do we? So we just expose ourselves to the will of a drug-peddling—not forgetting armed—maniac and hope he plays nice? How about we go home and try the official route?"

I kicked up some dust and wedged my hands into my pockets. God, how I wished my parents had kept their filthy lie to themselves. It was the Catholic way after all. But could they? Nah. Not my old pair. Didn't even choose the noble route of dragging it with them for life to their graves. Nope. They may just have said, "Here, take this for a moment, Benjamin, will you? Hang this heaving millstone around your neck 'cause we can't be bothered lugging it around anymore. What's that? You didn't want it? Sure, you're eighteen now, and we've decided it was about time life properly badgered you. You'll be grand, boy, no worries. Oh, and by the way…happy birthday."

The bunch of liars.

"Can't do it, JJ. I'm done with playing nice. The whole world has dumped on me for the last twenty-four hours, and it's time I stopped being its whipping boy. If you want to go, then go. But I'm doing this, with or without you. Your call."

He looked me in the eye and slapped his hands together. "Okay, let's do it. But to be clear, if Apache wants us to knock somebody off and bury their dismembered body in a shallow grave somewhere, I'm out the gap. Got it?"

"Don't be so melodramatic."

On we stumbled over the mounds of debris. It was only a hundred or so yards to the building, but it seemed like miles. We sidestepped discarded needles that'd have you running for a vaccine if they stuck you, jumped over used condoms, beer cans and shards of glass that lay strewn on the ground. It didn't need much of an imagination to wonder what went on here.

When we reached the top of the stairwell, we paused and listened for a moment. A fan droned and rattled below us, sending a constant stream of steam hissing out and up towards us. Its serpentine trails weaved with the early morning mist that shrouded the building.

Looking up and down at the row of apartments, it seemed bizarre that anyone actually lived there. Every door had been kicked in; every windowpane smashed. The only signs of repair were crisscrossed boards nailed into frames with patches of tarpaulin and plastic sheets laced through the gaps. I scanned the place for any hint of movement, any glow of light creeping through the cracks. There was nothing but the constant shadows and noxious odours that had me sneezing and wrinkling my nose in disgust. Sweat. Urine. Vomit. They were all there, like one giant mushroom cloud of human excrement wafting around us.

The place had a presence to it, though, an eeriness that clung to my mind like some parasite gorging itself on whatever slip of confidence remained in me. It was the same sensation I'd experienced years earlier when I'd carried my granddad's coffin from the hearse to his grave.

I remembered it all—the crunch of gravel underfoot, the greyness of that day, the sodden mud piled high to the side ready to be shovelled in on top of him. As I stood in the shadow of the Tenns, death's touch clawed at my skin once more. I clasped the wall, felt the dampness in my hands and shuddered. Granddad wasn't my own. Even my memories of the man had been sullied forever.

"Doesn't look like there's anybody home," JJ said. "We should probably head off and mull it over. This doesn't feel right."

I tutted once and pointed at the far right end of the building. "If Apache is anywhere he's there. It'd give him the high ground with the emergency stairs close to hand, and it's the best vantage point to scan the sweep of the city. Plus, it's the only one with a door."

"Door? What door?" JJ ran up to where I stood pointing and followed my gaze. "I can't see any door. Just boards and sheets and tarp."

"That's what they want you to see. But have a side-on look at the one furthest away. Now, when have you ever seen a handle on a boarded-up hole where a door once stood?"

He squinted in the low light for a second. "That's a handle. They camouflaged the doors to make them look abandoned?"

"Ingenious, no? And if this is the only way in, I'd hazard a guess that the rest must only open out. I must say this Apache chap is surprising me no end. He's the man for the job all right. Come on, let's go and say hello."

We walked shoulder-to-shoulder towards the end of the building. With every rise and fall of step our shoes made a squelching slap on the tarmac. When we were halfway along the walkway, JJ froze and held an arm out to stop.

"What's up?" I asked.

"Listen," he said in a whisper. "No rattle. The fan has stopped." No sooner had he uttered the words than every door on the floor opened in unison, and a slew of shadowy figures ghosted out from the darkness towards us.

Bats...I had to give it to them. They were tough little creatures. Being upside down wouldn't have been my first choice in relaxing, but then again, having a bunch of hooded hard-shaws hang you by your ankles from a meat hook in the ceiling made it fairly obvious that choices were temporarily off the menu.

The whole confrontation outside had me fizzing for a few seconds in rage before they'd pinned me to the ground. We tried to struggle, but the hands that held us had us hog-tied and attached to a hook without so much as a word or grunt uttered between them. It was an odd experience watching them operate so fluidly, without direction, as if they were all symbiotically connected. They marched into the cell, hung us up on two rings screwed to the ceiling before filing back out again. The only sound they made was the screech of metal and clang of the bolt as they slid it home in the lock. They looked like cloned hoodlums—clad all in black with their faces obscured by hoods tied up over balaclavas and latex gloves on their hands; same height, same build, same precise military strut.

The room where we hung was square, white and windowless. A strip light flickered above, casting inter-mittent blinks that seared into my eyes. A drain ran the length of the floor beneath us and divided the room in two. Concrete walls, stark lighting, bodies hanging on hooks—it reminded me of a picture of an abattoir I once saw sprawled across the front-page of a vegan magazine.

I puffed out my cheeks and looked around once more, checking every inch and stain in the place. It was as if my brain distrusted my eyes and wanted to double-check that the body in which it resided was indeed attached to a hook, and that hook was most definitely in a room akin to a slaughterhouse.

I'd no real inkling as to how long we'd been upside down, but clearly JJ'd acclimatised to the lunacy of it all, because my buxom buddy was swaying gently back-and-forth sound asleep. How he managed to nod off was anyone's guess, though I had to give it to him—it was a genius coping mechanism.

"JJ," I said, shouting over the noise of his snoring. Honest to God, it was like foghorns mating. "Wake up will you, you lemon." Nothing. He must have been deep in his winks. I inhaled deeply and barked his name until my voice nearly croaked.

"Wha...what is it?" He blinked a few times and tried to move about a bit. He'd that bewildered look only the grogginess of sleep could produce—eyes puffed up, focusing on everything and nothing all at once, lapping at his lips with his tongue for some moisture. He looked ridiculous really, wriggling about like a chubby worm on a line about to be gobbled underwater.

A bolt slid on metal. The door opened inwards and two shadows stretched across the floor.

"Look," I said, whispering. "Whatever happens, let me do the talking. The last time you spoke to Apache he shot you in the head."

The silhouetted figures stood in silence on the threshold. I gulped when I spotted two carbon-black blades in their hands, reaching to the floor. As they walked towards us they tapped them on the ground in synch with their steps. The sound of metal skinning concrete grew louder. A cold shiver pricked at my skin. They stopped six inches from my nose, giving me a close-up of the blades. They looked even fiercer this near. My eyes ran up the blade to the hand and up into the face of a man who must been fed steroids since birth. He'd a bald and brutal head with scars welting his cheeks and well-worn skin stretched taut from the heft of the muscles beneath.

Apache suddenly stepped in front. He hunkered down on his haunches until his nose touched mine. He'd the same manic eyes and smarmy grin full of swollen gums and wonky teeth. Slowly, he drew his blade up and ran the blunt edge gently down my face.

"Do you know who the fella behind me is?" Apache asked.

"No idea," JJ said. "Judging by your positions I'd guess your booty call?"

Apache laughed for a second before hacking up some phlegm and spitting in his face. "You're a right funny boy. I should have remembered that. This, my friends...is a *shochet*. A mad wreck of a fella I picked up on my travels with the Rangers in the Gulf. Has a natural-born talent for carving things up and making them disappear. Poof..." He clicked his fingers. "Just like that. We call him Magic because he's so damn good at it, like."

"Never heard of it." I said.

"A *ssshhh-ochet*," Apache said, breathing the word on me. The smell that wafted from his mouth was putrid. I turned my head slightly and held my breath.

Apache stood and backed away, swinging the blade in perfect arcs and carving up the air. "JJ will know, won't you, boy? Being the smart arse who forces people to shoot him in the face." He took a step forwards and lunged at him, stopping the blade less than a whisker's width from his eye. Even with his arm and weapon outstretched the tip of the blade remained perfectly still. "And in a convent of all places. There was no need to make me do that with all that religion watching."

JJ sighed. "A *shochet* is a Jewish butcher who prepares kosher meat in the traditional way by cutting the neck of an animal and draining the blood from the carcass. Apparently, *shochets* are men of strong moral character. Not so pious now, though, is he?"

Magic growled and stepped forwards, but stopped when Apache shook his head. "Oh, he was as pure as the driven snow in another life," Apache said. "But, I'm getting off point now, so let me steer us back to my original thought." He turned to face me, his smile dialled down to nothing. "You two must be the thickest pile of twits in Cork. Don't you know who I am?"

"Of course we do, we—"

"That was a rhetorical question. I presumed you do because you managed to walk right into my back yard lolling about the place like tourists. I can't imagine for a second you found it by chance, and no one gets directions here without being warned to stay the fuck away."

He clasped his hands behind his back and walked up and down the length of the cell. "Which makes it even more of a mystery why you two fools are currently hanging in my house. And quite honestly it's the only reason you're not bleeding out in the gutter right now, because the curiosity is simply killing me." He stopped and sneered. "You see, I'm one of those guys who can't go to bed without knowing why the baddies did it."

He raced forward and grabbed me by the cheeks, pinching them hard for a second and slapping me across the face. "Now, I don't mean to put the label of bad guys on you. No, God no. I'd never besmirch your daycent characters like that. But I have to tell you, lads, I don't know whether to be impressed or depressed by the two of you. Because if you rocked up here thinking you could retrieve your possessions without losing your lives...well...you deserve to be stuck like pigs and quartered."

Without warning, he drove his fist into my stomach. Pain streaked through my insides, making me scream from the shock of it.

"Thanks for that," I said, wheezing. "Just what I needed."

"Well, would you look here. It seems the comedy is catching." He clenched his fist and hit me again. Harder this time. Vomit spilled out my mouth and splashed by his feet. He laughed for a second, before placing the sole of his boot on my face and shoving me away from him. If I could I'd have collapsed on the floor, I'd have wrapped myself up like a foetus and whined. But all I could do was close my eyes and pray he'd move on to JJ.

"You know...I'd be doing the world a favour really stopping two dullards like yourselves from ever spawning more dumb fecks. Call it natural de-selection." He took a step forward and grabbed me by the legs, stopping my pendulous motion. "So save me from my misery lads and tell me please—why in God's name are you here?"

I tried to talk, but he raised a finger hushing me. "And let me give you one warning—choose your words carefully, because if I think you're spouting bull, I'll let Magic here perform his trick."

The shame of it.

The sheer embarrassment of being lorded over by two of Ireland's skankiest bellycrawlers, and us hanging from chains like their masochistic playthings. I eyed Magic and Apache looming over us. A right pair of scuts they were. I'd have caved my own head in if I'd to listen to any more of their guttyboy talk or witness any more of that southside swagger. In the normal swing of things, they'd be gowned up in high-vis bibs plucking up weeds for the council down Pana Street, or hawking knocked-off tat down the Coalquay. Maybe in a year or two, with a stretch on Spike Island under their belts, they'd have caught a new trade and be robbing cars from the fancier pads down Douglas. Yet, here they were thinking themselves the berries, and less than a moment away from becoming our own personal reapers.

The unfathomable shame of it.

"Tick-ety-tock," Magic said, tapping his wrist where his watch should be. Its absence didn't surprise me. Judging by the way he lumbered through words, numbers would probably bring on a seizure.

"Give me a chance there, Kojak," I said. "Let me mull on the moment." Seconds ticked by. A nervousness in my belly zinged about in loops. I started to speak, but my mouth cradled silence. Stage fright. That's what it was. I, Benjamin Hackett, heir to thirty head of cattle, had come down with a dose of verbal constipation. I looked to JJ and threw him my back-me-up-buddy look. But like the heap of useless he was, he just shook his head and shrugged.

"Well…" I said, trying on a word for size. I liked it. It was a solid start to any sentence. "We need your help."

Apache's head jerked back for a second with the disgusted look on his face. JJ groaned, Magic sniggered, and I swayed away on the hook.

"I'll admit," Apache said. "I wasn't expecting any bit of that. Good on you for throwing me off my saddle. I respect that. But you're having me on, right? Spent too long in the womb, sniffed some glue or something?"

"Nope," I said. "None of that. We do really have a need of your particular...um...skill set."

JJ coughed once. I looked over at the serious head on him. He'd his eyes all solemn and sad, and he gritted his teeth until his cheeks flexed firm. He'd a want for a word, all right. If he were free to roam he'd have cocked his head high, clasped his hands and loped slowly about in full-out sermon mode.

"It's not as ludicrous as it sounds," he said in that seminary tone of his. "We've a need for your services. And in return we'll do whatever deed you want. Except for murder, of course."

"Heaven forbid," Apache said, slapping his forehead with the heel of his hand. He raised the blade and gestured around the cell. "It's the décor in here, isn't it? Too soft and friendly. Is that what's confusing you?"

"Again," I said. "We want your help, and we'll pay a fee in the form of a favour. Anyways, you owe us something seeing as though we didn't rat you out to the Gardaí down the station."

Apache spat. "You'd be dead men if you turned me in."

"Look. As far as I see, you've two choices. Use us to do what needs doing, or hack us up and hope that no one comes looking for us. Oh, and a word to the wise, JJ's mam is a complete nutjob. And I mean a certifiable, religomaniacal nutter. She'll scour the streets of Cork for you. It's hardly worth the hassle chopping us up really."

"Cheers for that, Benjamin," JJ said.

"No bother."

"Benjamin, is it?" Apache said, smirking. And without another word, himself and Magic huddled together. They cupped their hands over their mouths, but they needn't have bothered. When these lads talked native there wasn't an ear in the land that could decipher a single word out of all their garble. How Magic understood any of it was anyone's guess, but I presumed when you parleyed with enough of Apache's ilk it'd bleed into you eventually.

"Grand so, lads," Apache said. "We accept your offer. Cut these two scallies down, Magic. We're colleagues now."

We marched out of the cell like dirt-grey cygnets up the lough waddling after their mammy, choosing to ignore the obvious issue of it being a weensy bit too easy. When the door clanged shut behind us, JJ and myself looked at one another and shrugged. And that was that. No words were needed, because in that moment we'd decided to ignore the naysaying and go along for the ride. We paraded down the length of the building and halted by the door where we'd originally intended to knock.

"Now, lads," Apache said with his hand on the handle. "This is the nerve centre. Only a privileged few have set foot inside. I'll ask you to mind your manners and keep in my shadow. No talking, no pointing. Just follow me and zip your lips."

The room inside wasn't so much a room, more a tuck-shop for dope fiends. He must have knocked through each of the flats to create it. About thirty masked women stood behind tables running the length of the place, cutting and weighing, counting and packaging. It was a veritable production line.

"My Pucas run a tight ship," Apache said, patting the head of one of the hoodlums who'd tackled us earlier. There was one per table, and they ticked away in sync on the clipboards in hand. "None of them know the identity of the others. Hard to be snitched on when you're anonymous. It's a sweet little system."

It was one of those moments that left me dumbfounded. I'd expected to see ravers queuing up for their Mollies still twitching from the previous night's buzz. Or maybe some bleary-eyed junkies salivating over spoons full of H, rubber cord clasped in their teeth, hands tapping for a vein, itching for some brown. But this?

Apache looked at me and smiled a proud and indulgent smile. "A one-stop shop, Benjamin. A choice of product for all of my customers. White Doves, Oxos, Fido Didos, draw, gange; they're all here. Even the much sought after Flatliners, which aren't as rare as you'd think." He winked and clapped his hands together. "Business has never been better. If you control the quantity, people are more forgiving over quality. Now, tell me...what is it *exactly* that you want from me?"

"We need your help to break into Barnamire."

"You two want to rob nuns?"

"Without killing any of them, of course," JJ said.

"Murder this, murder that. Touch paranoid aren't you?" Apache clasped his hands together and held them to his nose. "Right. If you want in, they need to be out. There are only two ways to get nuns out of a convent. And the Pope isn't on my Rolodex. So we'll burn them out. Now calm your boots, JJ. There'll be no murdering. We'll start it close by in one of their outbuildings. The nuns will bail out to safety until the cavalry arrive. We keep the fire fed and you two duck in."

I had to give the man his dues, when it came to criminality he was masterful. I mulled it over for a while. How he was cock-sure the nuns would react just so was a stretch, though my choices were thin and our time was tight.

"Seems fair," I said.

"Banging. But first things first, can you handle a boat?"

Chapter 15

The dunes where we lay were our only protection. A furious wind whipped in off the sea, making me cough from the sand it spun into my mouth. The shore lay a hundred yards beyond, and our boat bobbed up and down in the breakwater. It was an old, tarred currach with a blackened keel and a wickerwork hull. By the looks of the waves, we'd have to give her dixie to make clear water. But currachs being currachs, we'd probably sink like a lead balloon in the shallows.

Make a move at nightfall was the plan. Row out, meet the boat and return with the parcels. "Easy as," Apache'd said. The whole plot stunk worse than a week-old carcass. Why he didn't simply have his Pucas wander out there was a mystery all right, but I was tired from thinking and weak from the journeying.

We'd travelled in a rusted-up Lada, with Magic chain-smoking Majors and JJ yip-yapping away like he'd come over all senile and mistook the trip for a summer's vacation. In the three hours it took us, I reckon we'd snagged every bump, hump and pothole in Munster. When we finally stopped we all bailed out, except for Apache who lay angling for a snooze in the back seat. We stomped across bogs full of sinkholes and tore through blackthorns that'd flail your skin in a second. We clambered over turf bailed high and wide until the land gave way to reeds and the beach appeared in front of us.

And no wonder it was a beast to get to. A gnarlier cove I'd never clapped eyes on. Rocks jutted up from the waters, black and craggy and sharp as flint. Water raged and crashed around them, sending walls of mist grabbing for the air. Next to the currach a riptide flowed backwards, foaming and chewing on clutches of debris. It was puck ugly, the shame of the Creator. But, it just so happened, a cracking spot to land a shipment of drugs.

"Where the hell is this place?" I asked.

"Britten Bay," JJ said, like the show-off he was. "Just inside the Kerry border. Never been here before, but I recognise it from those twee tourist ads. You know those diddly-daddly, isn't Ireland great fun ones."

"We're in Kerry? That's depressing."

"Depressing? Our current location is the least of our woes. Oh, and by the way...you look ridiculous."

He was right on the money this time. Apache, in his wisdom, had decided it best to glam us up like the Pucas in tracksuits and balaclavas. About as stylish as drop-crotch pants they were; and itchy as all hell. I glanced at JJ and shook my head in disgust. The Pucas weren't the best crowd for him to borrow clobber from.

"Says the man in a tracksuit that looks like it was sprayed on."

He laughed, briefly. "True that. I've been holding in wind for ages. It'd probably cause a cataclysmic failure of material and have my ass hanging out from my breeches if I gave it way."

"Still, now you can give your leisure suit back to the eighties."

"Keep quiet, watch sun, be ready," Magic said, clipping the back of my head. Not the most natural of conversationalists was the butcher from Baghdad, but when he spoke we decided it best to listen, given that he kept tinkering with that blade of his within an inch of our feet.

Finally, the sun gave way to dusk. The wan light was kind to the eye, but it chilled the air something awful. A snaking wind scooted over the dune and nipped at my skin. I shivered and sunk down into the sand, trying to absorb the remaining heat from its depths and ignoring the growl in my stomach panging for food. A whole day spent waiting on some dunes was taking its toll on me, all right.

When night fell in earnest, the rains fell too. Globs the size of marbles splotched the ground and soaked me through. A streak of lightning crackled and zigzagged to the sea below. By the count of nine, thunder shook the skies.

Magic stood and walked up to the top of the dune. He looked out to the ocean for a moment before gesturing for us to stand. We followed him out of the dunes where the full force of the wind tore across my cheeks. Magic waded without pause straight into the waters and grabbed the stern of the currach. With a quick yank, he pulled the anchor up and threw it on board.

"Come, now," he said, while trying to steady the boat.

"Not the wisest oarsman is he?" I said. "Pulling anchor before we're in." Watching the currach bob like crazy in the wild ocean made me shudder as doubt crept up my spine. "Should we do this, JJ? If you want, we can renege and head back to Cork. We'll always find another way. There's no going back once we get in that boat."

JJ turned and grinned, his eyes glinting bright with the remaining trace of light in the sky. "Row out, row in. We've paddled in the dark thousands of times in the past. Piece of cake. Plus, I don't think we have any other option here—what with the butcher over there. These boys aren't the kind of people to just give you a pass and say forget the whole affair. Know what I mean?"

Without waiting for an answer, he ran towards Magic, scything through the waves with ease, leaving me alone on the shingled shore. In the distance, a lighthouse sent a stream of white slicing through the night and fog-horns wailed a warning. The moon appeared briefly, just an arc of white, before disappearing behind unseen clouds.

I puffed out my cheeks and stepped into the shallows. The frigid waters sent a chill through my bones. Spray lashed my skin, and I tasted salt on my lips. I hauled myself up and sat in behind JJ. The oars were already set in their locks, and the swell rolled beneath us.

"Count two hundred, stop, wait," Magic said, pushing us away into the waves.

We dipped the blades underwater and thrust into the stroke. The currach bit and glided away from the shore.

"One...two...three...four," Magic said, smacking his hands together.

We set into the rhythm and steered towards deeper water. I turned to check our bearing and cursed. Even in the gloom, I spotted the waves buck up and snap back down. The first surge of white-water charged to meet us. All froth, no fury; a toothless pup. I tweaked us star-board and we eased through. The hull crashed into the next wave square. It jolted us violently up. The currach stuttered for a second before slipping on slowly. More bristle on the third. I hunched up; gritted my teeth.

"Same as before, JJ. Hold...hold...now go."

It hit us with pace, thumped and rocked us about. My arms burned and my grip slipped on the oars, but we held her firm. I turned once more. Another wave was forming. This one had legs on it. It popped up high and bulleted towards us.

"Row," I said, screaming over the whine of the winds. "Row, or we're sunk."

Chapter 16

If the "Bull" Goggin had seen us then, he'd have flaked the shins clean off us for prostrating ourselves like a pair of weak and wishy-washy weeds. We passed over the wave all right, rode up the face and slingshot down her back. But by the time we pulled the oars in, we were so worn out that all we could do was collapse back down on our backs, panting and heaving and spluttering.

As swift as the storm had landed, it left, routing the squabble of winds and rain away. Calm draped over the ocean, so we figured the currach could drift for a stretch. I lay there resting, with the gentle roll of the waters at the keel and the puffs of wind on my face. My breath calmed down and the fatigue fell away a slip. I opened my eyes and eased myself up. God, I was hanging. Hunger. Pain. Nausea. They were all there in equal measures. My hands were frozen and numb. I tried to move my fingers, but they stayed coiled up, rigid and waxen. I shook them out, cupped them to my mouth and blew some air to revive them.

"JJ," I said, smacking his forehead. It was hard not to hit him and even harder to miss. He opened his eyes and growled. "Were you counting?"

"Was I hell."

I glanced for the shore. In the blackness, it was near on impossible to pick it out. I squinted some more and caught the glint of white-water tumbling in. My eyes followed its trail until it poured upwards and stopped. There it was—a grey band barely visible through the murk—the beach. "Must be about eighty or so strokes, I guess. Though it felt like a thousand."

JJ hauled himself up and stretched for the skies. The sight of him wobbling about had my skin prickling from fright. What with the fifteen-stone heap of him and an arse that could tow the moon, just one slip and he'd wreck us.

I grabbed his tracksuit and yanked him back down. "You'll capsize us with your hugeness. Will you sit?"

He slumped into his seat. The currach juddered about, and water leapt up inside.

"You were rowing?' he said. "I thought you were just sitting there shouting encouragement like one of those coxswains?"

"Funny that, because if it wasn't for you and your generous proportions I'd have practically skipped out. No bother at all."

He swung around to face me. "The fat card…Already? It's wearing a bit thin, isn't it?"

"Suppose it is…Unlike yourself."

It must have been the salt in our brains, because like two half-wits we broke down in a fit of giggles.

"Anyways eighty's the guess," I said, when my meltdown had subsided. "But it's not an exact science is it? I'm sure if we keep going for another hundred we'll be there or thereabouts."

We grabbed for the oars, and JJ got into the count. With the currach gliding over the waters, we rowed on, and the rhythm bored me into a trance. I thought of my childhood self and the fear for the sea that'd been nurtured into me from an early age. I recalled those green-haired Merrows enslaving men, waveriders snatching deckhands, the Kelpie, the Bean Sídhe, the Pookas. They were all there those tales, taller and wider than life, and they spilled from the mouths of our elders with a richness to the words that'd strike a picture in your mind with no effort at all.

"And two hundred," JJ said. He set the anchor, boarded the oars and swivelled about to face me. "You're thinking again aren't you? I told you to leave that to the experts."

I kept still for a moment; heard the hush of water parting on the prow, the peal of a bell from a buoy nearby. Sounds unseen at sea were not to be trusted. I shifted forward, dug my hands up under my thighs and shivered from the chill settling over me. "Well, what's your take on all this?"

He bowed his head, his fingers steepled. "No idea. Well, no concrete idea. But I do know one important thing...It must be a tiny haul of drugs, because this currach isn't capable of trawling much."

"Not sure about that. It managed to carry you, all right."

We laughed a bit, relaxing. With the last few days hanging over me, laughing even for a moment was a relief. "Anyway why would they trust us with drugs worth a load of money in a boat designed in the famine. I mean, if you were looking to land a shipment in the morning you'd dig up something more seaworthy than this yoke."

"Well, we're here now."

I groaned. Vagaries. The lad thrived on them. The ah-sures, the God-knows, the you-know-yourselfs, the well-now-sos, the that's-about-the-size-of-its. Ready-made verbal filler for those who were too cute to speak their minds.

"That's profound stuff, JJ."

He glanced up and mumbled to himself before tracing the sky with his finger like he was scrawling a star-map in the clouds. "We'll give it an hour before heading back."

"You're not telling the time from the stars?" I asked, immediately regretting it. The minute I spoke, his face lit up. I'd seen it many times before. He'd force-feed you facts until you'd beg for saving. A coma. An aneurysm. A horde of cannibals with empty pots. An-y-thing.

"Oh, you can," he said. "It's called sidereal time. And you use the Saptarishi's relationship to Polaris—"

I raised my hand. "I'll have to stop you there."

"Don't know why I bother. I'd have to dumb it way down for you to understand even a fraction of it anyway."

I slipped off the seat and crawled to the side. With my back resting on an old nylon fishing-net and my legs stretched out, a heaviness set upon my bones. For the first time in days, I allowed my exhaustion wash over me. I looked to land and spied slivers of lights shining here and there. Houses, I assumed, with those turf-briquette fires that my granny swore had smoked the slyness into the locals' mouths—sleeveens the lot of them. They'd pinch the eyes right out of your head. However snaky Apache was, these boys, with their

Gaelic drawl and sniping eyes, would've sorted him quickly.

I fished out an old wax tarp from under the seat and wrapped it around me. It smelt of rotten kelp and diesel fumes, but it broke the breeze nicely.

"Think we'll have less than an hour if it gets any colder," I said. "Oh, and if we lose the anchor, feel free to dangle yourself in."

"What?"

"You know...because you're—"

"I'm fat...I know. I get it. The fish get it. And you're going to get it, if you mention it one more ruddy time."

I chuckled a bit from the state of him—face with a raging puss on it, hands blanched from gripping the seat tight. "Don't get your pulse going. You could burn calories that way you know. Ruin your look—"

"You're a shite hawk, Ben."

We sat in contemplative silence for a while until JJ spoke once more. "So? How's your head now? Has the frustration died down any?"

I fidgeted with the edge of the tarp. "You know I was there when Ella was born?"

"No."

"I never told anyone. Swore a vow of secrecy to Mam at the time. She felt ashamed Dad wasn't there for some reason."

JJ leaned back on his hands, the hint of a frown forming. "Had they fought?"

"No. That was the madness of it all. Dad was attending a farmers' association conference in the Gresham Hotel in Dublin at the time. Mam went into premature labor three weeks early, so there was no blame on his part at all."

"But she still blamed him?"

I smiled. "She did. It was the kind of night where she'd have bawled at the moon for daring to shine."

I pictured the night Mam had burst through my bedroom door with her hand clutched to the underside of her stomach. We barely made it to the Mercy Hospital when she collapsed from the agony. Within seconds, the surgical team rushed in and whisked Mam away for an emergency C-section. The beeps and shouts and pure speed of everyone terrified me. But they got Ella out all right, all eight and a half pounds of her. I never forgot the time she was borne—5:23 a.m. The nurses brought her out to me wrapped up in a navy cotton towel while Mam came around from the anaesthetic. "I'd the honour," they said, "of being the first Hackett to hold her." It left a mark on me then, even though I was only twelve years of age at the time. Her hazel eyes glaring sleepily at me. The smell and satin feel of her skin. The way she settled into the crook of my arm as if she were moulded to fit it precisely. She cooed the whole time I held her, and I smiled at the incessant babbling. Already a chatterbox with plenty to say.

Anger welled up inside me once more. How could anyone abandon their child and pass them on to strangers to rear? It must have taken some amount of cruelty in a person to be capable of doing all that—

A distant drone broke the night. We scrambled up and stared into the darkness. I turned towards the sound and recognised the continuous low thrumming of a ship making headway.

"That'll be our guys, right on time," JJ said.

"What do you reckon—a mile away?"

"Maybe. Judging by the engine, she's running parallel to us. Probably behind the headland. So at least that. A mile...mile-and-a-half."

Bang.

The night lit up in front of us. The headland appeared under the blaze of a flare. It hung in the sky, painting the scene in a lick of white. The shadows in the cliffs twisted and shifted, the waters below looked sick and alien in the artificial glow.

A second shot cracked, followed by a third and a fourth. Each flare whizzed upwards with a tail of smoke arching behind it. Each of the four hovered further apart. The zone of illumination inched ever closer to our boat, but for the moment we remained hidden in the dark.

"Someone's firing them from the cliffs," JJ said.

"Rescue flares? Someone in trouble maybe? They're burning for a long enough time."

JJ cursed. "They're not distress flares, they're army issue parachute flares. Battlefield grade. They'll hang for near on a minute up there. What did Apache say he was? An Irish Ranger?"

"An ex-Ranger. Maybe he's showing them the way into the cove?"

"Yeah, because smugglers just hate the dark."

"Still...let's give it a minute. I'm not rowing in until we grab the gear."

JJ sat and set the oars. "We should go...now."

"Just hang on and give it a second."

"That isn't our contact, Ben, trust me. Let's go now.

It's probably too late already."

"Well, if it isn't our contact, we've committed no crime, so quit whinging and wait."

A minute later, the silhouetted shape of the vessel rounded the headlands. Its engines slowed down to a slow hum. The glare of the flares had weakened. I struggled to see her through the shadows, but by the height of the bridge she was hefty enough. The ship's searchlight tracked left and right, before fixing on the last remaining flare. Its motor quieted down to a whisper.

"You see, JJ, I told you that—"

The high-pitched whine of a different sounding engine cranked up. The waters roared as propellers cut fast. A chill slipped across my neck. I twitched my fingers and instinctively stepped back. Whatever that was, it came too noisily, too fast, with far too much purpose.

Bang.

Another flare flew, but it exploded too soon. It illuminated for a second in a flash of phosphorous white. I gasped at the sight of the stone-grey skin of the ship, the red-and-white flag high on the mast and an inflatable rib boat bulleting over towards us like an angry terrier let loose off the leash.

"It's the coastguards," I said in a voice tinged with panic.

I jumped back down and set into the row, whipping the currach about. "They know we're here. Someone marked us. But there's no way they saw us clearly in the dark. The flares...that's what they're aiming for. Right?"

"They see with radar, not their eyes," JJ said. "They spotted this currach before we did."

"Rubbish...They knew where we are, not who's in it."

He paused and turned with that doey-eyed stare on him. "You can't outrun them, Ben."

"How long until they close on us?"

"Standard rib tops out at twenty-five knots. So in this chop...maybe two minutes max."

"Well, just shut up and row." I checked for the lights on shore. "Sharp right, now. Make a beeline for it."

We raised the right oars, and the currach nipped into the turn. She slipped to port and we set off fast. The thunder of the engines grew louder. The lighthouse lit up the rib for a second. It careened over the waves with its fire-red snout stuck up for the hunt and her belly heaving with guards.

"Enough of this." I slipped off the tarp and flung it to the side.

"Why d'you—"

"You hear that?"

"The boat?"

"No, waves. We can't be far out. Radar can't see underwater, right?"

"Right."

"So we keep underwater as much as we can. We'll split up, head for shore. Let them puzzle over an abandoned currach."

"No way, that's too far out. We'll never—"

"You're flabby, you'll float." I grabbed him by the arm and hauled him up. "Let's go...now."

I shoved JJ over one side and dived over the other. It normally would have taken a necking of whiskey to get us carousing in the Atlantic sea at night. Yet there I was, in the blackness and cold of it, sinking for feet and fancying them fathoms.

I kicked upwards once, twice, and took a gulp of air before submerging again. It was an eerie experience, surfacing for breath with the motor louder each time and not daring to sketch around. I was one of those *mozos* with the bulls on his back, clattering down Pamplona with no option other than continuing on. But I'd struck off too fast. Cramp knotted my legs. Muscles wilted on my arms. I surfaced once more with the noise of the rib's engine ticking over only yards away.

I held my breath and slipped under. I turned on to my back and stared up where the sky should be. I saw no moon and no stars. The engine roared closer, the water adding meat to its hums. It tingled my skin and groaned in my ears. I shut my eyes and found comfort in the act. When I opened them, a light on the surface washed over my spot. I descended a few feet more and watched the froth of the outboard motor slide past. It stopped, drifted a moment, and then they slowly began to circle.

They were upon me.

I flipped back around and swam blind through the water. I tasted the slickness of it and felt the sway of its current and the heaving weight of it above. My lungs protested, but I didn't dare surface. I scrambled on until they screamed at me. Lights popped in my eyes. Fleeting stabs pierced my ribs like a swarm of stinging hornets. A panic mushroomed up in my brain.

I arched my back, zipped above water and gasped a lungful. I must have looked mental then, feasting away on air with an asylum smirk on me. I blinked the sea from my eyes and spat its trace from my mouth. Waves crashed about nearby. A shout, closer still, sounded to my side. I turned and spotted the rib less than twenty yards away. The murk of the night cast a tawny rinse to its red, and it rose and fell from my view as it rode the whip of the swell. The whine of its engine had petered down to a purr, and the voices on-board came muted on the wind. Four kitted-up guards stood anchored to their spots. With every bob-and-dip of the boat, they mirrored her movements with a silky ease. The searchlight panned slowly around. I ducked back under and let it sweep over my position.

The light fixed elsewhere. I floated back up into the cover of darkness. The thumping in my chest faded fast, and I slowly turned for shore. Within seconds, something tugged at my leg. I kicked it away, but it snagged me again, harder this time. I swung in circles and stuck my face in the water. Fear paralysed me. My pulse pounded in my ears. Despite being wet, I'd have sworn I was sweating.

Guards to my right. Invisible critters beneath me. Adoption, nuns and scobies with guns. The whole insanity of my days erupted. Words gathered on my tongue. Bunches of them. Curses, blasphemes, rants and ravings, all queued up waiting to be released like a bunch of bricked-up hooligans at a police cordon. I needed to howl at everything and anything all at once.

JJ appeared with a limp smirk on him, and I punched him square on the nose. He sunk back under, popped back up, so I smacked him again for the shock of it.

"Quit it, Ben," he said in a whisper. "They're just over there."

"That wasn't funny."

"It was a bit, to be fair. Anyways, you'll love this."
He raised his hand and produced the old nylon netting
from beneath the water.

"You went back for the net?"

"May put the brakes on them a bit" He pulled a
drenched balaclava over his face. "Unlike you...I think
before I leap."

"So what? You're gonna throw a net over them and
scare them off with that Halloween rig-out you've got
on?"

"Not them, the outboard motor. No motor equals no
chase...simple."

"That'll never work."

"Well, it did in my head."

"I'll be honest, JJ, I don't think that's a shrewd
endorsement of—"

He was gone. He dove underwater and swam in the
direction of the rib, leaving me bobbing about on my
lonesome. For a moment nothing much happened. The
guards drifted with the motor trimmed, and waves
jostled them about. When I spied JJ surfacing to the rear,
I almost laughed. He was in full-out guerrilla mode. If
only Val could see her angelic offspring then—glammed
up like a terrorist, about to mangle a government boat,
and probably ruining his pants from the excitement of it
all. The boys in the rib tracked the searchlight. I watched
in disbelief. No way would the net stop a motor's blade.
It'd be shredded to bits with barely a bother. The guards
would swing around, spot JJ ghosting nearby, and club
him like the flabby seal he was.

JJ gathered the net in both hands and closed the last
few yards to the rib. He stopped and fed the net towards

the motor. Silence set over the ocean. The wind dipped its tongue, and the sea quit flapping. He was bound to fail. The net was too old, too frail, the plan too crazy.

The groan of a motor seizing up cut a nauseating chord. JJ sunk down, and the engine coughed and hacked a plume of smoke upwards. The guards cursed. One of them yanked at the starter, ripping it violently towards his chest, but the engine only screeched and puttered to a stop. More curses came then, more limbs thrashed about the rib. One of them swung the searchlight left and right, and I ducked underwater again. By the time I'd resurfaced, JJ'd emerged next to me, and we swam silently back towards shore.

When we reached the beach, we crawled out of the surf and lay on our backs, shaking. Sand stuck to my skin, gritty and clinging. A frigid wind bawled off the sea. My teeth chattered from the shock of the cold. Tracksuits, it seemed, weren't fit for night swimming.

I blew into my hands and wrapped them around my chest. There wasn't a shred of strength left in my limbs. "I wonder what that was all about."

"Haven't you worked it out yet?" JJ sat up, removed his shoes and poured out the seawater. "We were Apache's shills."

"His what?"

"Decoys."

Chapter 17

We walked lost in the night, skirting the coast in drenched clothes. Whoever had laid these boreens must have had a touch of the poet in them. With all the corners and rises and dips, it took us twice as long to go half as far in a direction we'd never intended. It was the standard Irish experience. Once the country had you in her grip, you'd wander the labyrinth of her charmed meanderings for days before she'd allow you back out.

"That's it," JJ said. He glanced at the sky briefly before stopping. "It must be ten p.m. already. I'm soaked and tired of this wild goose chase. I'm going home."

"Ah, quit your whinging," I said. "We're nearly there."

"Nearly there. Meaning where?"

"Apache. Promises. Barnamire. The truth about my mouldy parentage."

His eyebrows pulled together, furrowing his brow. "We're nowhere near all that. And anyway, it looks to me as if Apache doesn't want to help us. So what's the plan now?"

I ignored the question. It was always best to step quietly out of JJ's brain-maze, lest I get caught in the trap of putting logic to my feelings. Truth be told, the rage in me had been simmering since we'd landed on the road and realised Apache had scarpered.

"What will I do?" I paused and waited for him to catch up, before continuing. "When we get back to Cork?"

He nodded.

"I'll make Apache keep his word. I'll march right up to him and demand it."

"And if he reneges? What then? Will you finally allow us to go home?"

"If he reneges? What, like if he pulls a cute stroke and slips away, or lumps me out onto the streets with a big kick up my hole to wish me well? That kind of thing?"

"Yeah."

"Well then." I poked him twice in the chest. "I'll burn those nuns out myself."

"You won't."

"Just watch me. I'll gather the tyres, the pallets, the rubbish, and pile them high into a pit. I'll douse it in gas, step back with a smile and send the whole lot up in flames."

"Good man, you've got it all worked out—"

"You're damn right, I have. And after I've snuck in and swiped the info, I'll punch my goddamn abandoning parents plum in their mouths...repeatedly. And I'll laugh in their faces while they bleed and beg for mercy. Got it?"

"Or something like that."

"Yeah...or something like that."

"Though probably not anything in any way even remotely resembling that at all."

I laughed despite myself. In fairness to JJ, he could dampen the fuse in me with a swift few lines when needed. I grabbed him by his shoulder, and we set off once more. "The punching is a guarantee, though. Multiple bruises will happen upon them. Whoever them may be."

"I'll set my watch by it. Will I?"

"You do that, chief. You do that."

After a mile, I clambered up on to a mossy rise and stood for a while, studying the lay of the land. I yearned for a pub or a church, or even one of those shacks I'd imagined on the ocean earlier. Maybe we'd nick a bike, or hitch up a horse and trap. Even a mule with a gammy leg would do—anything to speed our exit back to Cork. But there was nothing but hedgerows and hills and ditches full of mucked-up puddles, and those piddling fields swollen with hay bales all patched together by dry-stone walls. I always hated those walls. Had the look of something built by drunkards on the job for a laugh. All quilted together in a higgeldy-piggeldy way they were, and not a straight line connecting a single run of them.

"Any sign of life?" JJ asked.

"Not a jot." I sat on the grass and pulled the cuffs of my tracksuit down over my hands to warm them. I glanced down at JJ. He'd been tramping in my wake for miles now, with a doom-filled huff to him and his shoulders slouched down.

"You all right there? You seem a bit down in the mouth."

JJ drove his hands into his pockets and rolled back and forth on the balls of his feet. He went to speak, but all he managed was a twitch of his cheeks. There were only two occasions my giant friend fell silent; when he was hungry or snoozing. And I doubted he could have been this annoying in his sleep.

"I am a bit peckish, actually," he said.

I laughed at the admission. "I knew it. How long's it been now since your last feeding?"

"Well, I managed a ham sandwich back in the station, but—"

"They fed you in the station? They gave me nothing there. And what about the bags of crisps Apache gave us?"

"If it's not on a plate, it doesn't count."

"Ah, you poor thing. It must be awful for you, suffering in silence like that. Come on in here, and I'll give you a hug."

"Seriously, Ben. I'm so famished I'm imagining weeds for salads and rocks for buns. I've been licking my wrists for the salt since we left the sea. Hell, I spotted a verge with a sprout of dock leaves up the road and I'm still salivating from the shape of them."

There was a brief swell of silence, and then we chuckled. "That's pure gold, JJ. Thanks for that. Come on, come here, get under the wing, you poor sorry soul ya."

He wandered up and I grabbed him in a headlock.

"I promise...next town we see, I'll find some trough for you to park your snout in—"

We heard the car before it appeared. The creaking and cranky groan of a gearbox scarred the quiet of the night. I leaped down onto the tarmac.

"Here we go now, JJ. Get down in the ditch. People rarely stop for one man hitchhiking, not to mention two drenched blow-ins."

"No one ever stops for hitchhikers at night."

"They'll stop." I prodded the air with my thumb and angled my good side out.

An old, rusty Ford pulled up and stopped right by us. It'd brakes like a banshee's wail on it, and it towed a trailer brimming with tosses of hay lashed down with net and rope. I walked to the driver's side door and tapped the window twice.

"Scully's the name...What's it ye be needin'?" the man asked, with a screechy whine to him.

However needling his voice was, it was the best of the rest. A wet, mouldy stench wafted up from where he sat. With trousers dug into his boots and baling twine tied around his waist, he'd the look of someone who'd just climbed down off a scarecrow pitch.

"We need a lift," I said. "The tour bus left us stranded."

"Tour bus is it?"

"Yip."

He stared at me hard and sniffed. "Ye be lyin' to me, boy...dat right?"

"No, no, we—"

"Well...I've no need for knowing yer business, but I'll ney leave two pups astray on a night full of spit. Jump in, I'll get yis as far as I'm goin' as I'm goin' nawt further than dat."

"That'll do us fine, thanks."

I wandered around to the passenger side.

"The dag sits up front. Lay both yer asses 'n' the hind of us."

The seats squelched when we sat on them. The inside had a whiff of damp dog. I ran my hands along the frayed leather covers and found tufts of moulded-up horse-hair for lining. I flicked them away, but they clung to my skin. I shook them again, yet still they remained. It was as if the car itself was intent on infesting me. I shuddered from the thought of it crawling over my skin and ferreting into my person until I emerged the other side talking queerly, humming of feet and with a massive appreciation for the beauty of cute-hoorery.

"Keep a sketch for Sé here," Scully said. "With ye two fancies, he may take a shine a yis. So keep yer hands in yer pockets...Fair warnin'?"

"Fair warning," we said in unison.

"Now, where ye two boys headin'?"

He jabbed at the gearstick, and the car juddered into the hill. The exhaust wheezed and rattled, and the radio leaped to life.

"We're a hopin' to get a lift back to Cork a ways see," I said, getting into the lilt of him.

"Cork? I was close to it once. But there's dust atop those years now. Had me nose touchin' the border and the whole stretch of your county blushin' in the height of summer. Rode up the tailwind from Dún Chaoin, I did. With a sling full of food. A four-hour trot it cost me. And the aul' nag was fluthered, but a few swigs put steel back in her flanks."

"That's terribly sad, but—"

"Anyways, so I says to myself, 'Scully, get up the saddle, the day'll be driftin' and the ache in yer belly needs a look at these lands.' See, I'd an eye to broadnin' me future those days. And hadn't I so many poets and seanchaí notes in me head that I'd a cravin' to wander. But..."

He fell silent and threw a hand over his pup's head,

patting it twice. Growing up in a house full of Catholics, I'd seen the wistful eyes of regret many times.

"So you might like another go?" I said. "Take a wander with ourselves. We'll show you the sights."

"At this hour in the night? Not a chance. I'm headin' to Ballymaughan myself. Ye can call into Dooleys, see if any soul's drivin' the graveyard route to Cork. But I'd say nawt will stir tonight."

"Why's that?" I asked.

"Féile day, lads. At midnight we start the annual celebrations. They'll be chompin' mad until Thursday. Won't be a sober soul for miles until then. Ye take a drop yerselves? Two hardy bucks with two hardy stomachs...dat right?"

"That's right."

"Now boys. The lassies will go all gooey for two dapper-dans like ye. But I'll give a second fair warning. They'd lie down in nettles for it up here. So don't go off wasting yer cartridges on any howlers."

In fairness to this caffler, he'd a manner to him that'd have you forgiving him for his trampy ways. I shuffled forwards and Sé leapt into my lap. He coiled up snugly, and I held his chin in my hand. He was a Jack Russell, small and genteel, but with a titch of the maniac about him.

"Is there any chance, Scully," I said. "That you'd allow us borrow your car for the day? We're in a bit of a jam at the moment and we really need to get back to Cork tonight."

His eyes locked onto mine in the rearview mirror. The hawkish squint, the cobalt blues, the thin skin creased up at the sides. I'd no doubt about it. He'd a decent set of lie detectors on him all right.

"Get yerself tangled up in a tizzy there, boy. Dat right?"

"That's right. Can you help us?"

He went to talk, but instead sparked up a tab and smoked it down, butt and all. I could tell by the way he kept scratching his stubble and murmuring that he was in the midst of plotting, so I decided to let him to it and relaxed for a bit.

We crested the lip of a hill and snaked along a ridge. Far below lay a village with thatch houses and a church spire stabbing the sky like some divining rod for the heavens. Ballymaughan, I presumed. It had me coming over queasy from the picture-pretty quaintness of it all. We hit the flatlands and rumbled through a forest. I rolled down the window and stuck my face out, in that habit I'd formed as a kid. The wind licked my skin, and the headlights washed the night away in a blast of white. Birds, spooked from their perches, belted the air. The drone of the car sounded amped-up and anxious. I closed my eyes and saw Mam holding my head on her lap, and my younger self clammy and green from car sickness. "You need to follow the road with your eyes," she'd said. "Anticipate the turns and bumps and your belly will behave. And remember, Benjamin, it's the getting there that counts."

Oh, I'll get there, I thought. I'll find out the truth, wrap it up in a silver bow and present it to her on a silver platter.

We bumped over a humpback bridge and swept into the car park on the outskirts of town. Scully killed the engine, and, for a moment, we sat and listened to the cracks-and-clicks of the motor cooling down. He smacked his hands and turned around with a grin dialed up to his ears. "I tell ye what, lads. If ye help me out with a wee problem like, I'll be more than sated to give yis me car."

"We're listening," I said.

"Well, it just so happens there be a race on the village tonight, see. Annual event happenin' for near on centuries. Got a bet on a slip of a jackín. Twelve to one odds an' all he'll pay, if he noses home first." He aimed a sharp smile at me with his eyes sketching about. "But he's a bit on the spineless side yis see, and that be where you two bucks come in."

"You want us to fix it so your chap romps home first?" JJ said.

"Aye, that be the gist of it. Had a man lined up, but he could be groping both sides, if ye catch my drift. So if me man Wimps wins, yis get me car. Sound sweet enough for ye, lads? It's on in ten minutes or so. Ye could be away up the country in a jiffy."

I looked at JJ, and we both smiled. "We're in. But, how are we going to rig the race tonight with such short notice?"

Chapter 18

There was the hum of madness in the square of Bally-maughan. A bonfire burned in the green, and hundreds of locals jammed together roadside with burgers and pints in hand. Yellow-and-white bunting draped from eaves in a token nod to decoration. Judging by the cut of the men, though, that'd be as frilly as these boys got.

I stood to the rear of the crowd, standing as arranged near the start-finish line. "Stay apart," Scully'd said. "Don't let anyone cop-on dat yis know one another. And don't go drawin' any eyes yis ways."

I looked about me and laughed at the notion. That was all very well in theory, but being as goddamn gorgeous as I was, it was hard not to stand out amongst this sea of ginger. It was like a convention for the hope-lessly freckled in there, save for the occasional deep-teak tan some of the women had rubbed on. One of them kept barging into me and throwing weird shapes that in her drunken and deluded state she must have thought were sexy. Every time she flicked her eyes my way she nearly fell over. Scully was right. They'd rub you up for the rind of your rasher down here.

I glanced at JJ who'd wandered up to the stall outside Dooley's. He'd togged out in the local colours Scully kept in the boot and had his hands dug into the pockets of his shorts. I watched as he chatted with the organ-isers, hoping Scully had managed to keep his end of the bargain and freed up a spot in the race. The organisers seemed perplexed at first until JJ set about it. An exchange of words, a wag of the head, the shrug, and that was that. The deal was done, sealed with a handshake and back slaps all round.

JJ slapped the number four on his front. Someone spared him a pint, and he guzzled it down. Another offered him food wrapped in newspaper, and he wolfed it away. No sooner had he latched onto a second beer than a horn sounded, and three men marched out of Dooley's.

The first two hardchaws strode out like a pair of gamecocks. Then came Wimps, no doubt. He minced out onto the road ponytailed and glossy with two willowy arms swishing back and forth. The nickname "Wimps" was perfect for him. He'd have washed away in a dribbling shower.

The crowds from the four parishes screamed for their man as they passed. Wolf and Wa-Wa both looked as if they'd take a few smacks. They'd that Neanderthal finish that was a must-have in the country—sloping foreheads, ox-thick thighs, hands that'd crush rocks. And then came Wimps, sauntering behind JJ, with the burden of the damned in his eyes.

A bass drummer marched in front, leading them for the ceremonial lap of the square. He snapped out a boom-boom riff on the skin, and they moved in sync with the beat. Flags and hats were raised aloft, and cheers rolled around the square like a tsunami. When they returned to the start, a brass-and-reed band struck up in the centre of the green. The opening bars of *Amhrán na bhFiann* blared out from the bandstand.

Everyone fell silent and gazed towards the tricolour fluttering high overhead on the flagpole. With hands on chests, they belted out the national anthem, soaking the square in song. At the final bars, a man walked to the middle of the road mere yards from my spot, clutching a bullhorn, pistol-style.

"Now, genteels and gentles," he said, sending a hush through the streets. "The rules are...One lap. First to finish wins. Boxing at the start and the halfway point only. No biting. No weapons. No eye shots. And no tripping. Fight until one falls and run on the second horn. Other than that...have at it."

The crowd erupted in a din of whistles. The starter raised a hand and they dampened back down.

"And I'll ask ye good spectators to holster all projectiles and keep behind the tape. We don't want a repeat of last year's disaster. And, yes, horseshoes *are* a projectile and not a tool for well-wishing. So without further ado..." He raised a horn into the air. "On your marks...get set...go."

Wimps and Wolf set upon Wa-Wa with a flurry of punches that had the crowd sucking teeth at the sounds. Wa-Wa took a drunk-step back. Hands hanging limp. Eyes glazed over. He clattered back into the crowd, but a web of hands kept him upright.

JJ lurched forward, grabbed Wa-Wa's ears and drove in a knee, snapping his head back. He followed it up with two jabs to the nose and a swift uppercut to the chin. The crowd winced, a tooth whirled out, and he flumped to his back with a thud.

A cheer erupted, the horn sounded, and the three still standing took off up the street. They reached the halfway point, but I couldn't see anything through the fire blazing away in the green. Judging by the thuds and jeers, though, someone was taking a few years off another. A chant swelled in the crowd opposite and rolled towards us. With every thump, they screamed out a name. "Wolf, Wolf, Wolf." Their voices bristled with urgency. The horn sounded once more, and the victors emerged from behind the fire. JJ, it seemed, had fallen.

I cursed and slipped behind the crowd, keeping my back to the wall. I dug the balaclava out of my pocket and pulled it on. Wimps and Wolf streaked around the last bend, and the speed of Wolf sent him haring into the crowd, spraying them like skittles. They shoved him back out, but Wimps had closed to feet.

The line was near. A bottle came hurtling at Wimps, but it sailed low and wide and smashed by his feet. Nearly forty feet remained. I slid in behind a group of local lads. I shoved to the front and ducked under the tape. All eyes were on the race, so no one noticed me standing out in front. Wolf's head barrelled forward. I crouched down low, dialled into his step and counted.

One.

Two.

I whipped my arm up fast and hard, catching him flush on the chest. The impact whirled me around. I spilled into the crowd, sending a bunch of boys with me to the ground in a tangle of limbs. Pain seared through my shoulder, but I shook it off. I clambered back up and spotted Wolf laid out flat and Wimps hoisted high on the crowd. I looked around at the remaining faces. Old Wolfie's lot, I assumed. And my, how fondly they regarded me. They'd their fists clenched white and a communal look of murder blazing in their eyes.

"Skin that little shit," one said.

I ran down the alley with the horde chomping mad behind. The alleyway ended by the docks. I swung right and skirted the cars lined up by the boat club. The racket to my rear was frightening. The smack-and-clap of their feet, the breathing and panting, the howls for my head. I spotted the spire less than a hundred yards away. I leaned forward, pumped my arms and stretched out away from them.

A short spurt was all I'd in the tank, but it was enough to lose eyes. I swept around the corner, jumped the gate of the church and ran around to the vestry door. I knocked once, and it opened. The priest looked out and yanked me inside.

"Change as we walk," he said. "And get out the front."

We exited the sacristy and crossed the altar. I pulled off my mask and top and put on the jersey hidden in my trousers. It was maroon-and-white, the Wolf's parish colours. I had to give it to Scully, he'd catch a greasy pig that fella. We genuflected by the cross and strolled down the aisle to the front door.

"You ready?" the priest asked.

"I'll be grand, Father. Thanks."

"Just act roaring drunk. You'll fit in nicely."

He slid back the bolt, heaved open the door, and I walked calmly out with the screams of my pursuers still bothering the night.

"And remind Scully I expect my ten percent tonight."

"Will do."

"For the roof repairs, of course."

I turned up the alley and passed a few of the chasers who streamed down towards me. They barely gave me a second glance, so I tipped away up to the back of Dooley's. I bowed my head low and wandered inside. By the bar an old fella sat hunched over, nursing a whiskey and holding court with himself. And there to my right was Scully, Sé and a dozing drunkard, all bunched up together on one side of a nook.

"Nice spot," I said, slipping in opposite them.

"Aye, it is dat. Down the back. Outta sight o' gawkers and earwiggers."

I nodded at the lad with empties piled around him. "I take it this is who JJ replaced?"

"Tis, the excitement got the better o' him, see." He clapped his back and laughed a triumphant laugh.

"Anyways, it's done," I said. "But it may be contentious, seeing as how I'd to clothesline Wolf only yards from the end."

Scully pushed and pulled his pint like he was blessing the table. "Ah, that kind of thing happens all the time. Rules are rules. First crosses the line wins. You did a grand job, the two of ye boys. Brought a tear to my eye it did, watching JJ beat those two bulls before goin' down like a Fenian hero." He fished about in his pockets and slid the keys across to me. "Here ye go, as promised. She's topped with juice, but a bit iffy o' the hills. So make sure you take a run at 'em."

"Will do." I spun the keys on my fingers and clasped them tightly. "D'you mind me asking, though. How much money did you actually win?"

"Yis the taxman boy, dat right?"

"No, I was just—"

"Just rootin' about for the fun o' it then?"

"Forget it. It's late anyway. I've to go meet JJ by the car." I shuffled to the edge of the bench, and he grabbed me by the wrist.

"Before ye head away, boy...yis have made an aul man glad. A lifetime o' laments have been righted in our parish tonight." His eyes glistened. "I couldn't be prouder if yer were me very own sons."

I stood and sculled the dregs of his pint. It left a tang of rust on the tongue.

"Go easy there, Scully. I already have two dads. Three would be the end of me."

Chapter 19

We parked outside the Tenns after pulling an all-nighter drive from Ballymaughan. We'd have arrived earlier, if it weren't for the pips from the motor every time JJ leaned on the gas. Thankfully there was a little murkiness left to the night, so we still had time to convince Apache to help us. But I knew it wouldn't be long before dawn lit the city, and breaking into a convent in the height of day would have been exponentially more difficult.

Despite my horrific few days, I managed to catch some sleep on the way up. I'd balmed out in the back of the car, leaving JJ to do the chauffeuring. And what a sweet little snooze it was too. The grit of tiredness was gone and my mood was honey. JJ, on the other hand, looked raw. Wolf packed a bit of a punch by all accounts, and he'd landed a half dozen or so of his sweeteners on him.

I shuffled up and rubbed the fog from the window. Something caught my eye, followed by a metallic clatter and a whine. A fox skulked across the shadows, tipping his nose into bins and spraying the ground. I glanced at the clock glowing green on the dash. The digits blinked once and flicked to 4:31 a.m. I'd never seen such an ungodly hour before, and I didn't care for the look of it then. No wonder there wasn't a single soul traipsing the streets around us. They'd more bloody sense. It was far too early for the ill heads of Cork to meet their hangovers.

I stared at the grey drudgery outside. "Nah, it's complete and utter claptrap, JJ. Distance doesn't make the heart grow fonder."

"It's absence."

"What?"

"Doesn't matter. Anyway, I know I said this before, but there doesn't seem to be anyone about."

"Ah, they'll be inside chopping up the haul with rat poison or whatever it is they do?"

"Yeah, I suppose, but—"

A hand slapped twice on the driver's window. JJ rolled it down and a hooded head poked in.

"Name's Jesus," said a young fella astride a bike two sizes too small for him.

He was that spunky gurrier-type with the bizniz buzz about him. With a shaved head, emaciated face and chintzy studs blinging up the ears, his wasn't too difficult a breed to spot.

He leaned on the door and stared at the inside of the car. "This is some manky ride. I'd say it'd be safe enough to park her around here all right."

Not a hair on his chest, and he was already capable of stripping wallets and shiving ribs. "Praise be," I said. "Now, can you cycle away and leave the grownups in peace?"

He shot me a look. It was that perfect loutish stare, deadpan and glaring. He twisted the end of a rollie, sucked it and sparked it up. "Are you two beauts Benjamin and JJ?"

"We are."

"Well, you're late." He took a drag, left the smoke gather around his mouth, before sucking it deep and blowing it back out his nostrils. "Apache's waitin' for ya up by Barna. He says to get up there pronto, like, or he's gone."

"Apache's expecting us?" I asked. "Doubtful."

"Honestly, I don't know why he's any mass on ye. Course he was expecting ye. Fact is he said there'd be three of ye. And the chief's never wrong." He pushed JJ aside and peered in the back.

"What you looking for?" I asked. "Smurfs?"

He glared at me again. "Funny fiend ain't ya?"

"Well, what do you suppose we'd have hiding in the foot wells?"

"Ye'd be amazed how easy it's to hide something big in a place so little."

"So your mam said."

JJ and myself broke down. Our shoulders shook, our eyes streamed, our mouths went soprano with the squealing. God knows what Jesus did, because for those brief few moments that half-penny line became comedy gold and it had us bent over from the pain of the meltdown.

"Ye two finished?" Jesus asked, eventually.

I wiped my eyes dry. "We are ya."

"Well, let this be yer first and final warning. If ye diss me or me ma again, I don't care what the boss says, I'll put holes in both yer eyes...Got it?"

"Oh, yeah," I said. "No worries. Sorry, Jesus. Slip of the tongue."

"So, where's Scully?"

"Scully?"

"Yeah, boy. Scully. Talks too much and runs with that mutt of his Sé. Meant to collect you two and drive straight here. You should have been here hours ago. Been freezing my nads off all night waiting for you two bogmen. Thought ye for no-shows, like."

That godforsaken country tramp had been tied to Apache all this time. I could see him tittering away down in that hokey village of Ballymaughan, buying mucker's liquor for his muck-savage friends in his mucky little tavern.

I clipped the back of JJ's head. "Where were you on that one? I thought you said you'd a sixth sense or some other hippy, chakra crap for lies and...what's that word that has you coming over all funny?"

"Subterfuge."

"Yeah that's the one. Sub-ter-fuge."

"Didn't really get much time to study him, now did I?"

I slumped back down and chewed at my cheek. "That sneaky so-and-so, though. I mean Jes—"

"I'll stop ya there," Jesus said. "Don't go disrespecting my name, like."

The brassiness of this lad. All attitude, like a copycat of Apache, and him probably still being tucked in at night by his mam. I shunted forward in the seat. "Go away and cop on to yourself, half-pint. Jesus, Jesus, Jesus—"

His hands moved liquid smooth, darting into his jacket and whipping out a spike.

"D'ya know why they call me Jesus?" he said, darting through the window. He jabbed the point at me. "It's 'cause I crucify any gowel who disses me, you see?"

I stared at the puce red face of Jesus. He'd that gagga-eyed temperament of a glue huffer about him. Cool to apoplectic in under a second with little more than a prod.

Normally, the threat of an eye-spike would have rattled me off of my peg, but the last few days had skewed my compass for sure. I was either numb or dumb, but no matter, because my pulse and nerve steadied me through. I pushed his face away and shoved him sharply back, sending him and his bike sprawling onto the tarmac. A flood of curses came hurling from him. All those four-letter specials.

"Let's get up to Barnamire, JJ. Before this guy calls his mammy."

"Can do." He inched the car away, leaned out and shouted out after him. "In reality, you should adopt a Roman name to reflect the historical accuracy of your claims. The Romans were the ones who crucified Jesus. So maybe Pontius would suit?"

Jesus scrambled back up and pedalled along broadside. I rolled my window down and poked my head out. He cut an odd figure, riding limp with his razor head fuzzing with rage. He hopped off his bike and cupped his hands around his mouth to shout. "You'll get yours, baiys. I'll spike both yer eyes. Ya shower of goms."

I blew him a kiss and slumped back down into the seat. "I tell you what, JJ. His vocab is prison-ready. He's miles ahead of his peers that fella." I glanced once more at the clock ticking near five. "Put some weight on that pedal."

We raced through the narrows of Barrack Street.

There was nothing else doing. We were in the shallows of the night, and it wouldn't be too long before the sun rose. If we didn't get to Barnamire and start the fire soon our job would be near on impossible. There was something about darkness that amped up the fear of fire in man. Something primordial or innate I assumed, but a blaze in daylight was more likely to draw a crowd into song than frighten nuns enough to vacate their hidey-hole.

We pulled up outside Barnamire and waited with the engine idling in neutral. There wasn't a soul around. No corner-boys, no kerb crawlers, no walk-of-shamers, no all-night revellers and, certainly, no Apache. We were about to get out and have a nose, when Magic strolled out of a bush and waved.

"An unusual sight that," JJ said.

Magic tapped on the window, and JJ rolled it down.

"Lights off, follow in car," he said in that poetic way he had to him.

With the walls of the convent to our right, we crept along behind him through gates and on to a dirt track. A tingle in my stomach kept me silent. It'd set upon me like a rash the moment we left the backcountry of Bally-maughan and headed east. Call it nerves, call it fear of a fire-fuelled thieving in some Holy Josephine's recluse, call it the glorious thrill of finally getting my hands on the information of my birth. Whatever it was, it put a turn in my stomach right there and then.

Five minutes later we arrived waterside. Apache and a brace of his Pucas stood with two large bags slung over their shoulders. And just past them, right in the glare of the headlights, was a boat moored to the river wall, pulling at its tether.

"He can't expect us to get in that," JJ said. "I don't think I can handle another rowathon."

I had to agree. The notion of whipping about in the River Lee in a flimsy looking rowboat wasn't very appealing to me just then. I shifted forward and slapped him on both shoulders. "Final hurdle, JJ. We're on the home stretch now. We can manage another little paddle, can't we?"

He sighed and squeezed the steering wheel. "I suppose."

I felt a smidge of pain for JJ, truth be told. What a wreck of a few days. There wasn't another man alive that'd have followed me through it. "You know you're a living legend, JJ. Right?"

"Don't plámás me."

"We'll get back to Whitehaven in time for the match. I promise. And I'll personally whip the knees off of every one of those Glenbridge boys until my hands bleed from the effort. Deal?"

He laughed and opened the door. "You'd probably pull something just by trying. Don't play like such a girl again, and I'll be happy enough."

We jumped out and wandered up to the bank. I clambered up on to the wall and perched on the edge for a moment. A low gale sang in my ears, and the boat slumped gently against the pull. The river looked slick and black, and its steady flow seawards grew hypnotic in the scant light. It brushed up the walls and splashed back into itself, spinning little eddies of foam in its wake.

However unruly and savage the sea was, the constant wash of the river looked simple in comparison.

"How now, fellow criminals," Apache said.

I jumped back down and strode towards him. A few muffled laughs came from his cronies. I couldn't really deny them their fun; two wide-eyed lads from the sticks were on the cusp of losing their innocence after all. And by robbing nuns of all people. It was, to be fair, a rather asinine way of cutting your criminal teeth.

"It must seem like amateur night at the thieves' guild for ye boys," I said.

"Ah now, Benjamin. We're only yanking your chain. We all had to start somewhere after all."

"Yeah, well mine is morally robust, whereas you're only profiteering off of the addiction of misfortunates. That's a chasm of a difference in my book."

"Ah, po-tay-to, po-tah-to. Anyways, I see Scully pulled a swift one on you."

I couldn't really make out his expression in the dark, but by that smugness of his voice it was certain he was smirking. "I suppose he did. We should have guessed it really. He was far too willing to get us into the car."

"Yeah, that's Scully. Old school, but as sly as they come. Anyway, Benjamin, we'll make an absolute bomb with the haul we pulled in tonight, so the least I can do is light a little fire for you two. Man of my word and all that."

"That'd be you all right, Apache. Honest as the day's long. And where was that moral gumption earlier when you set us adrift in the sea as a decoy? You couldn't have warned us, no?"

"Nah. Worked better this way. Fair bouts to you for

dodging the coasties. Magic here said you pulled a quality trick on them. In fairness, I'd have bet against you."

"God, that just warms my insides. I do have one niggle about this whole thing, though."

"Go on."

"Do we really need another boating trip?"

"You do."

"Because I don't imagine nuns would be the most on-guard bunch in the world. Couldn't we scoot around the back and hug the wall?"

"You could, but it leaves too much to chance. The boat is bullet-proof."

I glanced at the four-foot wide slip of a currach with the tar chipping away from her ribs and the water already puddling her insides. She looked nervy and fragile. "I have to say she doesn't look up to much."

"She'll do just fine. Now then, we've got it all rigged up. The shed to the rear of the building will be our fire source. The lads here have already drenched it with diesel so all it needs is a light. No one will burn. So don't sweat it, JJ. We'll start it this side, but you two need to paddle around to the boathouse. It's the safest and quietest route in. The nuns' assembly point is towards the courtyard. So no one should see you enter."

"And how will we break in?"

He rubbed his hands together. "Now that's kind of my thing. We've every tool for any occasion. Hook them up, Magic."

The Pucas slung the two holdalls down in front of us, and Magic unzipped them both. He sieved through the items, holding them up and cataloguing them out loud.

"Torch, crowbar, masks, screwdriver, rope, gloves, trackies—"

Apache pinched my top. "To replace that bogger-chic style ye two are wearing. Couldn't help yourselves, could ye? Loving the GAA jerseys boys, but it's probably best to dress down for the shadows. On you go, Magic, show them the juicy stuff."

"Mace, scalpels...chains." He fondled them gently in his paws and ran them through his fingers, before placing them back in the bags. "Cuffs, flick-knife, knuckledusters—"

It was a toolkit for the mentally deranged. All it needed was a manual—a million ways to murder—and we'd be set.

"Hang on, hang on," I said. "We don't need the knives, or mace, or any of the rest of that crap."

"You sure?" Apache said. "There *are* nuns in there."

"Exactly...nuns. Elderly religious types. Not psychotic gangbangers ramped up on Ketamine."

He grabbed me by the shoulder. "You tell me," he said, layering the slyness into his voice. "Which one is worse?"

I shrugged his hand away and knelt down by the bags. "No weapons. I can't imagine a single possible situation where I would need to kill or maim or tie up a nun. No matter how nasty they are." I removed the arsenal and chucked them on the ground. They made for a horrific little pile there in the dirt. "Tracksuits, masks, torch and crowbar. That's all we'll need." I stuffed them all into the holdalls.

"'Never say never' is my motto," Apache said. "And besides it's not to kill them. It's more to coerce them."

"I'm sure the balaclavas and brawn will suffice. And anyway, isn't the point of the fire to lure them out? If you do your job correctly we shouldn't run into anyone."

"Fair enough, have it your way."

JJ and myself grabbed a bag each and stepped into the currach.

"Right so, ladies," Apache said. "Oar up." He unravelled the knot mooring the boat and walked with us as we drifted downstream. "A fire will be served in five minutes. If you don't have a watch, listen out for the whoosh. Those nuns will scuttle out in seconds. Give it two minutes and go for it. And, lads, whatever you two fools are taking in there, we won't be hanging around once the blues come flashing down on this place. You got me?"

He paused and pulled in the rope. The currach jammed up against the wall. He strode forward and bent down on his haunches to speak to us. "This is a one-time deal. Call it my charity for the year. If you mess it up—which you probably will—and get collared by the brass, make sure you zip those lips. Nothing good will come from dobbing me in. Trust me. But if you do, remember this—rat catching is a favourite pastime of ours. Wherever you go, I *will* find you. And JJ's mammy won't have to search for him, because I'll post him back to her in parcels, a pound-of-flesh at a time. Sweet?"

"Got it," I said.

He pushed us off into the current, and we drifted downriver. We grabbed the oars and feathered them in our hands. The strength of the current shunted us downstream. A quick flick of the wrists was all that was needed to control the drift. We rode close to the walls of Barnamire. They rose to only five feet tall at best, but with the added drop to the water we were certain to avoid the eyes of any curtain-twitchers. A hundred yards later, we swung right and rowed up to the boathouse pier. We guided her in to the steps, and JJ jumped out and laced the rope around the handrail leading up them.

"Come on," he said. He grabbed the bags from the currach. "And walk softly."

We shuffled up the steps and along the pier. Its concrete pilings had blown out millennia ago. They were nothing more than crumbling masses sandblasted by the winds and rinsed by the rain. The wharf sat nervously on top of them rattling with each step. Moss carpeted the planks, turning the whole boardwalk into a slip-and-slide ride. Our shoes squished in the sodden wetness of it all. However softly we trod, we still sounded like a bunch of hallions splashing about in a bog.

The boathouse attached to the gable end of the convent like a big, boxy umbilical. We paused by the entrance. The doorframe looked rotten. It would be easy to open.

"Should we leave the bags?" JJ asked, whispering in my ear. "There's hardly a need for them."

"We'll bring them with us, just in case someone's out for a pre-dawn stroll."

We changed into the tracksuits and pulled on the balaclavas, shoving the jerseys back into the bags. I tested the door handle, and it opened.

"That's a spot of luck, JJ."

"Do as we were told and wait for them to clear house?"

To the east, the first blush of dawn gathered on the horizon. Its pink light was no more than a slither in the night, and yet already it'd diluted the darkness. The wind changed direction and whipped about our feet, swirling a soft drizzle in on its tail. The mist shrouded us and set a chill on my skin. Nerves rolled down my spine, and I shivered, briefly.

A sudden whoosh stole away the quiet. Within seconds, bright and burning tongues leapt up from behind Barnamire. It swelled up fast into an orange-and-white glow. The brighter it grew, the darker it made the building. A series of cracks came quickly in succession. I closed my eyes and soaked up the sounds. I saw the wooden shed charring and warping and spitting out resin, and nuns fleeing for their lives. I saw the panels, all sanded and oiled and lovingly tended, creak and collapse into a charred tangle. I saw the agonised faces of my parents staring in shock at the convent laid to waste by my hands and the gavel of a judge slamming me down for life.

My mind was a stew of noise. Thoughts spun inside me, tornadoing into a weight of doubt. For the briefest while, I wanted to run around to the sheds and rip the fire away. But then I remembered all those lies and deceptions, all the half-truths whispered to me by my parents. The birthdays, the cakes, the candles and the infinite cards. All of those lost chances to tell me. The more they waited, the deeper the cut.

Eighteen years.

Eighteen birthdays.

Eighteen brand new lies.

I opened my eyes and stared at the sight; the fire was up. There was no going back now. I gave the thumbs-up sign to JJ who nodded once. "Once the nuns vacate, we take what's rightfully mine."

Chapter 20

An alarm rang out. Even from outside it sounded like a speed-drum ramped up to mental. If any ravers were in earshot they'd have legged it up here, dropped some tabs and melted into their trance-dance shapes. It'd have been a weird spectacle all right—seeing a bunch of nuns running for their lives with their habits barely on while a group of men had an impromptu dance.

Within seconds, lights flicked on in an upstairs window and dominoed along through the building until the entire top floor was alight. It didn't take long until a door crashed open, and panicked steps crunched on the gravel out front. I patted JJ twice on the shoulder. "Let's go."

I opened the door, and we inched inside. The interior of the boathouse was dank and dark and hummed of must. We paused for a moment, allowing our eyes to adjust. Cardboard boxes emerged from the shadows, piled high on both sides with a walkway through the middle. We moved to another door, and I tested the handle. Locked. I pulled out the crowbar, but JJ brushed it aside and held his finger to his lips. He clasped the handle firm, butted his hip and shoulder against it and heaved. It opened with a pop.

"Solid lock, rotten housing," he said, shredding the wood of the frame in his hands.

We moved on into the main building, ghosting through a utility room and out into the corridor of the internal quad. Sash windows ran the length of it, facing out onto a central courtyard. In the confines of the convent, the alarm blasted out a near deafening din. Already, I could taste the trace of smoke on the air, sulphurous, bitter and gritty.

We hunkered down low and crab-crawled along the wall to the corner. I laid the bag down and peered around. My skin prickled from the sight of Mother Superior ambling down the far end of the corridor. She glanced in each room as she passed, slamming the doors shut and locking them. Then she released the key chain, letting it spring back behind her frock, before ticking on a clipboard and moving onto the next.

When she reached the main exit, she paused, held the clipboard behind her back and gazed straight in my direction. I ducked out of sight and held my breath, certain that I'd hear the snap of her step bearing down on us. I pictured her craning her head around the corner and her cackling at the two of us. I saw those thin lips pulling tightly into a sneer. Lord knows what she'd actually have done, but I instantly regretted not grabbing a knuckle-duster. Women were sacrosanct to me, but if that wizened old witch had poked a nose round right then, I'd have taken her jaw off, no doubt about it.

Time passed, but no footsteps closed in. The only sound came from a heavy set of doors swinging shut. I looked again and my nerves retreated. She was gone, spirited away outside as if by magic. I nodded for JJ to follow, and I gathered the holdall in my arms.

"I assume you know the route to the office?" I asked.

"I do. Straight down, up the stairs as far as it'll go, then left, right and right again."

"Nice, JJ, nice. Glad to see your memory's intact. Even after Wolf gave you such a hiding. Now let's get a move on. I reckon we've about ten minutes tops before the emergency services make their way across town."

"They'll tackle the fire first. We've got shed-loads of time."

"Still, the sooner we get out the better."

We tipped down the corridor past the rooms where we'd once lain, cautious all the while for any stragglers. The last thing we needed then was for some poor old nun who hadn't heeded the bell, shuffling about with her hot water bottle hunting down the toilet.

We ran up the stairs and wound our way through the maze of turns, stopping outside Mother Superior's office. Right next door stood the file room with a padlock shackled to a meaty bolt. I knelt in close and peered at it. The lock was hardened steel and had a single-dial combination mechanism. There'd be no jimmying this one. The code lay in Mother Superior's head, and I feared no amount of torture or cajoling would release it from her.

"We'd need an oxy-acetyline torch to burn our way through it," JJ said.

"Yeah. That and about a two-hour stint. The door hinges are our only chance. I doubt we'll be able to lean our way through this. Brute force is required, I fear."

I stood and drove the crowbar between the frame and door as far as it'd go. I grabbed the handle with both hands and pushed with all my weight. The only crack came from my spine and hands that sounded like they were going to snap any moment. I yanked it back out and shoved it in further from the lock, to try and get the door to bow a bit. The crowbar slipped its purchase and flew from my hands, sending me cracking against the door on the way down.

"I did it," I said, half stupid from the knock on my jaw.

JJ laughed. "You did. If taking a splinter out of the frame is what you were after."

I glanced up and cursed. A tiny gouge in the wood was all my effort produced. It was less than a slither— probably no deeper than the layer of varnish.

"Should have brought Apache's arsenal after all," I said, exasperated. "We could have shot the lock off."

"And alerted anyone within a mile of this place in the process. Give me that thing." JJ picked up the crowbar. "Time to change tack."

He weighed the bar in his hand and moved in to study the run of the lock. His fingers caressed the hinges. He ran them along the edge of the panelling, tapping with his knuckles as he went. "Deadbolts, top and bottom. We'll never break in this way." He tried the office door. "Locked as well. But not so tough this one." With a heavy kick, the door swung in and he strode inside.

"Not really any further along, though. Are we?" I said, walking in behind him. Dawn had arrived. Streams of light sliced through the blinds and basked the room in a hazy glow. I sat in the chair opposite the desk, watching JJ pat the wall down. "What are you doing now?"

He ignored me and continued tapping. "Strange that the office doesn't have an internal door to the file room," he said. "Normally they'd have had direct

access, especially in these Victorian buildings." He
paused behind the desk, put his ear to the wall and
tapped once more. The wall made a hollow, clunking
sound. "Jackpot." He held the crowbar like a hammer
and swung. It sank in with ease. He jabbed until he'd
mapped out an outline of a door in the wall. Digging the
bar in, he pushed at the plaster like a lever. The dotted
partition groaned. He clawed at it once more, prising it
away in a single lump from the wall. It fell in a heap,
smashing against the desk.

The plasterboard disintegrated and whooshed into a
white mist. Dust itched up my nose and coated my
clothes and face in talcum-like powder. I sneezed twice
and fanned away the cloud. The swirling settled, and I
stepped up to the recess.

"You lucky so-and-so," I said, staring at a door
behind criss-crossed batons.

He pulled them away and tested the lock. It opened
outwards with an arthritic creak to it. "No...*that* was
lucky." He kicked the plasterboard on the opposite side
of the doorway. It gave way with ease, and we stepped
into the darkness of the room beyond.

The air inside the file room was stifling. Thick drapes
hung drawn on the windows, and blackout blinds kept
the light at bay. I fished out the torch, rattled it and
switched it on.

"Point it at the floor or away from the windows," JJ
said.

"They're blackout blinds. Nothing gets in or out."

"Just humour me."

I held it against my palm, the glare of the torch setting
my skin alight. "Anything stirring down below?"

JJ moved to the curtains and peeked out. "Nope. Just a bunch of nuns looking...nunnish."

The torch's soft glow was enough to find my way. Five filing cabinets stood hemmed up in a run against the wall opposite. The room was vacant besides them. Not a pen, not a sheet of paper, not a chair, nothing. Not even the usual cross or picture of Himself looking empty-handed and doleful.

I brought the torch up a smidge and inspected the cabinets. Each one had a label written in swirly, calligraphic writing. The nuns must have been at this game for decades. Every cabinet accounted for ten-year stretches. Fifty years of filthy secrets lined the walls. Fifty years of deceit and lies. There must have been hundreds of stolen or forgotten or discarded babies detailed in these drawers. Locked away behind thick doors with padlocks and bureaucracy and nuns as their wardens. No wonder there wasn't any religious iconography in this place; it was a room brimming with shame.

I aimed the torch low and let the backlight guide my eye. I shifted down to the third cabinet in line; 1970 was the year on the insert. I yanked the drawer out and shone the torch inside. Tabbed files were neatly arranged, girls on the right, boys on the left, and alphabetised according to birth names.

"Do you know your birth name?" JJ asked, gawking over my shoulder.

"Mine?" I shrugged him off. "Should be under Benjamin."

"Seriously? That's not very imaginative."

"Apparently, my parents thought it best to keep my actual birth name when they adopted me."

"A nice sentiment then."

I laughed, dismissing the idea. "I'd have gone for bone idle myself."

I flicked through the folders and raced down the letters. My fingers twitched, and I fumbled a few times. Sweat beaded my top lip, and the pit of my stomach grew nauseous. I swept down the list from Eoghan, to Daithí and Cathail. Reading the names, I'd a twang of sadness for my fellow adoptees. Forget the fact we'd been marred as the unwanted, we never stood a chance with these titles.

Three more files and there it was. My full, undoctored name stared back at me. I pulled out the file and held it in my hand. The first name was mine and mine alone. A familiar foe. Benjamin. I wouldn't have noticed it for a moment. But the surname? It jumped at me, practically flung itself off the page and screamed at me, it did. I felt detached staring down at it, like some amnesiac looking at his reflection with new and uncertain eyes.

My name. My real name. My bona fide birth-name: Benjamin Dowling.

I balanced the opened file on the top of the drawer and held the torch in my teeth. My eyes darted from page to page, and a coolness wafted over me. I'd a hunger for the information within. The file was my oasis, my life's blood. I speed-read lines and scrolled my fingers down them all as if I could absorb the content by osmosis from the mere touch of its ink.

"Slow down," JJ said. He laid his hand on my shoulder. "We can pour over them later when we're clear of here."

"Just give me a second."

I breathed deeply and focused. The words stopped swirling, and I studied each of the pages within. They'd the usual plethora of information I'd imagined—medical history, details of inoculations, current address, copy of the adoption certificate—and there near the end, on a piece of yellow and tea-stained paper, was my original birth certificate. I paused and stared at the details, before turning to the last page.

I picked up the admission form and waved it at JJ. "Bingo!"

"You found what you needed?"

I held it at arm's length and shone the torch at it. "I...Benjamin Dowling...Was born at nine twenty-three p.m. on June the thirteenth in the year of our Lord 1978. And my real mother's name is Emily Dowling of 26 Cappa Street, Moortown."

"And your dad? Any sign of him?"

I read the forms again, back and front. "Nope. That line is empty on the birth certificate."

"Not unusual in those days, though. We've all heard the stories."

"But we've my mother. I'll assume she's an inkling who impregnated her. We'll root him out."

With the file clutched in my hand, I moved to the window. A strange indifference stole over me. I'd discovered the name of my mother. Fished out the facts of my birth. The anger in me had quelled all right, but something was off. The whole thing was incomplete, blunted.

"Anybody about to raid the place?" JJ said, sifting through files and opening clutches of them at once.

I stared down at the nuns as they stood huddled together on the gravel. "Nope. All's quiet. Still no sign of the fire brigade or Gardaí. Not surprising, though, it's a bit too early for them as well, apparently."

"Ben, come look at this…"

I didn't move. The whole reality of my situation turned to rot in my head. I'd imagined euphoria, or that sweet hug of finality people natter on about when they've attained what they so desperately sought. I pictured my surname once more, rolling the full title around in my consciousness. Benjamin Dowling…

Nothing. I felt zilch. It was foreign to me that name. It could've been anyone's plucked out randomly from the phonebook. It meant little without a face to my parents, without a history, without explanations as to why Emily Dowling had ejected me from her womb and cast me astray to a bunch of complete strangers. I wanted to hunt her down and watch her face change when she realised who I was. I wanted her to know I'd tracked her; that she couldn't hide me away in her past like a dirty secret skulking in her memories. I wanted her to suffer for the mistake she'd strived to bury in the bowels of Barnamire. I stared at my birth certificate again. Numbness, that's all there was to it. No tears welling up the eyes, no raptures of delight rattling in my throat. I needed more than that. I demanded to have more than a damp squib of un-feeling.

"We need to find her," I said. "And I need to do it today."

I flicked open the file again and fingered through the pages. "There's an address in her admission's form. People didn't move too far afield in those days. There's a good chance she's still there. Or at the very least some of her kin are still residing in the homestead. What do you reckon?"

"Ben," he said again, more anxiously this time.

I groaned. "This is kind of a heavy moment for me, JJ. The least you could do is focus on the issue to hand instead of nosing about."

"None of these files had their requests accepted."

"So? Mother Superior probably returned the ones that did."

"I seriously doubt that. She's not the kind to forego keeping photocopies at the very least."

"And how's this our problem?"

"That yoke who calls herself a nun has not once allowed a single adopted child to meet up with their real parents. Even when both sides requested it."

"Ever?"

JJ flicked through some more files. "No, not one. Not a single one. It's all here. Genuine requests answered by rejection letters all full of blatant lies. As far back as they began too. Far as I can figure, she stonewalled them all." He held up a bunch of files above his head. "This is a scandal of monumental proportion. We have to do something."

"Grand. Grab what we can carry—as many of those files as possible. Fill both bags and we'll decide what to do with them later. After I've door-stepped Emily Dowling, though."

I pulled back the blind an inch and stared down at the nuns. Mother Superior marched back and forth with her hands clasped, gouging out a trench in the gravel of the forecourts. She'd the walk of a colonel parading up ranks. The nuns were lined up in two neat rows with their heads bowed low, avoiding her stare. There'd be hell when she'd discovered what we'd done. I could see her lashing out, screaming for divine intervention and doling out punishment with that cane of hers.

I stuck my face to the glass and stared hard at her as if my very gaze could combust her on the spot. Just as the thought lingered in my mind, she stopped, swung around and glared straight up at me. She took a step forward, and I jerked back. The torch slipped from my hand and flashed across the glass. I tried to catch it, but my hands missed and flicked against a switch on the wall. The blind swished up and the day rushed in. I thought of ducking away, but it was already too late. The stiff walk of indignation, the pointing and shouting and gesticulating at the window—she'd spotted me.

Chapter 21

"She's seen us, JJ. She's on her way up here. Time to vamoose."

"Just a few minutes more."

I moved to the doorway. "Forget it. Let's go."

JJ stopped and held my stare. "And how would you feel if you never discovered the truth of your parentage?"

I wanted to tell him to keep his questions to himself, that their lives were not the issue here, and that I'd come for my story, for my information. Not to ruin it all for the hopeless cause of strangers. But the rat had gone and infected me with some of that pre-mixed conscience he carried about for just such an occasion as this. It was a well-travelled act of his. Put a dollop of the doe-eyed stare on top of it and, hey presto, one large serving of guilt.

"All right, fair point," I said, unzipping my holdall.

I rushed over and pulled files out of the drawer, wedging them into my bag on top of my own. There was no time to sieve through them all and filter out the dead from the living. They all went in, and as many as my arms could carry at a time.

"That's enough," I said after a while. Any moment now, I was expecting Mother Superior to tear through the door, howling.

JJ ignored me and kept layering them into his holdall,

all neat and tidy, one on top of the next, perfectly aligned and arranged in lengthwise stacks. "Only a few more handfuls. Each second means another truth told."

By the time we'd filled the bags there must have been five or six hundred of those case-files spanning half a century hemmed into them.

"All right, JJ, that'll do." I closed the holdall, slung it over my shoulder and hauled him up. "Let's get out of here."

We stepped through into the office and crept to the door. I paused and listened for a moment, before moving out into the hallway.

"If she's on her way up the stairs, we'll have to hide and—"

An explosion thundered through the air. Glass fractured from the windows behind us. The bulb overhead burst on its cord, showering shards down. The floor bucked up for a second, and the whole heft of the building shuddered in the shockwave. The brutality of it all made my knees quiver. A dark plume of dust and smoke swirled up, tipping the hallway into darkness. I staggered forward, hands fumbling in the void out front. The shaking ceased. I regained my footing and spread my arms out to my sides to balance. "What the hell was—"

A second explosion came, fiercer this time. It swayed me sideways. I crashed against a wall and walloped the ground chin first. My teeth slammed together, snipping the side of my tongue. Blood warmed my lips. I spat out the iron trace of it and turned to find JJ standing above me. He was either speaking or shouting or screeching. It was hard to tell. Couldn't really see him through the dust, couldn't really hear him. The sounds came muffled as if my ears had cotton balls wedged inside. I remained still for a moment and shook the dizziness from my head.

JJ slapped me twice across the face; real cheek-strippers too. But they'd the desired effect. My senses rallied, my ears cleared a smidge. The background fuzz faded some more, and the tinny whine in my ears dampened down. I heard the alarm and a roar nearby. The noises rushed back all digital sharp.

JJ grabbed my arms and hauled me to my feet

I picked the bag up. "What was that?"

"Doesn't matter. There could be more explosions. We need to get out...now."

"What's with the roaring?"

"The fire's inside. We need to go now."

We ran down the flights of stairs, skipping down four steps at a time. When we reached the end, we stopped at the door leading on to the quad. I grabbed the torch and shone it out in front. The battery waned, and the room tipped into darkness. But I'd seen enough. Rubble coated the floor. Two of the walls had a jagged crack running right through the block-work. A crashing noise came from beyond the door. I grabbed for the handle and opened it an inch. The fire snarled and air rushed in. Smoke billowed up, hot and acrid. It rushed up my nostrils and burned my lungs.

We fell flat to the floor and belly-crawled along, pushing the holdalls ahead of us. I couldn't avoid breathing the heat and choking ash. My mask filtered out the worst of it. It was a small relief save for the heat, which came just as fierce and from every angle. The floor, the walls, the ceiling, they all had a hand in it. The air roasted my skin, cocooning me in its swelter.

My breath came in sips, and sweat bled onto my skin. It seemed, for a moment, as if every bead of moisture was being sucked out of me by the fire nearby. In my delirium, I pictured my charred remains collapsing into a pile of dust and being scooped up onto a shovel. I saw them being thrown onto a heap, before being whipped away by a scattering wind.

I snaked along on my stomach and slithered down the hall. Inches grew into yards, seconds ticked for years, the hallway itself seemed to stretch out for miles. We made it past the first corner and manoeuvered down past the front door where the ash and smoke thinned out.

We stood and bolted down the hall, exiting through the utility room and into the boathouse. JJ slipped past the narrow channel first and staggered outside. Wind rushed to greet us, fresh and cool. I pulled up my mask, opened my mouth and gulped a lungful.

"Ready when you are," JJ said. "Last few steps."

I slipped the holdall sideways and waddled my way out when the faintest trace of a whisper pricked at my ear. At first I thought it nothing more than the tricks of the fire inside. A fire like that could conjure up any matter of sound—the whine of its flames as it purged on oxygen, the spits of wood as they cracked fast along the grain. I ignored it and set off once more, but a few steps further along I heard it again. I stopped and cocked my ear towards it.

"What are you doing, Ben? Come on, let's go—"

I held my hand up. "Pipe down a second. I heard something."

"Heard what?"

"Someone crying. I think."

I slipped back into the store room and listened. The cry came again, fainter still. It sounded weak and desperate, but it was no ruse of the flames. I grabbed the crowbar and threw JJ my holdall. "Take this."

"Ben, we don't have time for a detour. We've got to go."

"Someone needs help inside. Probably Mother Superior. She was on her way in the last time I saw her. However much of a wench she is, I can't just go and abandon her. Stealing's one thing, but manslaughter? I can't live with the guilt of that."

"You're codding me, right?"

"Nope." I pulled the balaclava back down. "And don't go ragging on me because of it. Get the bags in the boat and wait for me. I won't be long."

I quickstepped it back into the utility room and tipped a basin of filthy water over me, drenching my body from head-to-toe. It'd a bite to it, but if it saved my skin the misery was worth it. From hellfire hot to Baltic cold. It'd been a strange few moments. It felt as if the lads upstairs were straddling both sides of purgatory and having a knockabout with my soul. I pictured Himself sitting in judgement and me hairless after being scorched to death in the flames. "Burning a convent. Tut, tut. Bad form on the whole," He'd say. "We'll mark you down for that. Fair enough? Oh but here, I see you went back and rescued a nun. Truth is, we don't see that as often as we like. Well done, you."

I drenched myself a second time and set off through the door. The smoke came thicker and grittier. It smelled of tyres toasting on a bonfire. I turned the corner where umber flames crackled wood overhead. I couldn't see far through the haze, and the heat made walking intolerable. I hurried on my elbows and knees down the hallway. Every few feet the cry came weaker somehow. I reached the main entrance and paused once more. I held my face flat on the tiles and listened.

A cry whispered from a room to my right. I crawled to the door and tested the handle, but it wouldn't budge an inch. I hauled myself up into the cloud of smoke swirling above me. The temperature doubled. Its heat immense. Flames licked the sides of the door and hot splodges of burning plastic dripped from the ceiling. I jammed the claw of the crowbar between the frame and door and heaved. The wood creaked and groaned but held.

Wooziness swirled in my head. I needed to get to air. I dropped to my hands and sipped a dirty breath. It caused a fit of coughs and offered little relief. I cursed, stepped back and flung myself forwards. The frame splintered, the door swung in, and I collapsed onto the carpet inside.

The air in the room came crisp and unspoiled. The sealed door clearly acted as a fire-break. I savoured it for a second, sucking it deep into my lungs. It was an instant fix. I jumped to my feet and kicked the door closed, but it flapped straight back, wobbling drunkenly on its hinges.

Already the fire rolled hungrily across the ceiling, and smoke chased it in. I turned and spotted Mother Superior lying under a collapsed roof beam, face down and clutching a bat. I rushed over and tried to pull her free, but she just moaned in pain. The weight of the timber had trapped her leg.

"Help me," she said without a glance in my direction.

"Are you hurt?"

"Ankle...maybe more. I don't know. The table took the brunt of it. I can't move."

Tar black smoke engulfed us. The fire spread, devouring all the air in the room. She coughed violently. Her breaths came in shallow, panicked pips.

"I can't..." she said quieter now. "The weight...it's too much."

"I'll try to shift it."

I dipped my shoulder under the rafter and pushed with my legs. Nothing budged. It'd take ten men to lift it. I angled the crowbar under the edge closest to the ground and wedged the leg of the collapsed table underneath it for leverage. I pushed down on top of it and grabbed her by the scruff of her shirt.

"When I say 'now,' I'll lean on this and try to give you some space. You pull; I push, both at the same time. Got it?"

Nothing.

I checked for her pulse on her neck. It was still there, beating away. Not dead, just unconscious. I gripped the bar with both hands and shoved it down, gritting my teeth until blood whirred in my ears. For a second nothing moved, but then when my grip was about to falter, I thought of Ella. I saw her sitting in the stalls of the courthouse while the judge surmised what we'd done. I watched her gulp back tears of confusion as the Garda carted me out of court, shackled and bound for a life behind bars. And with her image floating in my head, strength grew in my arms, and I pushed sharply down. The beam cracked and lifted an inch. Keeping my weight on it, I dragged Mother Superior quickly towards me with my free hand. I released the crowbar and the wooden beam crashed back into place.

The room was pitch-black now. I fell forward and found her on her stomach, immobile. Without hesitating, I pulled her up and slung her over my shoulder. Smoke filled my lungs. I held my breath and drove through blackness. It was too risky to try to get as far as the boathouse. Too much chance of getting turned around and lost. The front door was my only option. I stumbled out the doorway and drove left, hands leading the way by touch.

The heat in the hallway enveloped me. My eyes streamed with tears. I swung around the corner and into the porch. Rafters fell to my rear, and ranks of flames jumped up in front. I covered my face with my arm and dashed forward. Fire caught my clothes. The shock of burn on my skin. I barged out the front door and spilled onto the gravel. Twenty yards later I collapsed to my knees, and we both careened to the ground.

Hands patted me down and rolled me over. A sickly sweet smell crept up my nostrils. I lay there for a moment smouldering and coughing up smoke, burnt and frozen all at once. Hands touched my stomach, and I winced. I gathered up my top and glanced down at the red welt spanning the width of it. It was as if someone had branded me with an iron and slopped hot pitch on top of it for good measure. The skin looked white and raw, and the pain quadrupled when I spied it. I'd have cried right then. Floods of the stuff. There wouldn't have been a trace of shame in the shedding either. And if I'd any drop of water left in me at the time that was exactly what I'd have done.

Instead, I felt for the mask. It was still there; they hadn't touched it. I glanced at the nuns who just stared open-mouthed in shock at me as sirens wailed in the distance. Barnamire burned overhead. Smoke bloomed from every window in thick curling plumes, and tongues of fire grabbed for the skies.

A pang of guilt struck my insides. I never meant for this to happen.

The whoop of sirens grew louder. It was time to go. I looked about to get my bearings, when Mother Superior came to. She crawled towards me, dragging her mangled ankle through the dirt. She reached to pull the mask off of my head. I batted her hand away and tried to stand, but she curled her fingers around it and yanked it up to my nose.

"I knew it," she said, hissing through teeth. "I'd recognise that birthmark anywhere." She lunged for me, drawing her nails across my cheeks. Pain seared my flesh, and I cursed. I threw my arms around her, trapping her in a bear hug. She flailed and screamed at me in words I'd never have expected to come from a woman of the cloth. I breathed heavily for the effort, wheezing from the smoke still nestled in my lungs.

"Now, Mother Superior," I said, whispering in her ear. "Let's say we know exactly what you and your order have been doing here. And if you want to keep your honour and veneer of dignity intact, you'll listen and pay careful heed to what I have to say."

"You burned our Barnamire," she said. "You burned

our life's work. You'll do time for this. They'll lock you up for life."

"You're missing the point." Some of the nuns closed in, but I growled, and they scattered away like witless sheep. "If you squeal on us, we'll squeal on you. We've hundreds of files as evidence of your behaviour. If I get so much as a sniff we're implicated, I'll send copies to everyone concerned. It'll be on every news channel, every paper will run it—every radio and biddy in the land will be pouring over the details. Your name will be dirt. It'll be the scandal of the century, and you'll be damned as the demon you are."

The fight seemed to falter in her. Her muscles relaxed, her writhing stopped. "No one will believe a low-life degenerate like you. You'll die in jail with the rest of your ilk."

"In case you hadn't noticed, I'm kind of committed to this project, so what will be, will be. And anyway, with the public outcry and my mitigating circumstances, I'll probably have my sentence whittled down to the bare minimum. Hell, I'll probably make a mint from the publicity. You know how it goes these days. Everyone loves a good-boy-gone-bad story. I'll be as right as rain. Probably be considered a bit of a hero. I'll be stood drinks for decades for this. Whereas you?" I brought my face in closer until my nose almost touched hers. "You. Will. Be. Ruined. And *that's* a fact. Your choice."

"You'll burn in the fires of hell for this, Benjamin Hackett."

"Maybe." I jumped up and backed away. "But I'll have you to keep me company, now won't I?"

Chapter 22

Over the wall, I leapt. I grabbed my knees, tucked them to my chest and bombed into the waters. Lord, the cold. It enveloped me instantly like I'd fallen into a suit of snow. My heart pounded so hard it I feared it'd explode in my chest. If it weren't for the coolness of it, I'd have swam up fast. It was just the tonic for the burns on my tummy. A few more seconds would sooth my skin, so I decided it best to remain submerged for a moment, surrounded by silence, cocooned from the maelstrom above. I'm sure Freud, or one of those other quacks, would have said it was all foetal, a clichéd attempt to return to the womb, an existential reflex caused by my yearning for my mammy, or some other such tripe. But nuts to them and their kind. It was peaceful down there, plain and simple, and I'd been short-stacked in that recently.

I resurfaced with my teeth chattering and my limbs rigid from the cold. I carved my way through the water to JJ who sat perched in the currach, shaking his head at the sight behind me. I reached up, and he grabbed me by the arm and pulled me on board.

We rounded the corner into the flow of the mainstream, its pull seawards speeding us away downriver. I paused mid-stroke and stared at Barnamire's bell tower. It glowed like a small sun in the flames, and I couldn't help but feel a trace of shame at the sight. A building that stood through centuries, through crippling rains and sleet that'd rinse through granite, through rebellions and wars and barrages of English cannon, was ruined.

"What have we done, JJ." I laid back down with my hands clasped around my head and watched the brightening sky scoot by.

JJ ceased rowing and hung his head. "Wasn't our intention to gut the place; something went wrong."

"Yeah, and that something is me. Since we set off a pile of doom has been waiting for us. Sooner we get to the end of this the better. We could have been killed or arrested about five times in three days. That's some going, in fairness."

"So," he said, twisting around. "I take it you embraced the hero within and pulled Mother Superior from the jaws of a scorching death?"

I sat back up. Pain shot through me belly, and I grimaced. "I did. Just about."

"And did she recognise you?"

"Of course. Vicious snipe that she is."

JJ groaned.

"Don't worry. I reminded her if she shopped us to the Gardaí, we'd have no option other than going public with the files."

A smile twisted on his lips and grew into a wide grin. "I bet that went down well. But how are going to help the people she hoodwinked all these years? If we can't use the files to expose her?"

I grabbed the oars and dipped their blades in the water. "I thought you were the self-proclaimed genius of this outfit. Use those smarts of yours to figure it out.

And when you do, please tell me. But until then, we lay them low."

"Leave it with me, I'll not disappoint. So what's the next move? And let me remind you the match is tomorrow, and you promised to play."

"I remember. Let's wait a few hours before we head back for the car. Let the heat die down. Moortown's on the way home anyway, so it's no skin off your nose if we take a quick detour."

"Thank God for that. After the hiding Wolf gave me, I don't think my nose has much more to give."

I laughed despite myself.

About a mile or so later, we hitched up the currach and hauled ourselves up on to the river wall. Nothing but parklands surrounded us. This scrap of land, full of ripening fruit and leafy trees and hosts of flowers, would have been sheer, godlike perfection—if it weren't for a lad leading his mutt on a leash for a pee and the winos bedded down on the benches.

We changed back into our jerseys, threw our masks and tops into a bin and slung the holdalls over our shoulders. A path wound up through the park, and we followed it along until we reached the main road. I sat on the curb while JJ leaped over a wall to loot some food. He trotted back with two pint bottles of milk clutched in his hand.

"There were six in the crate on the doorstep. So no harm done," he said.

He sat next to me and offered me one. I took a deep slug of it. The chill settled into my stomach, and my mind perked up with the moisture. I finished the bottle and rubbed the glass against my scalded brow.

"Cats," a voice said. "The two of ye have to be the jammiest cats around. How many lives have you two lost by now? I count four, so loads more to go, ye jammy cats."

I looked up at the face poking out from our car parked opposite and immediately flung the bottle at it. It flew wide, glanced off the windscreen and smashed on the road. "Apache...you son-of-a–"

"Now, now, boys." He raised his hand and waved the snub-nose pistol at us. "Don't go having a fanny attack. The fire got a bit out of hand. It happens."

"No, it doesn't." I clambered up and went to rush him, but JJ hauled me back by my shoulders. "You nearly killed us...and a nun."

"But I didn't. And they're insured. So where's the harm?"

"You said it'd only be a little fire and no one would get hurt."

"Well, I did say that, fair enough, like." He opened the door and stepped out onto the curb. "But the Pucas didn't check the contents of the shed. That's where the nuns kept their gas supply. Who knew? An honest mistake. And I can tell you they're very sorry for it. It'll keep them up for days. Anyway, here ye go. I'd the fore-sight to collect Scully's car. Had to hotwire it, mind you, so there's a bit of damage to the wiring, but the keys should still work. And all things being equal, I feel ye owe me something."

"Owe you?" I said, nearly shouting.

JJ grabbed me, pulled me towards the passenger's side and shoved me in.

"Let it go, Ben," he said. He jumped into the driver's

seat and gunned the engine. "We've been down this road before."

"Listen to your buddy, would be my advice," Apache said, his smiling flitting away to a frown.

"You can stick your gangster logic where the sun don't shine. We don't owe you a goddamn thing...Mossy Deane."

His eyes twitched, his face reddened and every sinew on his neck pulled taut at once. He raised the gun, cocked the trigger and aimed it straight at my head. "You've had a fright, so I'll let that one slide. But a word to the wise, you know my form, so you should muzzle that mouth of yours. And just so you know, I'll be calling down to you two in the next few days to clear the slate. Sweet?"

"Oh, yeah, sweet as. We'd be delighted. Wouldn't we, JJ?"

"We would. We'd just love to meet up for a few suds or something and see what other crimes we have on our to-do list."

"You're taking the mickey now, lads? I like that." Apache lowered the gun and leaned in the driver's side window. "Giant pairs on the two of you. Off you go so, but remember—you do owe me a debt."

"We don't owe you jack," I said, snapping back.

"Well, my son says you do, and like his old man, Jesus never lies."

I groaned at the revelation. "We only pushed him into his bike *after* he tried to spike us."

"Exactly...so you admit it. You owe me."

"Did we?"

"Well, I'm glad we cleared up that little puzzle, 'cause

for a moment there, I thought there'd be ructions." He rubbed his hands together and stood back. "Oh, and, lads. It's a dangerous, unforgiving world out there, so buckle up and safe travels in your rusty little mucker's truck."

I watched him in the rearview mirror as we sped west. His smirking face shrunk to a speck, before disappearing into the traffic behind. But even as we turned on to the motorway and ticked up the miles from Barnamire, Apache and his Pucas and his distorted code kept replaying in my brain. A feeling of dread jostled about in my stomach, and I knew right there and then, there'd be no shaking free of it.

"Think he'll actually follow through on that promise?" I asked.

JJ glanced at me and laughed briefly. "About coming down to Whitehaven?"

I nodded.

"Well, Ben, I would say it's guaranteed."

Chapter 23

There wasn't a brush or comb on the island of Ireland that'd tease my hair down. For the first time in days, I studied my reflection parked up outside twenty-six Cappa Street like some nervy virgin about to rock up to collect his date. My face, Lord help us, was mullered looking. My eyes had sunk back into my skull, leaving puddles of black underneath them. My cheek had welts from the various slaps, and a trail of scrawls stood proud on the skin where Mother Superior had gouged her nails across them. I licked my palm and tried to settle the hair sprouting tall on my head, but it kept pinging back up and scattering at all sorts of angles.

"I look like a tramp, JJ."

He laughed a childish laugh. "You do a bit. But it'll have to do for the time being."

"Not exactly the finest way to meet your mother for the first time in decades. She'll hardly regret her decision when she claps eyes on me."

"You all worried now about what she'll think of you? I thought you said you were going to march straight up there and punch them in the nose...multiple times."

"Yeah, well...that's still on the cards. Depending on whether she gives up the old man or not. You coming?"

"You really want me there? I figured you'd prefer to go solo on this one."

I fingered the file in my hands and flicked through the

papers for the umpteenth time, checking again that all the bits of proof were there. If Emily Dowling played it cute and tried to connive her way out of the revelation, I'd need these pages as evidence. "Not really, but I know how easily boredom sets upon you."

"Nonsense, but to spare your blushes, I'll probe no more. Come on then."

We stepped out of the car with my head tangled like knotweed. Was there any etiquette formally agreed upon for meeting birth mothers? It'd have been nice if there were, because JJ would've probably known.

We crossed the road and a car whizzed by, honking the horn and nearly flattening me in the process. I barely flinched, though. Just a few feet more, and I'd be knocking on the door, face-to-face with my real mam. If she were there that is.

God, I hoped she wasn't home. It'd have been nice if she'd bunked off to the States, or been hit by an asteroid, or caught a cold that turned out to be fatal. Anything really, rather than dealing with all of this right then.

I became conscious of my limbs and stumbled on the curb. They were definitely moving weird. Why were they moving weird? My legs seemed longer, my arms not my own, like I'd borrowed the body and hadn't quite broken it in yet. I'm having a seizure, I thought, or a fit. One of those petit or grand mal ones. I'd be rigid on the ground any moment now with epilepsy. Another thing to blame her for.

I sensed someone shadowing me. I glanced around expecting the Reaper to be tip-toeing along, his scythe at the ready with hollow eyes deeper than space and a poacher's smirk on him.

Soon we stopped by number twenty-six. Her house was a quiet, dull affair—terraced with flaking windows. I stepped onto the doorstep and grew faint from the stress. This was it. The Big Man's moment to knock me off the mortal coil. I'd bet it'd be a hoot up there if He did it.

"Are you going to knock?" JJ asked. "Or try to communicate psychically with the ghost of her womb?"

"What? Oh right, no...I'll knock."

"Good man."

"God, I'm all over the place. What time is it anyway?"

"Just after ten; or as I like to call it, a lot later than it should be...o'clock. So cop on to yourself and quit stalling, it's embarrassing. She's likely to have moved years ago anyway."

I wiped the sweat from my hands on my top and rattled the knocker once against the plate. Footsteps closed within, hands fumbled a chain free, a latch snapped back, and hinges creaked. The door swung open, and an old woman in sight of eighty limped out.

"What can I do for you, lads?" she asked with a weary trace to her voice.

"Sorry to bother you, ma'am," I said. "But does an Emily Dowling live here?"

She pushed her hands into the pockets of her cardigan and wrapped it tightly around her. "Emily? She did. Up to a few days ago, anyways."

"A few days ago? So do you know where she's moved? Do you have a forwarding address?"

The old woman smiled, her eyes both happy and sad. Her lips twitched once before sitting still on her face. She shook her head. "No use to you, my lad. You'll not be going there for good a few decades yet. You see, Emily is dead. This is her wake." She blessed herself and gazed skyward. "May the Lord God have mercy on her soul."

"She's dead? As in...*dead* dead?"

The old woman knitted her brow in confusion. "Have you two been at the sauce?"

"But...I've only just found her."

"I don't have time for this," she said and went to swing the door closed.

JJ jammed his foot under it. "Hang on a second, ma'am. Apologies for my friend and for your loss. But he's had a strange few days."

"Haven't we all." She gazed at me then, up and down, drinking me in with her eyes. "Do you mind me asking...how did you know my daughter?"

"I do," I said.

"You do what?"

"Mind."

Her laugh was short and haughty. "It's true what they say. Death attracts crazies like a carcass does maggots. Word to the wise, though, boy. Stop getting hit in the head, it doesn't agree with you?" She pulled the door open once more and beckoned us in. "So are you coming in or what? If you want to pay your respects you're more than welcome. Half of the county have been traipsing in and out of here for the last few days. But you'd better hurry because we'll be removing her for the funeral within the hour."

I didn't talk to JJ; I didn't even blink. I was in autopilot mode. I simply puttered along behind her with my plans scattered to the wind and my mind frozen. She led us into the living room where the body lay. A mix of smoke and incense hit my nose. I remained by the door waiting until my eyes adjusted to the darkness within. Every scrap of carpet had some auld fella or biddy trodding it down. Everything was devoid of colour. Black suits and dresses in a room of pure shadows, and each of them strangers to a man.

The room was set up in the usual way with the curtains drawn, the mirrors covered and the clocks stopped. By the hearth, two women keened away to some old-time lament and candles stood either end of the coffin with their wax cooling hard near their base and casting a wan light.

Despite seeing plenty of graves, it was my first official wake, and judging by the general roughness of this lot, it wouldn't take much to upset one or two of them. I watched them for a while hoping to pick up a few cues, but whatever the decorum was there'd be no telling from these folks. The old woman waved at me, and I pushed through the sweat and the hypnotic hum of whispers. I nodded when they nodded. I shook my head when they shook theirs. I'm certain they figured us to be all kindred spirits, like we'd some huge insight into the seriousness of the day, but to me their gestures seemed mere reflexes, nervous ticks, nothing more than habit. The old woman took me by the hand and led me to a man sat off to one side of the coffin.

"Emily's husband, Seamus," she said to me in a whisper.

I stood over him in silence, feeling awkward and ignorant. No thoughts or words sprung to mind. This man was a stranger to me, and my intrusion into his mourning struck me as fake. I was gatecrashing his sadness. A thought struck me then, swung in on a limb out of nowhere. Was this man my father? And would I ever know for certain? I wanted to scream and howl obscenities. I remembered all the beatings, all the madness, all the violence—all for squat.

I stared hard at him, looking for some resemblance, some familiar sign, a sense of belonging. The light cast a jaundiced hue to his skin. His shirt was open to the chest, and a long-forgotten cigarette hung limp from his lips. By the length of his stubble and his haggard face, he'd been hard at it for days now. He reached out and grabbed my hands in his, never once looking up, never once shifting his gaze. It was a solid and practised grip, and we shook firmly once.

"I'm sorry for your loss," I said, surprised that my words materialised in my mouth.

His fingers went limp and our hands slipped away. He lit another cigarette, clasped it again in his teeth and let the smoke curl up above him. Lost in his trance, he stared at the pile of butts and ash dirtying up the carpet; his was a genuine soul all right.

The old woman kissed his forehead, and with a nod to the coffin, she gestured me forward. I stepped towards it, clasped the side and closed my eyes. I listened to the murmurs and sniffles, to the flapping of the curtain flicked back by the wind, to a laugh nearby that seemed out of place, unnatural and bold, to rusty lungs with phlegmy coughs and to the maudlin tones of the keeners' song. They played strange in me those noises, so varied, so vibrant, the anthem of life spinning away without pause. And the only person who could sate me lay dead on a table. Coffined up and about to be sent underground, fully pardoned from punishment, immune from any questions, free from the burden of me.

In fairness to Himself; He'd checkmated me all right.

I opened my eyes and stared down at the corpse of my birth mother, Emily Dowling. She'd her hands clasped over her chest and wore a lemon cotton dress. Her skin had a waxwork hue to it as if the pallor of death had been buffed away and hidden under a heavy hand of rouge. Despite all the mortician's efforts, though, she still looked strange, inhuman really. And I thought how final it was, how unnatural and grey a body really looked without the spark of life flowing through it.

I stared at her face some more trying to cut through the strangeness of the moment. She'd a curling mop of greyed hair and carried a few too many pounds. Not fat mind, but edging there. Her face had a kind enough demeanour to it. There was a slight twist to the corners of her mouth as if she died on the cusp of a laugh, and the crinkles near her eyes hinted at a happy enough life. And at the thought of all her laughter and fun and moments I'd never been privy to, a ball of sadness struck high in my throat, and I cried.

The tears snuck up on me, but by God they must've been plotting for a while because they poured out of me right then. I guess it was the last few days that did it, that and the body of my birth mother stretched out in front of me like the ultimate cosmic stitch-up. The hurt and injustice of it all released through those eyes of mine, and I let it come. My shoulders never shook, my voice stayed silent. Only to my front would the signs have been evident. A minute or so slipped by, and the tears ran dry. JJ appeared next to me and slung his arm over my shoulder.

"If you keep this up they'll think you were her fancy man," he said.

I smiled a lazy smile at the jibe and wiped my face on my sleeve. "You're really going to have to work on that bedside manner of yours if you plan on being a doctor. Anyway, nobody can tell."

"What are you going on about? There are puddles by your feet."

I laughed faintly and stepped away for the coffin. I had to give it to him; he'd a way to lighten the load. The old woman waved us out. We wandered into the kitchen and took a seat on a bench by the range. A cup of tea was shoved into my hand. It was treacle thick stuff. I took a sip and coughed at the burn of poitín scalding my throat.

"That'll stiffen you up good," she said, wedging in between us. JJ stood and wandered away to the other end of the kitchen. The old woman took a sip from her cup and stared at me. "As much as I respect people's right to mourn in private, I have to ask again. How did you know my daughter?"

"I think she was my mother."

I don't have a notion why I blurted it out like that. It was rash and foolish to reveal such a thing in the middle of a wake with emotions already sweating up a fever. For a few seconds, I expected the old woman to throw a nod at the big jungle animals above me who'd mooch on over in their suits and boots, drag me outside and give me a hiding for being such a stirrer. Instead she laughed, almost had her tea in her lap from the fit that burst out of her.

"Her son?" she said, trying to dam up her mouth with her fingers. "That's hilarious. You don't really think you're her son, do you?"

"I do. I've the evidence and all here with me."

"You can't go around making statements like that. You know the place is teeming with our relations. They'd lynch you on the spot if they heard it." She placed the cup back on its saucer and laid it down on the table. "Tell me the truth now. Is it an eye on the inheritance you have? Is that your angle? Because take a gander around, why don't you—there's not a stick of furniture worth more than a farthing in this place. You're on a con to nowhere with this one."

I pulled the file out and showed her the admission slip. "I'm not trying it on here, honest. You see…here's her name, here's her admittance form to Barnamire, and here's my birth certificate with *her* name and *this* address on it. I'm not just winging it and making stuff up off the cuff. I genuinely believe Emily Dowling is my birth mother."

"Ah, quiet down with that kind of racket, will ya, for the love of God. There's no chance. Not in a million years. I think someone must be pulling your leg." She sat back in the seat and sighed. "But thanks all the same for lightening the mood. I tell you, if Emily's up above watching this now, she'll be wetting herself."

Her glib manner confused me. Despite the irrefutable proof in my hands, she'd this calm indifference that both surprised and annoyed me at once. "And how are you so sure of yourself? It's all here. Isn't it possible she kept it a secret from you?"

She crossed her arms and fixed me with a hard stare. "Nope. It may be her name on the forms, but there's no way my daughter gave birth to you. Not in a month of Sundays."

"You can't be so certain."

"I can, and I am. It's a case of simple biology. You see, you need a womb for a baby and when Emily was fifteen years old she'd hers removed after a car accident."

I shook my head in disbelief. "You're lying."

"Honest to God," she said, holding her hands up. "She suffered blunt force trauma to the abdomen. Ruptured something or other, so they'd to operate and cut bits out. And one of those bits was vital to you coming out of her. Truth is, I think the surgeon was a bit too eager, bit of a cutter. Nobody went under his knife without coming out a stone lighter. So you see, unless you're the Second Coming and my Emily the Virgin Mary—which she wasn't, let me tell you—there's not the faintest chance that she gave birth to you." She clasped my face in her hands. "Thought you'd it all worked out, hadn't you? Well, I'm sorry to set you back, but it's the truth. Whoever put her name on those forms was lying; it's as simple as that."

I paused and stared at her eyes, searching for some sign of lies. There was little reason for her to invent this story. "But why would anyone want to?"

"Not unusual in those days. If the person never wanted to be found, a red herring like this was a good way. Pick up the phone directory and pluck any number of names and addresses out. I doubt they'd have done any background checks on those poor pregnant misfortunates up the convent. Ireland's drenched in secrets like you, I'm afraid. Emily's been in a wheelchair with a broken back since nineteen sixty. The poor creature never had a normal life since then. And she certainly didn't have you."

She twisted around and pulled on the jacket of a man standing above us. "Michael, pass me the picture album you've got of our Emily."

I slouched forward in the seat and stared at the flagstones, at the polish worn into them from slippered feet, and the blankness in my mind swallowed me whole. I glanced at JJ who'd been holding court with a group of men. For a while, I'd imagined they were my long-lost cousins or brothers or family friends, but now I saw them for what they truly were—a pack of random strangers. Their laughs screeched in my head. The walls of the kitchen squeezed in on top of me, and I recognised that familiar anger swelling in the pit of my guts. It spread quicker than poison shooting through veins. Another dead-end. I needed to get out of there.

I went to stand, but the old woman grabbed me by the hand and pulled me down.

"Here you go," she said, "The life and times of Emily Dowling."

She opened a photo album on her lap and flicked through the pages. She brushed each picture with her fingers as she went and her eyes grew sadder with each stroke. She flicked on some more and paused on a page with wedding snaps.

"You see," she said. "Here she is on her big day. Emily insisted on sitting in the wheelchair for the formalities. We tried to convince her to sit on a wall or a chair, but she was too proud for that kind of nonsense." She peeled back the plastic cover, removed one of the photos and held it in her hands. "And the hoot of it was no one really noticed the wheelchair at all. She was such a stunner that day. I couldn't take my eyes off of her from morning to night."

I felt like a right intruder then. And despite me wanting to hare away, the sight of the old woman all cut up about her daughter kept me rooted. She offered me the photo, and I took it as a courtesy. It was an old sepia shot of the wedding party in the standard set-up outside a church, with confetti still stuck on the bride and groom's shoulders, top hats in hand, and a haphazard bunch of guests jammed into the scene.

One figure caught my eye, though. If it weren't for everyone else's smiles, I'd hardly have noticed the stern, formal stare of a woman to the left of the bride. It was those eyes that had me transfixed, sending a shiver slipping down the nape of my neck. I recognised that woman. Younger, yes. Fresh faced, no doubt. But there was no mistaking her. The sombre eyes, the hooky nose, the air of absolute contempt. It was Nell of all people. My mother's sister and chronic alcoholic. The one who fed off of our lives like an insatiable leech. My Aunty Nell was somehow at the wedding. But even more damning, what really shook the fog from me; she was heavily pregnant. And I knew for a fact she'd no children of her own.

A brooding deja-vu stole over me, full of doom and

blood-curdling clarity. I bolted up and turned to the old woman. "When was this?"

"It's on the back of the photo. What did you see in there?"

I turned the photo over. Scrawled across the top-right corner was the date—the eighteenth of April 1978. Two months before I was born. The date was a key. It unlocked the jumbled pieces of the puzzle in my mind and rearranged them all in an instant.

Nell was my mother.

How was that even possible? The thought bulled into me, threw its talons into my mind and wouldn't let go. I wished for someone to come and blindside me, whip a spanner into my skull, induce amnesia with immediate effect. No way was that wreck of a human my biological mother. There had to be another explanation. I was jumping the gun. She could've had a child unbeknownst to me. Secrets were ten-a-penny in those days. But the dates, the photo, the bump, the way she'd hung around despite not being wanted, the drinking.

Slip, slip, slip.

More and more of the pieces slotted into place. It was like trying to touch the same poles of two magnets together. The harder I fought the notion, the more impossible it became to dispel. I gave the old woman the photo and jabbed a finger at Nell. "How did Emily know this woman?"

"Who? Nell? Oh, they were best friends. Went to the same secondary school, St Mary's. I think they worked together in the post office in town for a while. She was a bit of a tearaway. Always had an eye for the lads. Disappeared fairly soon after this, though, it was all hush-hush. Emily seemed concerned for her about something." She stared at me briefly, before looking back at the photo. "You know her...don't you?"

"She's my aunty."

"Well, son," she said, slipping the photo back behind the plastic and closing the album on her lap. "Taking everything you just told me into account, she may very well be more than that."

Drunk—that's how I felt. Her words seduced a kind of trippy intoxication into me. I needed to get out, get to Nell. I staggered back and clattered into a table behind. The tea-caddy swayed and fell, followed by glasses and plates and platters of ham sandwiches. The whole mix of it swept like a tide across the boots of the men, and a brace of curses came my way. A hand grabbed my shoulder, but I shrugged it off and barrelled through the thick of them towards the kitchen door.

"Have some respect," one of them said.

I ignored him, nodded at JJ, and we belted out onto the street and into the car. He fired the engine up and we sped away out of town.

"Would you mind telling me," he said. "What the hell that was all about?"

"Nell."

The heat on my neck rose up even more by the sheer mention of her.

"Nell, Nell, Nell," I said again, as if by repeating her name I could exorcise the spitting rage in me. I slumped back and roared.

"Christ, Ben, what's got into you?"

"You remember our dear Nell? The one who's been masquerading as my long-suffering misfortunate aunty?"

"Yeah."

"Well, I think she's actually my goddamn, please-shoot-me-in-the-face-right-now, birth mother."

Chapter 24

It was a long journey back to Whitehaven. Scully's car needed four hill starts, and we lost the front bumper somewhere around Bantry. We normally would have laughed at the whole trauma of it all, but the trip back was a silent affair, with JJ trying desperately not to say a word for fear of stoking another psychotic moment in me. It'd deep roots my anger, and my thoughts kept feeding it until my head was so stuffed with murderous intent I felt fit to burst.

By rights, when we arrived outside Nell's on the tip of Madden Head the day should've been drawing in on itself. The sun should've been clocking out, the birds should've been roosting, the windsurfers down below should've been sitting around their camper vans smoking joints and cracking into their tinnies. But the evening had a mid-summer's stretch to it, where all the drizzle and sogginess, all those wild winds and weeks of non-stop greyness were immediately forgotten.

In another life we'd have grabbed a flagon of cider, followed the goat path down to Sheep's Bay and sat on the stones until we'd a lobster's sheen. Stocious drunk and pinking up nicely. Now, that was my own personal snatch of heaven right there. But I'd only an eye for one thing—Aunty Nell.

"Is she even in there?" JJ'd asked, when we'd swung into view of her place. "A day like today she's probably off drinking down the quay with the rest of the grown-ups."

"She's in there all right. It's not dark yet. Nell rarely sets off until the witching hour—even in the summer. Soft candles, dimly lit bars, alcohol turning the dial down on some chancer's standards. That's more her scene. She doesn't really have the kind of face that's licensed for day-wear, you see."

No sooner had JJ killed the engine than I leapt out and strode down the path and up to her front door. I didn't pause to knock. I didn't even call out as a courtesy. I simply walked in like a general with my head held high and more questions on my lips than an Inquisitor. I stood in the centre of the kitchen, hands on hips, and bellowed for her by name. I moved through the bedroom, the pantry and the toilet, but there was no trace of her. Nell, it seemed, had scarpered.

"Any sign?" JJ asked, still standing near the doorway.

"Nope. And stop wasting good manners on her and come in, will you?"

He looked around and checked the back of the door. "Not exactly security conscious is she? Leaving the place open and unattended like this."

"And who'd bother with her up here? Anyway, knowing Nell she was probably too hungover to remember to lock up."

I picked up the quaich on the table. Her two-handled cup was essential for those early morning eye-openers, especially when the shakes had her firmly in their grip. I sniffed it, and my eyes streamed from the trace of cheap whiskey still inside. I'd watched her drain gallons of this stuff over the years. "Only fit for lifting rust," Dad had said. I left a drop dribble onto my lips and winced. It was like swishing acid.

"By the looks of things," I said. "She's already had her evening snifter. And if she's downed some of this stuff, it can only mean one thing—she's out on the razzle for the night. And knowing Nell, she'll tend not to hunt in the same place twice in succession." I placed the cup upside down on the table and sat in the rocking chair with a huff settling over me. "She could be anywhere."

The only sound came from the ting of water drops on the sink. JJ glanced out the window. "Let's go. We'll come back whenever she resurfaces. I'm starving and knackered and probably going to be grounded for the next millennium whenever I get back home. I've been missing for three whole days now. Mam'll be livid when she gets to me."

JJ and his mam. Given half a chance, she'd still have him latching onto the breast. "You know," I said. "The thing with Nell is she's a right hoarder. Never throws much away. I bet you if we snooped we'd find some proof of it all. I bet you under a floorboard, or hidden in a drawer, or wrapped up in some bedding somewhere is a reminder of her brazen secret."

"Well, if you're right, and she is your mam, *and* she gave you up, *and* you ended up with her sister...you'd have to feel sorry for her. No matter how dubious they were back then, they'd never have knowingly placed you with her sister's family. If they knew who she actually was, that is." He wrenched the tap on the sink until the drips stopped. "It must have stuck in her craw a bit when she realised you were her child. It'd explain the drink."

"Sorry for her? And what about me? I'm the victim here, not Nell. She's the one who gave me away, lied for decades and used someone else to throw me off the scent. Seriously, JJ. Sorry, for her? No chance. She made her choices, and now I'm left dealing with the fallout from them."

"If it indeed is her."

"Well, seeing as though she's not here to answer our questions—there's only one way to find out."

JJ rested on the edge of the kitchen table, arms folded, throwing his eyes over the place like he had a clue where to look. "So, where do we start? Shouldn't take long to rifle through the drawers. It's only a bolt-hole of a place really."

I closed my eyes and went with the sway of the chair. The wicker creaked and cracked, and the storm in my head seemed to find solace in its rhythm. I calmed down a notch then, and, in the quiet of the moment, a single memory slipped into my head.

"Pandora," I said, leaping out of the rocker.

"Ah, yes, the infamous Greek mythological tale of—"

"Calm yourself down there, magus. We all know the story."

"Well if you do, why is it relevant?"

"Because that's what Nell named her trunk at the end of her bed. She used to call it her Pandora's Box. When I was young, she was always herding me away from it, joking about it, telling me it was her Pandora, and if I knew anything about that story I'd do well to leave it alone." I paced about the place and rubbed my face. "Herself and my mam...they're all the same. Sisters I mean...in general, like. Probably read the same books about the same teenage girls, hiding the same terrible secrets and all that dross."

"So?"

"You see, Mam always stores her keepsakes, knickknacks and photos in her trunk at the foot of her bed. I'd bet my life if there's anything worth finding here, anything that'd prove me right, it's wedged deep down in Nell's trunk."

We entered her bedroom, and I made a beeline for the trunk. JJ, though, seemed distracted. He wandered around the place fawning over the décor and the tidiness of it, amazed how a drunkard could render a room and house so perfect, as if now was the time to wax lyrical. I watched him then lost in his philosophies, nattering on about the dichotomies of life, and I was struck by how much of a pure fool he could be at times.

"The inner sanctum," he said, pawing at her quilt and running his fingers over the pillows. "I must say, Ben, I never expected her to be so house-proud. Not the Nell we know."

"As I said, she's obsessive about two things—booze and housework—both in equal measure."

He plonked himself on the bed and bounced up and down like he was angling to buy it. "Think this is where the magic happened?"

"Have you seen her recently? The tide wouldn't take her out."

"Not now...then. When she bedded some young fella and nine months later you popped out?"

"I doubt that. She didn't live here back then. And will you stop playing the fool and pay attention. This is a big moment for me. It'd be nice if you looked like you gave two hoots. So stop with all the questions about the specifics of my birth. Nobody wants to relive their passage from the womb. And even less so if it were Nell's I slid out of."

JJ grimaced. "That's just nasty, Ben. Still, this mattress has got some nice spring-works going on underneath. Not a squeak or a squeal from them." He paused and looked up. "Not sure about the cross, though."

I glanced up at the crucifix nailed to the wall above the bed. It looked all out of place hanging there. The simple shape against the sweeps of walnut, the crown of thorns against the velvet sheets, the face full of anguish against the soft plushness of the surroundings.

"I'll give you that. There should be something in the Rule Book about subjecting Himself to the goings-on in here."

JJ laughed, and I knelt down by the trunk. Many a time I'd been in the same position about to yank back the lid and spill the goodies out, but Nell always turned up to spoil the moment. I flipped up the catch and waited, convinced she was about to burst through the door, catch me by the ear and threaten me with the wooden spoon again.

But nothing happened. No drama yet.

I opened the lid and rummaged inside. "Socks, silk stockings, hats, scarfs." My stomach lurched at my mouth. "Frilly knickers." I kept on going, pulling the entire contents out of the trunk. "Nothing but clothing and underwear. I don't understand it." I stared into the bottom of it, ran my hands along the edges and tapped it with my knuckles. It made a distinctly hollowed sound. There was something else there. A false bottom; but there wasn't any catch, or pull, or finger hole or anything else to get in underneath.

"I think there's a hidden compartment here. But I've no way in."

I knew I didn't have to say any more. JJ shouldered me out of the way and peered inside until his nose nearly touched the bottom.

"This is slick craftsmanship all right," he said. "Only bits and pieces in on top of it right?"

"Seems so."

"Well, what you've got here, I reckon, is a pressure-lock mechanism." He placed a hand flat and pushed sharply down. A cushioned click sounded. The bottom swung up and folded neatly to the right.

I pulled him away and stared at the brown leather folder tucked neatly inside. I picked it up gently and weighed it in my hands. It had a sweet fragrance to it as if it had been perfumed, like the Bible Mam'd pull out and handle with reverence for Easter sermons. My fingers slipped over its skin. The spine was still in decent enough nick, but the cover was cracked and split at the edges. There was dirt in between these leather pages all right, whole cemeteries worth of skeletons.

I waved it at JJ, and my face erupted in the first real smile for days. I laid it on the bed, untied the ribbon and opened it up. Piled on top were hundreds of photos, and all of me. From every year of my life, cataloguing my every move, every birthday, every Christmas, every outing to the beach.

"Fairly damning stuff, JJ."

"It's not unusual to keep pictures safe."

I grabbed a handful of them and fanned them out as

proof. "There are only photos of me. This doesn't strike you as strange?"

I skipped past the rest of them, spreading them out on the bed. Near the back were dozens of letters, still in their envelopes addressed to Nell and with an English stamp on them. The paper had yellowed with time, and each one had been surgically opened across the top of the envelope. By the dates, the letters started in nineteen eighty and stopped two years later. I slipped the earliest one out and unfurled it flat on the bed.

"Should you do this, Ben," JJ asked. "What if they're personal? They could be love letters."

"And what else would they be? I doubt Nell gets much in the way of fan mail."

"It doesn't feel right, rifling through her stuff like this."

"They began when she returned from England. I heard little about the whys and the how. But I've heard enough discussion about it between the parents over the years to warrant my looking at it now. Okay?"

"Fair enough, I'm just saying."

"Well, don't."

I picked up the first and read it. It was full of pitiful pleading from some desperado called James from Dagenham, wondering where Nell had gone, and so on. And no other clues about anything, bar the fact they were engaged, which was strange enough on the whole. I read on, speeding through them, until I'd consumed them all. It was hard work being privy to the nauseating beggings of an English fella. But one thing was certain: Nell had absconded back to Ireland and given James the old heave-ho for no known or discernible reason. The letters were nothing more than a fluffer. I scoured the bed for anything I'd missed. There had to be more.

"So?" JJ said finally.

"It seems our Nell ran away from a fella called James six months before their wedding and set up her stall in Whitehaven."

JJ shrugged. "That kind of thing happens all the time."

"I don't know. He was a surgeon and from good stock. They'd a house in England and she'd a decent job. She was feathering her nest for good over there. There's no way she'd drop a catch like that, not the Nell I know. She sticks to moneyed-up men like glue."

I looked back in the box and tapped the insides again. No more secret compartments. I kicked the box in frustration until it toppled over, revealing a sight that made me gasp. In the corner was another envelope taped into place without a name or stamp. A fresh manila mystery. I released it from its catch, pulled out the letter inside and unfolded it. I read the first few lines, and my pulse roared in my ears. "It says, 'Dear Benjamin...'"

JJ shifted toward me with his eyes widening in disbelief. "It does not."

"I'm telling you. It's a confession, it's a bloody confession." I read the first line again. Dear Benjamin—"

"Holy crap."

I clenched it in my fist and waved it in the air. "I knew it. This is it JJ. This is what I've been looking for all along. Let's retire to the kitchen and open a brew. I need to get comfortable for this."

I strode out and rummaged through the cupboards until I found a half-empty bottle of Nell's cheap single malt. I placed the letter on the table, slumped down into the rocking chair and took a deep slug. Despite the nasty taste, it was liquid gold that stuff, splashing a tonic in me like a right nice calm-me-down for the moment that was in it.

"Right," I said. "I bestow on you, John Joseph, the honour to read, without pause, the entire contents of this here letter."

JJ picked it up and flicked through the pages. "Wouldn't you prefer to read it yourself?"

"Nope. I've hunted long and hard for it. You've been by my side throughout my quest. We've bled for those words. I want to be free to absorb each and every syllable of her confession. So please, and without further ado, crack on."

Chapter 25

Dear Benjamin,

You've just bulled out the gate with Ella, and I wanted to write this down before I lost my nerve. If you are reading this, though, one of two possible scenarios has likely occurred. Either I'm dead, or you're a sneaky filcher who has been rooting around in my drawers.

If I am dead, your first act should be to head to Margareta's place down the Grove and tell her the money she owed me is now rightfully yours. If, and when, she finally cobbles together the five grand she borrowed and returns it to you, make sure you have the decency to waste it all immediately. I leave it up to yourself to figure out the best way, but if you want a tip: gambling, girls or a drink addiction should have you blasting through it fairly rapidly.

Also if I'm dead, you might consider taking a match to the house because the insurance will be worth more than my entire estate. There's a leaky gas hose with some duct tape under the cooker. Yank it out, wait ten minutes and flip on the porch light outside. For some reason when the porch light comes on the rest of the lights do to. It should go up with a boom. If you duck in time you should be quids in.

If I'm not dead, though, and you have found yourself in possession of this letter, then put it back immediately, close the trunk, step out of the house and run your cotton socks off home. Because if I catch wind that you read this, I will break you into bits and bury those bits in the garden.

The truth is, I've been struggling with whether or not to write you this for near on a decade. The revelations in store are shocking in a way, so if you haven't the stomach stop reading now.

Still here? Grand.

To make a long story short, I'm your mother.

Sorry about that.

I know you were hopping about the place trying to track me down, and that this will come as a shock, and more probably a disappointment, but it is what it is. For the record, never refer to me as Mam. I carried you and gave birth to you, but your mam's your mam, and let that be the end of it.

And now, I suppose you'll be wanting to know why.

Well, a while ago, a couple I knew were not in the best place. They'd been trying for children for years, but nothing was taking. I'd always had an eye for the husband (we'd a fling before he'd met his wife) and being the complete eejit I was, one night, when he was roaring drunk, I took the chance and seduced him.

And who'd sleep with me, I hear you say. Well to answer you, I wasn't always this old. In fact, in my heyday I was quite a minx, but that's another tale and your stomach's probably still a bit too queasy. As for your father? Well, he is a man after all, and I've always suspected there's not a single one of them who wouldn't stray if it were presented to them on a platter. Anyway, it was a one-off. He told his wife straight away, and I left. I'm making it sound very matter-of-fact. There was a lot of suffering, a lot of dark days. I moved to Cork, and a few months later found myself pregnant with you.

Fact is, I wasn't mother material. Not then anyways. I knew it was his, and there was no way in hell their marriage could have survived that, and less chance I was going to raise a child by myself in Ireland. So I planned to abort you in England.

Harsh and selfish I know, but at least you now have a notion who you got it from. And I would have followed through, if it weren't for my friend Emily. She begged me to carry you to term. She knew all about the sordid details, knew I couldn't take care of a baby, knew I could barely manage to take care of myself. She was the one who convinced me to go to Barnamire, to give you up for adoption. She allowed me the use of her passport and details. Nobody, not even her, wanted this kind of secret to come out. We looked similar in those days and nobody cared to probe too deeply, so it was easily done.

When you arrived I kept you for ten days. I fed you, changed you and slept with you. I even named you Benjamin as you were born in Cork. It means "son of the south" in Hebrew, or so the nuns there told me.

Those days after your birth were the single most beautiful moments of my life, but I didn't realise it until later. I struggled with it then, but what were the options? Keep you, and eventually have you asking about your dad? No, a clean break was best for all concerned. So I gave you up and moved to England, and it would have worked out perfectly, if it weren't for fate.

I'd a grand life across the pond before I met you again. I was engaged to be married, had a nice job, plenty of money coming in and a bright future. And then, I sent a letter to my sister. A few lines scribbled down asking her how she was. I'd left without a trace, you see, and I felt she was owed an explanation. As the weeks passed by, the anger of my disappearance faded, until eventually she invited me back home to visit. I was reluctant at first, too embarrassed, too ashamed of my actions, but James forced my hand, bought me the ticket and packed my bags.

I arrived blind back in Whitehaven. I'd no idea they'd adopted a child and certainly didn't expect to see you sitting in the playpen with food stuck to your hair and face, flinging blocks at the fire with the birthmark as red-raw as the day I left you. At first, I thought it pure coincidence, but then they told me your name and the date they adopted you. Hell, Father Brogan even told me the name of the convent one night—after a few too many sherries. It was as if the heavens had conspired to give me a second chance. By the end of that first day, I'd decided two things—I'd keep you close and keep it all a secret.

It seemed as if the Lord himself had forgiven me. I forgot about James, ignored his letters, ignored his calls and settled in Whitehaven. And it was grand for a while, for about a month or two, until something in me changed. You see, I fell for you big time, boy. Never thought it possible. Always imagined myself immune to those instincts. But nature is a brazen teacher. It crept up on me, slowly at first, but it wasn't long before I was completely smitten by you. I held you, played with you, washed the dirt from your cuts and scuffs, read to you and sang you to sleep. I did all the normal motherly things. And then along came Ella. And I saw the bond the two of ye had and the way you took care of her, despite thinking yourself too tough to be kind. It was impossible for me to ruin that for you and to heap the misery of my decision onto Ella as well.

Well, that was the kicker. I knew then I'd never be able to tell you the truth while alive. I knew I'd never have you call me Mam. It cut deep, Benjamin, this realisation. It cut to the marrow of my bones, and it was only then I figured out the truth of it all—I wasn't forgiven. I hadn't been given a second chance. I was being punished.

Anyway, that's the long and the short of it. You've been rampaging about the country for the last few days now, and the damage it's done to your poor parents is frankly disgusting. The truth is, we all make horrible mistakes in life. But I learned my lessons too late. I was born with blackness in me, and I've suffered under the weight of it. But your parents, your real parents, the ones who reared you, who held you, who kept you safe, who taught you how to be a man, they've no need to suffer. Nor Ella for that matter. Not because of me.

Now, in case you haven't figured it out yet, let me clarify certain points.

<u>Your dad is your dad.</u>
<u>Your parents were the couple.</u>
<u>They do not know I am your birth mother.</u>

Sorry for the underlining, but you've been known to have a few thick days in the past.

So before I go, let me say this—you were my purgatory. The way this has eaten my soul was my penance, my cross to bear, mine alone to suffer. Please, don't condemn them to the same. They don't deserve it.

It's your move now.

Nell.

Chapter 26

Dad was my dad, my real one, not a made-up one, not one of those fair-weather fellas who gets landed with a bub of another because his little fishies lacked the mettle to get the job done. I'd say I was a right sight then, sitting stock still on the rocker, with my mouth agape. I never thought he'd it in him to stray, never thought he'd do battle with Nell, beered-up or not. Tagging sisters. The downright filth of it. My dad was my actual biological father, and a bit of a player by all accounts.

"What a belter. What a corker of a letter, JJ," I said. "I'd say it was about as good as I could have hoped for, even if I'd penned it myself. Wait until I tell him the news." I stood, grabbed the letter and stuffed it into my pocket. "He'll be chuffed. Can you imagine? However shocking it is to us, he'll be bowled over by the news."

"You're going to tell him straight away? Why not sleep on it for a day or so?"

"No chance. There's only one person this news will damage, and that's Nell. And as far as I'm concerned, she deserves what she gets."

"Not necessarily true though, is it?" he asked.

His eyes narrowed, and his shoulders rose an inch. I cursed silently to myself. I could tell by his expression alone that he was about to open his mouth and fire pins at my happy little bubble. "What isn't true?"

"The letter is a wrecking ball, pure and simple. And

245

you're just the dope to release it without even giving it a moment's thought."

"Hang on a second," I said. "Why are you raining on my moment with your sanctimonious ways? They already know Nell and Dad slept together. There's only good news here for everyone—bar her."

"Wide of the mark again, Ben. Will I tell you what'll happen if you storm on down to your parents and reveal the truth held in those few pages?"

"Go on, then…tell me. Not that it'll make a blind bit of difference."

"First, they won't believe it."

"They will."

"No…they won't. It's a parent's default setting. They'll think you are full of crap and look for confirmation. They'll hunt Nell down and confront her about every sentence in those pages, and your mam will feel like the whole affair has only just happened. That's the thing with news like this. It may have occurred years ago, it may have been forgiven. But when the old wound is reopened by you, it'll be as if your dad cheated on her yesterday. Your parents will suffer the whole episode again, and this time with the added benefits of years of marital resentment. Nell will be ostracised, she and your mam will probably never repair the damage that's been done. Plus think of Ella. She's a smart kid. She'll wonder what all the arguing is about, and when she finds out…"

His words made me pause for a moment. "But Nell…I mean, she deserves it."

"She may do. But Ella doesn't. Nor does your mam. She'll lose a sister. And not only that, but she'll also realise her sister is actually your mother, and how will that wreck her sense of motherhood? Add an affair revisited, and it's a melting pot of domestic fire. Who knows where it'll end."

"And Dad? He'll be over the moon. Any man would be to discover the son they thought he'd adopted was actually their own flesh and bone. It's hardly fair to deny him the truth because of a few hypotheticals."

"Your dad will be happy. No doubt about it. But I don't honestly think he'd change one iota, do you? He's not going to suddenly turn into Superdad, because, as you well know, he's as close to that as humanly possible already. He loves you regardless of whether you're adopted or not. It's the kind of man he is. So go on and tell your story, but it'll bring devastation to your door. There'll be tears and fights and screaming, and months, or even years, of pure poison. And eventually, and mark my words on this, when the fog has cleared it's not beyond the realms of possibility that they may even point the collective finger of blame at you. You'll regret it, one way or another. It's guaranteed, Ben."

I grabbed the bottle of whiskey and stepped to the door. "You couldn't simply let it be, could you? Couldn't just butt the hell out for once. You had to wade in and ruin the moment like the big, party-pooping gom you are."

JJ sighed loudly. "Hang on a moment will you."

I ignored him and stomped out of the house and up the path. "Go on away home to your mammy," I said, when he caught me up.

"Don't be such a cry baby and get into the car. We've had a hectic few days, and it's a bit of a walk back to yours."

"It's only a few miles. Anyway, the walk might do me good."

"You know you'd have come to the same conclusion—if you gave thinking a go for once."

I stopped and stared at him. "Well, maybe I'm done with all the lies and deceit of the adults in my world. Why should I be the one to live with this? He's my dad, and I'd like to tell him. Is that so hard to understand? All the rest of this muck is pure speculation. And anyway, they may react completely different to your doomsday prophecy. They may be so chuffed with the news that they forget to turn into the usual bunch of selfish, angry adults. Ever consider that when you were doing all your thinking?"

JJ put his hands up in surrender. "Listen, Ben. We've been friends for years now. And as the last few days prove, I'd follow you to hell and back. I'm on your side in this. Of course you can do whatever you want. And whatever you decide is cool with me. I get it. My dad was a complete ass, who snuck off with some floozy and abandoned us all. So trust me, I really get it. But this is an unadulterated nightmare in the making. Promise me you'll think it over first before you go traipsing in and telling all and sundry."

"I'll give it until I get home. So unless you want it to be in five minutes you should bugger off and leave me walk it in peace."

He climbed into the driver's side, and I walked up the lane.

"Come get me tomorrow for the match," I said, shouting over the groans of the engine.

He rolled the window down and stuck his head out. "You're playing?"

"I am. A promise is a promise. Anyway, I may need an excuse to skive off, depending on how things go on the stroll back."

He crept alongside me with an arm hanging out the window and a kerb-crawler's grin on him. "All things considered. It's been emotional."

I watched my friend then, with his mashed-up face and his off-centre nose, looking more beat-up than I remembered. "That's one way of looking at it. Oh, and best of luck with Val. Tell her I was asking for her."

"I won't. It'll be tricky enough without mentioning you. Every time I utter your name it's like chucking gasoline on a fire with her."

"She's fairly immune to my charms, all right. Either way, if she keeps lashing the salvos at you, feel free to blame me for the whole thing. Tell her to post me a poison pen letter or something if she feels a need to vent."

He revved the engine, and the car screamed for a gear change. "Will do. But, I'll be honest, on balance I may prefer your situation." And with that he slammed the accelerator and trundled away into the distance, leaving a cloud of dust spewing up behind him.

I kept still for a while just then, deep in the dregs of the day. I'd no notion as to which way my mind would tilt. There were troubles in my head, but with a half-bottle of whiskey in hand and some warmth left in the sun, I did what came natural to me and decided to let the drink solve it.

I jumped the wooden stile and followed along a path

until I reached the cove far below. I picked my way over the stones to the shore and sat with my back against a rock.

It was grand and quiet there. The sand, still hot from the day's rays, warmed me. I pulled out the letter again and looked at Nell's words. In fairness, she must have tempered the shakes when she wrote it because it was the most perfect looping handwriting I'd seen. I read it over and over again, until I could recite the whole thing verbatim. For the next long while, I laughed and cried and sighed and argued with myself like some half-witted simpleton. I watched the evening splash its streaky good-byes across the sky and the grey of the night fill in from all sides, and for all the calm around, for all my debating and deciding, I was none the wiser for the worry.

My brain was well and truly flummoxed.

When the night's chill set in, I shuffled down on my back and tucked into the whiskey. By two fingers in, I understood JJ's point clearly. I saw the logic in it. I wholly understood the effect these words would have and how it was best for me to suffer in silence. I laughed and congratulated myself for such insight, and was so beside myself with joy, I decided I deserved another few swigs to mark the occasion.

By four fingers in, though, I thought to hell with the lot of them. I'd round the whole troupe of scoundrels up. Mam, Dad, Nell, even old mutton chops himself, Father Malachi Brogan. I'd corral them into the front room and regale them with each and every sordid detail until they wilted from shame, and I'd swing for anyone who dared contradict me. And after laying them out cold, I'd high-five Dad for being such a goddamn, king-of-the-county legend. And with the zany idea playing rings around my mind, I lifted the bottle and decided to drink it dry.

As the last drop slipped down my throat the sky began to swirl. I found myself wondering when the stars had started zipping around like dragonflies, and how far I'd get if I swam straight out from shore, and I couldn't for the life of me remember what all the fuss was about.

It must have been around midnight when I called a halt to the whole proceedings and headed home. The walk back up the cliff became a Herculean effort with the last few days' antics weighing me down. However tricky it was to come down, the way up was murder. Each step conquered became a victory of monumental importance. Each wobble overcome became a chance to celebrate with a dance and a song. By the time I'd hit the road and swayed my way back home the night had long settled in and my hangover had turned up early.

I walked in through the back door into solid darkness. I stood in the kitchen for a moment and listened. Dad snored in the bedroom, and the carriage clock chattered on the sill. I moved into the dining room and flicked on the light. There on the table sat a plate with my cover on it. "Benjamin's Nosebag," it said on top. The lime-green lettering scrawled in kindergarten donkey's years ago seemed tacky to me just then. Never to Mam, though. She'd have bawled at anyone who'd the neck to pass comment on it. Ever since I'd waddled home with it clutched in my hands and presented it to her wrapped in newspaper and tied up with twine, she'd cherished it like it was the finest piece of cut crystal ever produced.

The sight of it then, the run-of-the-mill normality of it all, the sheer thoughtfulness of her setting a place for me without being certain of when I'd return. God, it smacked me sharp, right in the gut, and I recognised the feeling for what it was. It was guilt, that well-seasoned trickster, the black belt of emotions, and it had seen enough apparently because it flooded me with its voodoo ways.

I slipped down the hall on the flats of my feet and stepped into their bedroom with thoughts yanking me each and every way. Dad and Mam were sound asleep, oblivious to it all, snoring their hearts out. They looked happy and content, and it riled me no end. How easy would it have been to wake them up, tell them the whole nasty business and scarper off to bed with the security of my drunkenness there to lull me into oblivion?

Let them take their fair share of the worry, I thought. Let them wring their hands and say, "Ah now, what are we to do?" Why shouldn't they have a slice of the big, guilt pie? After all, they did have a hand in the baking of it. Unlike myself, who was destined to catch diabetes of the soul after being forced to swallow the whole, sickly lot of it. I smiled at the thought. Now, how would that have been for a finish? Here lies Benjamin, gorged himself on a pile of dirty lies until his pancreas withered and died.

And I nearly did it. I'd my hand on their quilt cover and was on the verge of whipping it away, when a tide of memories jammed into my brain with flashbacks of days gone by. All those times when I'd played the maggot, when I'd bunked off on the hop from school, when I'd being caught rapid robbing apples, when the Gardaí dragged me home for giving Johnny Gibbons a belt, knocking his central incisors out into his hand after he taunted me for days about the cut of my runners.

I remembered all those moments of drama, all of them caused by me, all of them unnecessary tortures for the two of them. In truth, they did make a bit of a to-do and scolded me some, but always in a measured way. They never lifted a finger, never raised a hand, unlike the rest of the savages around us who'd be dying for a genuine excuse to leather their kids, to show them what's what, to put some serious manners on their brazen children's heads.

I remembered when Dad crept up to my bedroom after Mam had sent me there without dinner. He smuggled me in a bag of crisps and some Tanora on the sly and told me not to dob him in to Mam. He reminded me how us men had to watch out for each other, especially in a house with tough women, not that he was disrespecting them or anything, only he'd been a wild young fella himself, and he knew there wasn't any badness in me, only a lack of talent for boldness and a serious dose of bad timing. After he slipped away downstairs, I climbed into the duvet cover as I'd a tendency to do. With my snack and my book and my torch as standard, I'd stay in there until the air grew tropical and my feet sweated up my socks.

It was amazing in a way the clarity of those thoughts and my brain still marinating in booze. For a second, I'd the mad notion of slipping in beside them, but instead I turned and wandered upstairs to my bedroom. There'd be time to talk soon, not then, not when my words would come out slurred and nonsensical. Nope, this drunk was too drunk, not-the-full-shilling drunk. Plus, I'd no real inkling as to what my move would be anyway. And there was nothing worse than a highly emotional man mullered from drink, screaming at some ungodly hour in the morning in sentences devoid of vowels. No, it was best to get the head down.

I tipped upstairs and headed for the bedroom with nausea beginning to ripple through my insides. There by the foot of the bed was my gear-bag with the hurley and helmet shining like new stacked to the side. I unzipped the bag, pulled out my gear and, with that drunken logic, sniffed it. It'd the familiar reek of Mam's beloved detergent. I must have been drunker than I ever imagined because when the traces of lily hit my nose I'd to gulp the sobs back down.

I saw it all there and then, how she'd included me in the to-and-fro and daily grind of the house without me even being there. I felt shame and anger and sadness in equal measure. I leaped under the covers of the bed and sank down into the mattress, its sides wrapping around me.

The softness of the sheets, the freshness of the pillows, the shrieking turmoil in my brain; if I'd just woken up I'd have sworn I was in purgatory. I fished the letter out of my pocket and held it in my hands as if the words inside were a charm that'd ward off memories and grant me a moment of calm. But when I closed my eyes and drifted off, I was abroad in a land full of fear; of screaming nuns and gunned-up scobies, of flaming gates and demons' heads, of feral beasts and banshee cries. My sleep was a palace of nightmares.

Chapter 27

Never again. Never again will I touch a drop of the poison drink for as long as I live. I'd one of those mornings where I kept waking, suffering and flitting in and out of snatches of sleep. Lord only knows what time it was when I finally thought about committing to the day, but it was well into the midst of it because my parents had long gone. I lay on the covers still dressed in the same clothes as yesterday, wondering if the boys in my head would ever quit their jackhammering, when in breezes JJ with a look of panic and him mad for business.

"Look at the cut of you." He yanked me straight up on to my feet, causing a dose of nausea to leap up in my throat.

"Slow down there, JJ." I reached under the mattress and retrieved the letter. "Any more of that sort of thing and I'll have last night repeating on me."

"It's four p.m., you fool. The match is on in an hour. Get your gear and let's go."

"Four already? I must have drunk more than I remember." I collected my bag and helmet and hurley and we headed downstairs. "I'll just go to the parents' room and get something of Mam's for the migraine."

"No time. You'll just have to suffer on, little prince."

It was one of those glorious days with a sun that was pure murder for a man as hungover as me. We crossed the drive and climbed into the car, and JJ had the engine gunned and wheels spinning before I'd even a chance to tuck my shirt in.

"So did you tell them?" he asked.

"Nope."

"Are you going to?"

"I might do. It depends on how I feel when I see them."

"And the files in the boot?"

"Funny you mention that." I sat up and rolled down the window to let the freshness of the day blow some holes through my fog. "Far as I see it. The deal with Mother Superior is we don't expose her hand, right? So what I suggest we do is simply post every person who requested the information the last known contact details of the others, and vice-versa. We'll drip-feed them, anonymously of course, over the next few months, so as to not to build up a flurry of noise. And then we simply keep the files as collateral in case she gets wind and forgets we didn't actually implicate her. What do you reckon?"

JJ glanced at me with surprise widening his eyes. "That's actually not half bad. When did you manage to come up with it?"

"About four fingers in. And on reflection, I should've stopped there."

By the time we wandered into the dressing room Bull was in full swing; head beet red, face drenched in sweat and with a sting of hot words flying out of him. He kicked it up a gear when he spied us traipsing in late.

"Two bould gossoons we have here," he said. "Farting about the place with your airy-fairy ways with less than ten minutes to the throw in."

I didn't utter a word. I'd seen many a teammate giving him lip only to get a belt from him for their efforts. When dealing with pre-match Bull, a slip of the tongue could get your throat cut sharpish.

"Tog off and do it quick smart, ya pair of last-minute blackguards."

"Yes, Bull," I said.

"Yes, Bull?" He screwed up his face mockingly and sighed. "How is it possible you can derail my thoughts with nothing more than a curtsy? Two show ponies looking to be led on parade. Is that about the size of it? Is it? Think yourselves too talented to show up on time?"

"Sorry, Bull," we said.

"Shut up, will you. Now, throw on eight and nine, the two of ye are midfield. I'll talk tactics to you in a second after I address the team."

I left him to it and threw on the shorts and jersey and laced up my boots. It took me less than a minute, but the Bull clearly had a daily quota of words he needed to off-load, because in that time, he'd raced through every member of the team, lashing out orders, screaming about the Village, and being generally hateful towards Glen-bridge people.

He was in rare form all right. And he was only building up a head on him.

"Right, lads," he said. He held the centre of the room clutching a net bag of sliotars and the usual bottle of tap water. He paused for a moment, checked the clock behind him against the digital stopwatch hanging around his neck.

"It's a light and dusty sod today, lads, so don't go picking it up," he said. "When it comes, give it holly and let it fly up the field. Because today's all about speed, about keeping the sliotar moving. If I see anyone outside the forty-five trying to pick it up more than once—I'll pull you off, no exceptions. And don't go trying to break the stitching when you're striking it. Hurling's a game of skill, not brawn. You with me, lads?"

We answered yes.

"Good...now, they're a handy enough side, as ye know, but they're no Allstars. And they can't do much if they don't have the ball. So look for the free man, no hospital passes, and be first to the ball if it's played to you. If you do all that, we'll be bringing the silverware back to the parish for the first time in decades. And we'll be able to lay the curse of the place down for once and for all. Are you with me, lads?"

"We are," we said, slamming the walls with the hurleys.

"Let it all on the pitch, boys. I want to see sweat and tears and smashed sticks and bloodied noses. I want to see the scoreboard ringing up the points and the bunch of bowsie boys from Glenbridge racing back to their mangy village, ruing the day they ever had the misfortune of meeting us."

A roar shot out of us, but Bull was like our puppeteer. He waved his hand, and we calmed. "There'll be time for that," he said, cooling his tone with our mood. "Just let me say one more thing...I love this club." He walked up and down the room, patting the crest of his jumper.

"Everyone grab their jersey and smell it. Take a deep breath of it right into your lungs. Do you know what it is? It's the smell of failure. I haven't washed these since the last match when you tramped about like a bunch of gormless hatchets and stank the place up to high heaven. Smell it again, lads, go on. It reeks, doesn't it? Smell that failure? It's worse than death. A rank, wretched, shameful thing you did Sunday, and you'll not repeat the favour, boys. Will ye?"

"No, Bull."

"You must refuse to settle for mediocrity, for second best, for taking feckin' part. Because no matter what your parents tell you, life ain't no picnic, it ain't got the stomach for carrying burdens around. And when you're cold and dead in the ground, it'll be days like this that define you, that'll pay homage to you as men when you're good for nothing but fertilising fields."

His breath failed him. He stopped talking, turned away and rolled up his sleeves. "You see this, lads? Flesh. They're only skin and bone those boys next door, the same as you, they're nothing special. Are they?"

"No, Bull."

"You're not going to leave them come into your house and bully you, shame you in front of your family, your friends." He plucked rosary beads out of his tracksuit and showed them to the heavens. "In front of God Almighty Himself, who bestowed on you the gift of being Whitehaven born, who gave you legs and arms to beat and chase and hound those buckos. It's winner takes all today. So tell me, do you want to win?"

"We do, Bull."

"Well, get out, get out, get out." He opened the door

and the team filed past him. But just as JJ and myself were leaving, he gestured for us to hang back. "A quick word?"

We stood in silence as the rest of our team ran out on to the pitch to the roar of the crowd. The Bull sat us down and kneeled in to talk. The rage in him was there still, you could sense it in his manic stare, but he'd put a leash on it for the moment.

"Had a rough few days?" he asked.

"You could say that," I said.

"Well, just do the business out here today and I won't give a damn, but if you're struggling you'll be substituted. I don't care how important you two think you are to the team."

"Fair enough," I said.

"Now, lads, I want to give you a little job. A different role to play than your normal ones. Is that all right with you?"

We nodded.

"Benjamin...the Humphreys fella. He's their main man, their superstar. Everything they do goes through him in some way. And without him they're average at best."

"I know. No worries, though, I've got his number today."

The Bull smiled a winsome smile. "Now, I don't doubt it for a moment, but let's consider a different tack. You see, he gets in your head, bullies you the minute he's on the pitch, and you spend the whole game darting about the place trying to shake him off, hoping he doesn't get a chance to lamp you. That about right?"

"It's a fair analysis," JJ said, like the big brown-noser he was.

"Hang on a second, Bull," I said. "You calling me a coward?"

"No, not at all. It's just we all have a button and he's been hammering on yours for some time now. And we can't be having that. So when you line up out there today, I want you to lay into him when the first ball's thrown in. Get up in his face, hard but fair, nothing that'll get you red-carded. Don't avoid him, seek him out and shadow him. You're faster and fitter than him. If you do one thing today, just spoil his game. Hell, in fact I don't want you to even bother yourself with the whereabouts of the sliotar. Your sole job is to castrate him, metaphorically speaking. And, JJ..."

"Yeah."

"Your job is to make sure Benjamin here doesn't lose a limb in the process. You got it, lads?"

"Got it."

"Right then, let's go play hurling."

Chapter 28

The bank surrounding the pitch heaved with supporters. The sheer weight of their voices made my whole body hum at once. We lined up on the halfway line, waiting for the referee to throw the sliotar in. He'd more nerves than the rest of us with all his ticks and tweaks. He pulled at his cuffs, swept his hair back and kicked out both feet before checking both sides had the legal number of players.

Humphreys had locked eyes on me the moment I stepped on the turf. Normally, I'd have found some interest in the blades of grass by my feet, or had a sudden dose of the jitters, but not this time. No, I strode out deadpan and indifferent, throwing him a wink when I came level with him. For all the last day's madness, all the running and scheming and violence and lies, he was nothing more than the local bullyboy in a speck of a parish.

The ref clicked his stopwatch and bit the nib of the whistle. Humphreys leaned into me, throwing his elbow and the boss of the hurley into my ribs. I kept staring at the sliotar in the paw of the ref until his arm hung down and swung back.

The sliotar came bouncing in towards us. Humphreys made a dart for it, and I went with him. He went to swing, but his timing was off. I met the ball on the third bounce, right in the meat of the hurley, and followed through whipping across Humphreys. No sooner had the sliotar sailed away downfield than the stick broke across his shins, and we both crashed to the floor.

For a second there was silence, followed by an almighty cheer, and a thirty-man fight broke out on the field. Humphreys howled and grabbed me by the bars of my helmet. By the twist in his face, I'd done some damage all right, but he must have been made of steel because he came at me without the trace of a limp.

If the crowd were in fair spirits before, they were practically euphoric then. The ref wasn't a fan, though. He blew his whistle and screamed, his skin turning purple with anger. When the madness died down, he pointed at Humphreys and myself and gestured us over to the sideline.

To be fair, it should have been a yellow card at least. I could've been sent off the pitch without a moment's notice—if the ref decided he'd seen some intent. But today wasn't a day for rules. Not when the championship final was only ten seconds done. Not when an entire parish stood less than ten feet from your sweaty old head and would be looking to cave said head in if any local boy was sent to the showers for little more than a momentary over-exuberance. And certainly not when I'd played the ball first, and if the fool of a ref did a drastic mad thing like following the rules, there'd be little left of whatever car or van or truck he'd the misfortune of arriving in. No, there was no doubting what he should have done. And even less what he was about to do then. If he didn't want to be abroad in the car park, looking for a lift home that is.

"Right, lads," he said. "We'll have no more of that

kind of nonsense. I'll presume you got a bit carried away with the excitement and all, but if you pull high and wide like that again—you'll both be off. Got it?"

"Both of us?" Humphreys asked. He hacked up a gob full of phlegm and spat it at the boots of the ref. "He shinned me. Have a look at my leg." He pointed at the red lump swelling on his ankle. "What do you call this?"

"He played the ball first," the ref said, slipping in between us. "Far as I could see. But I don't care about all that. Any more and you're both off. Now, get back to your positions."

He blew the whistle and signalled for a free for Glenbridge, and even this paltry gesture was enough to send the local crowd mental. Boos rose up from the meat of them, and they flung crushed up cans and coins at the ref, until all he could do was run back to the centre of the pitch, sending the pea in his whistle baloobas from his non-stop tooting.

"You'd better run, little patch," Humphreys said to me. "'Cause when I catch you, I'll rip your scrawny head off."

I strode up and butted my helmet against his. "There'll be no running away today, Humphreys. If you fancy your chances, you won't have to look past your shadow. Because that's where I'll be, right behind you, ruining your day."

I beamed at him then, giving him both rows of teeth. And in that moment, with less than the bars of the helmets between us, I saw a change in him. The cockiness was there all right, but there was something off in his eyes—a quick widening of the pupils and a flicker. Nothing more, but it was enough for me then.

This man mountain. This decade long pain in my side. The fella who'd bullied me, cajoled me and chased me out of the dances. This man who'd spent his childhood inventing ways to embarrass and shame and hurt me wasn't afraid. No, he'd never be scared of anything. Not his type. He was too thick, too familiar with violence, too used to waking up with bruises and gashes and a swollen brow where he put the head on some poor misfortunate. Humphreys and his kind could never be afraid—but neither was I anymore. And he was starting to see it.

The first half flew past in a jiffy. I'd kept my promise and didn't even bother myself with the ball. Everywhere Humphreys landed, I swung in to up scupper him. I stood on his heels when he went to run. I tapped his elbow when he tried to solo away. I dove in to land block after block on his strikes for goal. By halftime we were a point up, though it should have been more. If it weren't for their keeper being a hero on the line, we'd have been ahead by a cricket score.

Into the second half we went, and, in fairness to the Glenbridge boys, they turned things around. The ball fizzed up and down the pitch, and point after point was exchanged. It all became a blur towards the end. The lads tired and grew ratty, afraid the game was slipping, afraid to be the ones caught in possession. We'd lost our way somehow, and, with only seconds remaining, they pulled into a two-point lead.

JJ ran over to me and pulled me aside. "Forget Humphreys, Ben. We need a goal. Break off into the right-hand side. When I get the ball I'll find you. You do your thing."

He ran short for the puck out. I crept back out from the shadow of Humphreys and tucked up close to the line by the crowd. JJ caught the sliotar and turned. He spied me in my position and sent a low daisy-cutter spinning towards me. It'd some of heat on it, but I was dialled into the moment. I controlled it on the hurley and into my hand with ease.

I turned and slipped the ball onto the boss of the hurley and sprinted forward. The few supporters from Glenbridge spotted the move and screamed for Humphreys to chase his man. I made it to the sixty-five. The centre-back cut across, tried to shoulder charge me into the stands. Just before he hit, I slowed, moved infield and flicked the ball over his head.

I raced downfield. Every step closer to goal, the crowd screamed louder. I hit the forty-five and two more defenders closed. I caught the ball, braced for the impact and accelerated through them. I spat out the other side and threw the sliotar back on the hurley.

Thirty yards out. The goalie crouched and readied. Everything dulled. My breath came in heaves. My thighs burned. I never looked back, but I heard the stampede of players chasing me down. I closed to twenty yards. The full-back rushed out. Someone grabbed my hurley, and another clipped the back of my heels. I stumbled forward. The sliotar flew up in front of me. The full-back spotted it and swung his hurley back to lash it away from danger. A hand pushed me violently. Someone cracked my helmet, and I stumbled.

Then I heard it; my name. Just before the defender volleyed the sliotar mid-air, I palmed it back overhead towards the voice and crumbled onto the grass, sliding into the full meat of the swing. A hard blow to my helmet. Heavy bodies landed on top of me. The shrill of pain in my knee. The breath crushed out of me. I slid to a stop with earth gouging my skin, as JJ hared past at full tilt. He took two short steps, threw the sliotar up and swung.

Crack.

The ball fizzed past the keeper, rippling the net. The umpires waved their little green flag, and a tumultuous roar rose from the banks. The ref stopped by my feet, raised his hand and blew the final whistle. We'd won. By a single point.

JJ rushed over, knelt down and screamed. "You legend, you're a goddamn legend. How'd you know it was me?"

I pushed him away and sat up. "Instinct. You talk enough. I imagine your voice must be branded into me at this stage."

He dragged me to my feet while supporters swarmed around us. Someone tapped me on my back. I turned to find Humphreys with his skin ashen and the cockiness long faded. He didn't speak or smirk or spit in my face. He simply held out his hand.

I yanked off my helmet, and the cool breeze wafted over my skin. I paused for a second, imagining the whole thing a ruse, as if he was going to pull it away last minute and laugh in his usual mocking way. But when I reached out, he didn't falter. We shook twice, two short shakes. Then he nodded, as if to say fair bouts, and he stomped off pushing over an old fella and grabbing a half-smoked cigarette from another. And that was that.

I focused at the usual spot by the flagpole where my

parents always stood. Mam had her hands up shielding her eyes against the blazing sun. Dad sported a beaming grin, clearly loving the drama of his son standing tall, sticking up for himself, doing it on his own half-baked terms. He'd have been feeling the poke of pride I'd say, all right.

My parents knew the history more than anyone. They suffered through the quiet moments when I'd sit in my room talking myself around from tears, hiding the torn jumpers, the ripped copybooks, doing everything in my powers to ensure they never found out. But they always did. Especially Dad. Despite his roundabout way of counselling, he could pluck at the edges of you until the lot of it flooded out in big, gulping breaths. Then he'd stay there in the room, telling me stories of his youth, about how everyone has to figure these lads out for themselves, how he'd been buried under years of the same story. And the two of us knew it was a complete fib, and that he was a notorious fighter who'd levelled many a lad for giving him lip.

And in that moment they both waved. In the rush of screaming fans and chaos and missiles and the Bull howling at me about how I'd just written my inter-county ticket, my parents were their usual sea of calm, an anchor for the madness in me. And I suddenly under-stood the hurt I could cause them. I saw it all play out in an instant.

"Where are you going, Ben?" JJ asked. "They're about to present the cup. The Bull will be making a speech, and you can't miss that."

"Sorry, JJ, but I've a more important thing to do. I've got to tie up some of those loose ends."

I pushed past the crowd of supporters streaming on to the field, past Don dressed up in the parish colours holding the club treasurer in a head lock, past Father Malachi Brogan who stood in the middle of the park with a nice bit of space around him as if his religiosity were a force field. On I went, out through the gate and up the bank, where Mam ran towards me waving her little flag and grinning widely.

"Well done, son, you played a blinder," she said.

And right there and then, in the middle of the entire village, she planted a kiss on my lips and fixed my hair with a lick of her palm. "What happened to your face?"

"Calm down, Mam, will you. It's nothing," I said. "Come here, Dad, and take her back."

But she kept smiling and hopped on the spot. For the briefest moment, she looked like a teenager again, stepping out for the night, blushing with nerves.

"It was tight there at the end, wasn't it?" she said, practically giggling.

"It was a close-run thing, all right," I said.

Dad appeared by her side and gently pulled her back. "Go easy, Peggy."

"I'm only congratulating our son for playing like a young Christy Ring."

"I know. But give him a chance to breathe."

She tutted and fell silent with the look of a youngster who was about to stamp her feet and storm off in a huff. But she rode it out and looked at me again, all serious this time.

"So?" she said, no more no less. But that single word had a thousand different meanings, and it sucked all the fun out of the air.

"So what?" I asked.

"Did you find what you wanted on your little goose chase up to Cork?"

"Leave it out, Peggy." Dad said.

"I will not."

And she wouldn't. Once Mam fixed on an issue there'd be no end in sight without her say-so.

Ella appeared behind them, dragging Boots by the leash. She stood by my feet with one of those ninety-nine ice creams in her hand showered with sprinkles and a chocolate flake plopped in the centre. I bent down to her level and gave her a hug.

"Did you miss me, Ella?"

She stared at the ground with a tinge of sadness in her eyes and scuffed the pebbles with her shoe. "I did. A bit."

"Just a bit?"

Dad patted her on the head, and she shied away from him. "She was watching the door all day since you left. Wasn't she, Peggy."

Mam nodded.

"Well I'm back now, aren't I?" I hoisted her up in my arms and tickled her up under her chin with Boots snapping at my ankles. A fit of giggles flew out of her, and she writhed until I put her back down.

"So go on, Benjamin," Mam said again. She folded her hands, cocked her head, and I knew then if I didn't give an answer, it'd be a wild night for Dad.

"Go on away up to the car, Ella," Dad said. "We'll be along in a little while. Give Boots a quick run off the leash to tire him out for the night."

"Okey-dokey," she said, and she clipped off the leash

and squeezed my hand as she passed with a huge smile etched on her cheeks. When she was away down the bank and out of earshot, I turned and stared at my parents.

"Only ghosts," I said. "Dead ends. Clues that went nowhere."

Mam folded her arms and ground the toe of her shoe into the dirt. "You sure about that?"

"I am. And I'm kind of done with all of it, to be honest. I figure with the trauma of you two, dealing with another set of parents would be torture. You're enough of a mam and a dad for me now."

She wept then, eyes glistening without a trace of sadness. She threw her arms around me again and kissed me five times on the cheek. Wolf whistles came from some lads nearby, and I knew there'd be a rash of mammy-boy cries whenever I wandered in for a pint in Brehon's. But I wasn't bothered. I left her linger. I didn't brush her away.

"You're just gorgeous, despite yourself," she said. "You know that? Just gorgeous." She held my head in her palms and smiled a contented smile. "You've the makings of a fine young man."

"All right, enough now." I peeled myself away. "I need to wash the dirt off."

Dad took her by the arm and led her down the grass, but she stopped and turned, eyes pulling tight at the sides. "You'll go and visit Nell now, won't you? She's in a strange mood. Gone off the drink even. If you'd believe that. Keeps asking whether you said anything to us since you got back. She's beside herself with grief about some-thing she lost, but she won't tell me what. So you'll go up and tell her you won. Give her a bit of good news, a bit of a gee up."

"I will, Mam. I was going there anyway."

"Make sure you do."

Chapter 29

By the time JJ and I'd showered and changed, the rest of the team were only just coming back into the dressing room. They were in wicked spirits, singing their heads off, with jerseys drenched in beer and taking turns to sip from the cup. JJ and myself slid on past them and out the door, leaving them to their revelry. The Bull was still outside soaking up backslaps and praise from the knot of supporters who swarmed around him. He'd been crying, of course, and he kept leaning forward with his head in his hands and swearing incoherent thanks to the Lord Himself, saying how he'd have been grave with the worry if the lads hadn't managed to pull off his last-minute tactical change.

Typical Bull, wallowing in other peoples' sweat and tears, but I'd no time for corrections, and, in a way, I thought he'd deserved the moment more than the rest of us. He'd go to his grave a happy man, forever remembered by a plaque on the wall of the treasurer's office.

We slipped around the corner and into the car park. JJ tagged along out of his usual sense of honour, but I could tell by the way he kept half-heartedly high-fiving everyone on the way out he was not a happy trooper.

"Don't fret," I said. "We'll be back down celebrating until dawn in less than half an hour."

And no sooner had the words left my mouth than a fire-red BMW swung in front of us and juddered to a stop blocking JJ's car. With its exhaust still pouring out fumes and the engine idling, four men jumped out.

"Hail, our heroes return," Apache said, slow-clapping us as we approached. "I tell you fellas can't half hurl the ball. Some high-risk move you pulled off there at the end, Benjamin. I'd say you'll be getting action off the local ones for months on the back of that performance. You'll be knee deep in them."

I groaned, and JJ cursed, but we continued walking to the car. "Now's not a good time, Apache," I said. "We've places to be—"

"And people to see. Yeah. I'd say you two shams are the embodiment of busy." He stepped around to the boot of JJ's car and pushed down on the back of it. The suspension gave an arthritic scream and something popped near the undercarriage. "Always rushing off without so much as a goodbye. Even when a good pal, who promised he'd come knocking, pops up to solve all your woes."

He left the words sink in. JJ and myself eyeballed each other.

"Go on...I'll bite," I said. "What problem do we have?"

"The car I took from you. And the debt left unpaid. Both, as it so happens, have a pleasing solution."

He pointed at the brand new sports car, purring away behind. The Puca saw his signal and revved the engine. It practically sang. Not a cough or hiccup in it and it'd a low, bass growl that said, unleash me lads and we'll have many a happy mile.

"And what do you want us to do with that?" I asked. "You looking to give it to us, is that the gist of it?"

"I am."

I laughed and turned to get into the car. "Come on, JJ. It's just more of his lies."

"It's no lie," Apache said. "You drive the contents of this car across the border up north, drop off the delivery, and the car is yours. And not only that, I'll wipe out your debt. You'll be free men. No longer kowtowed to Apache and his tribe."

"Don't believe a word coming of this gangster's mouth," JJ said. "There's bound to be a catch. There always is."

"So what?" I said. "You're going to set us up to take another fall, and we'll be arrested and chucked into Portlaoise jail with a bunch of freak-shows for the rest of our youth?"

Apache laughed. "Look, as I said before, you don't really have a choice. All I'm doing here is making it easier for your egos to accept your situation." He slung an arm over my shoulder, and I shrugged him off. "I tell you what...I'll make it even simpler. I'll give you a cash advance now."

He clicked his fingers, and a Puca flung an envelope at me. I caught it and stared inside. There were inches of notes in there, all fifties as well. A thicker wad than I'd seen in my life. There must have been twenty grand at least. I slid it across the roof to JJ, who stuck his nose in for about ten seconds before puffing his cheeks out and whistling.

"Twenty-five Gs, Ben," JJ said.

"So that's your vice then?" I asked. "Cash?"

Apache jabbed his thumb at the car. "And don't forget the motor, lads. It's worth thirty easily. Do with it as you see fit. Sell it, trade it. It's all legit, paperwork's in your name and everything. A few hours work and you'll be fifty-five thousand pounds wealthier. And, more importantly, debt free."

"And we'll definitely be finished with you, if we do this?" JJ asked.

"On my honour," Apache said.

JJ shrugged, retrieved the files from our boot and walked over to the Pucas who parted to let him pass.

"Where you off to?" I asked.

"We don't have much of a choice, though, do we, Ben?" He chucked both holdalls onto the back seat, before clambering in the passenger's side. "And because you played so sweetly, I'll give you the honour of driving."

I paused for a second and studied Apache—his eyes hungry, his greasy fingers pawing the paint, the way he bent over the boot of the car like he was going to give its tailpipe a ride. He'd all the look of the devil himself after sauntering up here to sign my soul to damnation for the price of an admittedly sexy looking machine. I'd a gnawing pain in my stomach, one that said, "To hell with this and scream out for those supporters over there who'll tear strips out of these blow-ins."

But however hard the sensible side spoke to me, there was one overriding fact—Apache would torture me forever if I didn't get out from under his shadow. And with that in my head, I strode forward and slipped into the driver's seat.

It'd that intoxicating new-car smell. I ran my hands over the wheel and felt the solid stitching underneath. The shine from the dash lit up racing car green, and numerals on the speedometer went all the way up to two hundred. I revved the engine, barely feeling any vibration beneath us. It'd about a million little horsies of power under the bonnet, and each one with manners on them. It was some machine, in fairness.

Apache crouched down on his haunches until his eyes drew level with mine. "Follow the road north to the spot marked on the map in the glove box, wait there until you're met by two lads from Lisnaskea. Don't ask any questions. Don't even talk to them. Those Skea boys are unpredictable types. Pop the boot, let them unload and get back down south. Cool?"

"Sounds dandy," I said.

"And one more thing. Neither of you two smoke, do you?"

"No. Why?"

Apache shrugged. "No reason. Just don't think of starting until the stuff in the boot is gone and you've blown air through the car for an hour or so. Hate to see another accidental inferno. Other than that, enjoy boys."

I slipped the gearstick into first, hammered the pedal, and we drove out of the place with the sounds of acid house bruising the ears, and I thought how the day had been kind enough to me after all. But when I remembered Nell and the showdown, I decided to head south for a little while, safe in the presumption a detour wouldn't be such a major drama.

"You still going to Nell's then?" JJ asked.

I was surprised he noticed the direction at all given how he'd his eyes swimming in the pile of fifty-pound notes on his lap.

"I am."

"So judging by the humongous smiles on your parents, you've decided to keep it to yourself?"

I nodded.

"I have to say; you've grown up over the last few days."

I scoffed at the statement. "We're delivery men for gangsters, JJ. Hardly an action that defines maturity."

"I suppose. And what about Nell? You going to rag her out?"

I didn't answer. I was too wrapped up in my thoughts. I wished for a fool's guide on this sort of thing, a blow-by-blow account on how to challenge a mother masquerading as an aunt.

When we pulled up to her house, I parked and turned off the engine. I stayed there in the moment, weighing up whether to hug her, race in through the door and unleash a torrent of abuse like a ten-gun salute, booming expletives until I'd wasted my words, or simply turn the car around and head north for the border. But this was one of those moments that couldn't be planned. "One of life's little testers," as Dad liked to call them.

"You want me to come with?" JJ asked.

"No, not this time. This is between me and her."

I opened the door and jumped out. I slipped my hands into my top and wandered slowly along the cliff as the dwindling sun coloured the skies caramel. Out on the horizon a storm was rising. Ink black clouds crunched together, and sheets of rain beat a slow march towards shore. The wind turned westwards. Its fingers slipped under my clothes and buffeted them out, raking my skin until I shivered.

I headed down the path and up to her front door. I knocked this time, but there was no answer. Nerves swarmed in my belly, and my thoughts turned to static as if my consciousness wanted no hand in my acts. I took a deep breath and walked straight inside. Nell stood by the window with her back to me, washing dishes in a sink full of foam. She didn't budge when I entered; never looked around, never spoke.

I settled in the chair opposite her, relishing the silence. I understood then how it felt to have a stay of execution, if only for a few short minutes. All my senses bucked up at the sight of her. I smelled the resin recently rubbed into the wood and the lime wax finish sheening up the floor. I tasted bleach and smoke tainting the air, but, more than anything, I sensed the pressure building between us.

I'd expected her to turn and howl at me for my actions, for taking the letter and ousting her in such a manner. The Nell I knew would have carved me up, chewed on the gristle and fed the bones to the crows. But there was no sign of the wily, old lady today.

I stared at her back, at the chequered apron tied twice around her waist, at the last spears of sun streaming in through the windows and the haze of dust motes zig-zagging in the glare. And I noticed her age then; the frailness in her frame, the greyness of her hair coiled up in a bun, the noises of the house as creaky as her bones. She always looked older than her years by some measure. And now I knew why.

We stayed that way for a slip, no more than a minute, each of us ignoring the other, delaying the inevitable. Her shoulders scrunched up, her head dipped slightly, and the faintest whisper of a sigh emanated from her lips. All of them were signs of her body betraying her. They played briefly and subtle on her, but I didn't need any more. I saw them for what they were right then; small, unconscious gestures of decades' worth of guilt.

In truth, I could have left the moment roll on forever, left the quiet hang in the space between us. It would have satisfied most, assured the secret was mutually known. I could have stood, backed out the door and left the details and the stress of it all there. I was certain she'd have lived with it left like that, words gone unsaid, drama nicely averted. It'd have been enough for many all right, no doubt about it.

I stood after an age and wandered over to her. Her neck flinched slightly when I approached. Up close, she looked even more withered, like the last leaf of autumn pulled ragged by the winds. I put my hand on her shoulder and studied her reflection in the window. In the wan light of the kitchen, she'd this ghostliness to her. Her cheeks were sunken, her skin ashen-grey, her wrinkles so deep and many you could have counted her years like the rings of a tree.

For a moment nothing happened, then she slowly looked up until her eyes met mine. And right then, right in the face of her, when the devil in me said, "Give her both barrels, boy," all the anger and noise and thunder fell quiet. I raised my finger to my lips and smiled.

Without a single word uttered, without a drop of a tear or a curse tripping off our tongues, I laid the envelope down flat on the table, righted the quaich and sat it on top. And just like that, we confined the drama of it to the shadows of our minds. I stepped back outside and cushioned the door closed with a soft, solitary click.

Everything returned to near normal; everything back in its box.

ACKNOWLEDGMENTS

Thank you to my mentor, Les Edgerton, for his encouragement and dedication to writers everywhere, without his help and sage advice I would still be fascinated with the smell of rain at dawn.

Thank you to my agent, Svetlana Pironko, for taking a chance on an unknown, her candid and expert guidance has been priceless throughout.

Thank you to my publisher, Eric Campbell of Down & Out Books, who showed such faith in this book from the very beginning and brought my dream of publication to reality.

Thank you to my editors, Lance Wright, for his dogged and proficient editing, and Síne Quinn, for her cool-handed judgement and eye for detail.

Thank you to my cover designer, Khent Rick Tobil, for his beautiful artwork.

Thank you to my stablemates old and new in our online writer's group, you have endured the torture of many drafts; my admiration for you all is boundless.

Thank you to my friend, Pamela Weaver, whose wisdom and critique in those formative months were invaluable.

Thank you to my English teacher, Sean Murphy, who lit the fire in me to write.

Thank you to all those authors, Maegan Beaumont, Paul D. Brazill, Janey Mack, Richard Godwin, Gerard Brennan, who selflessly offered me help along the way.

Thank you to my wonderful parents, Donal and Helena O'Connor, for everything they have done, without their guidance I would have never reached for the impossible.

Thank you to Nicole, Ailín, Daniel, Sorcha and all of my family far and wide for their love and encouragement.

And finally, thank you to Rosemarie, Tilly, Jack and Oscar. You make this all worthwhile. You are the very best of me.

Gerald O'Connor is a native Corkonian, currently living in Dublin with his long-term partner, Rosemarie, along with their three children. He writes character-driven novels of various genres by night and is a dentist by day. When he isn't glued to the keyboard, he enjoys sci-fi films, spending time with his family and being anywhere in sight of the sea. He is currently working on his second novel *The Tanist* which is due for completion soon.

CPSIA information can be obtained
at www.ICGtesting.com
Printed in the USA
LVOW11s0056070217
523425LV00002B/338/P